Breaking Even

Alejandro Grattan-Domínguez

Arte Público Press
Houston, Texas
1997

This volume is made possible through grants from the National Endowment for the Arts (a federal agency), Andrew W. Mellon Foundation, the Lila Wallace-Reader's Digest Fund and the City of Houston through The Cultural Arts Council of Houston, Harris County.

Recovering the past, creating the future

Arte Público Press
University of Houston
Houston, Texas 77204-2090

Cover illustration and design by James F. Brisson.

Grattan-Domínguez, Alejandro.
    Breaking Even /
    by Alejandro Grattan-Domínguez.
        p.   cm.

    ISBN 1-55885-213-1 (pbk. : alk. paper)
    1. Mexican Americans--Texas, West--Fiction.
I. Title.
PS3557.R2827B74 1997
813'.54—dc21   97-22172
                                                        CIP

The paper used in this publication meets the requirements of the American National Standard for Permanence of Paper for Printed Library Materials Z39.48-1984.

BREAKING EVEN

Alejandro Grattan-Domínguez

There are some things that cannot be learned quickly. Time, which is all we have, must be paid for their acquiring. But because it takes a lifetime to learn them, the little new that each man gets from life is very expensive and the only heritage he has to leave.

Ernest Hemingway

This book is dedicated to my
niece, Nikki, and my nephew,
Juan, and in memory of their
father, Tom, who all his life
brought me the two most precious
gifts a brother can bestow,
love and luck.
And also to Ilse Hoffmann, Kenny
Meyer and Linda Feyder, who each in
their own way greatly contributed to
the birth of this book.

PART ONE

Chapter 1

What Val saw as his long period of involuntary servitude was about to come to an end. In the prison-movie parlance he liked to affect, he had done his "hard time." He had finally reached his eighteenth birthday, and Texas law entitled him to make his own decisions now.

Further, only the week before, he had graduated, though just barely, from high school, thus completing the last of his onerous obligations. He was finally free to ditch the tiny West Texas town he had always despised, and set off for the Promised Land of California, which in that summer of 1955 was not yet sullied by smog, overpopulation and drug-crazed barbarians. This very day he planned to declare his independence, as well as his travel intentions. But first he would have to enlist the aid of the man many people considered the finest attorney in the entire county.

Yet even with the law and the lawyer on his side, Val knew that escaping from Big Bend, Texas might prove about as easy as swimming in quicksand.

Part of the problem was his mother.

Guadalupe Santana Teran Cooper Dalton. Those weren't all her names, but should suffice to indicate some of the scattered pieces of her past. She was a Mexican, though most definitely not of that timid Texas variety whose main mission in life back in the mid-50s was to quietly blend into the background.

Val thought his mother was more like a famous movie producer he once read about, who had been described as having gone through most of his life "demanding to see the manager."

In that summer of 1955, there were few Mexicans living in Big Bend. But what they lacked in number, Val's mother made up for in emotional fireworks. As the unofficial representative of the town's tiny Mexican community, she had stormed into City Hall more than once to demand their right to equal treatment under the law. She didn't always succeed, but she invariably tried, and that had made her a hero to her people. Lupe could have been a major personage among the Anglos, as well, but the wrong skin color and ethnic heritage had long since relegated her to more modest billing.

The little diner and motel Lupe owned had once been on the main road between Pecos and El Paso. Business had been brisk. But when Val was about twelve, the new highway came in, and much of their trade tumbled off. Some of the older truck drivers, though, still remembered the place and didn't mind rolling a few extra miles over to the former highway for country cooking that hadn't had all the flavor frozen out of it. So the business got by, but ofttimes just barely.

Some folks thought the stone-faced diner resembled an old frontier trading post; but to Val the place seemed more like a prison, and what surrounded it, almost worse than walls. It sat perched on a slight rise strewn with rust-colored boulders and parched little clumps of cactus. Out behind the diner, its five motel units were penned in by mouse-shaped foothills as barren of vegetation as a billiard ball. This part of Texas would never be featured in any travel magazine, and was so devoid of greenery, whenever anyone actually encountered a full-grown tree, their first impulse might be to touch it, just to make sure it was not a mirage.

But Val's mother was no illusion, and over her tiny chunk of desert domain, she ruled supreme: owner, manager and one-woman court of last resort. As if to further declare her sovereignty, she had painted or upholstered almost everything inside the diner red, white, and green, the colors of her native country of Mexico.

By seven o'clock the cafe was already jammed with their breakfast trade, always the busiest time of the day. That morning, the customers, mainly ranchers, farmers, and truck drivers, were being serenaded by Val's favorite singer. Frankie Laine's robust recording of "The Wild Goose" had long seemed to Val about the next best thing to actually taking a trip to faraway places.

Val punched up the song again on the jukebox, and having attended to that bit of business, he hurried over to pin another order on the shelf that opened back into the kitchen. Then he banged Floyd's order bell. He enjoyed hitting that bell, and now whacked it extra hard. After all, it was his birthday.

Inside the kitchen, Floyd stood bleary-eyed over a sizzling griddle, sweat pouring off his lantern-jawed face. For a moment Val thought of making some remark about his stepfather's usual morning hangover, a foolproof way to jump-start a conversation with Floyd; maintaining it, however, was always about as easy as busting boulders with a tack hammer. So Val simply banged the bell again and walked away.

His mother was holding court around the cash register, as he sauntered up to hand her a five-dollar bill and a customer's check. Val waited for the small group of admiring males to go on about their business, but none of them seemed overly anxious to accommodate him. Val's mother, along with Floyd's cooking and the rock-bottom prices, was the restaurant's prime attraction.

Now nearing forty, Lupe's features, as well as her figure, had started to sag a bit; but that didn't matter much to most of the men who came into the cafe. Her olive complexion, wavy black hair and thick-lashed green eyes made for a combination not normally found on the north side of the Rio Grande River; and to Val's continued amazement, her tart tongue and quick mind only made her more interesting to men who usually preferred dull and docile females.

But Lupe harbored no delusions about their true nature. The Anglos who stood bantering with her almost every morning were often the same men who tried to hire Mexicans at only half of what they paid a white worker, or who charged Mexicans higher prices for food and housing. Nor would these men, she knew, ever invite her into their homes, or allow her son to date one of their daughters. Yet Lupe was secretly proud that she had beaten them at their own game. Her friendliness was as feigned as theirs, but in her case it made her money.

As the group slowly disbursed, Val finally got her attention. "What's wrong with Floyd today?" he mumbled.

"His *estómago* not at the right place today," Lupe muttered, checking Val's addition on the customer's check. "And the noise from the jukebox is not the better cure for his hangover."

"Floyd should find himself a habit he can handle," Val said, belaboring the obvious. His mother's expression hardened.

"Listen, Val, we all try the best we can," she murmured, speaking low so that the customers wouldn't hear. "And your own father—may he rest in peace—never once do he start off a morning without first taking a drink. His 'corrective,' he call it, for the things that go so wrong the day before."

The memory seemed to please her. Chuckling, she handed Val his change and strolled back to her admiring public. They were still lolling around, tearing up toothpicks with their teeth.

Val walked over to give the change to his customer, who left him a nickel tip. Then he ambled back to bang Floyd's bell once more. This time Val got his stepfather's attention.

"Can create more commotion, boy, than a locomotive passing through shantytown," Floyd growled, laying out a couple of orders on his pickup shelf.

"Just trying to prove I'm still alive," Val mumbled.

His stepfather was not amused. "So try playing dead for a while—and you can commence by killing off that damned wild goose song of yours."

"Hey, I'm not the only one who plays that song," Val said, thinking to taunt Floyd into an extended conversation. "Don't you ever read the newspapers? Heck, that song is number one on all the music charts and—"

Floyd raised his fist, as if to inform Val exactly where he could stick those same music charts. Gathering up the orders, Val quickly scooted away.

Floyd, whom Lupe had married some eight years earlier, was the cook. Val did just about everything else, though whatever work he managed to avoid was usually handled by a toothless old Mexican woman named Juana. This made for a four-party pecking order, with Val and Juana always competing for third place. Most times, Val won.

When it came to dealing with his stepfather, however, Val never maneuvered much more than a tie. Floyd Dalton was about ten years older than Val's mother. Val figured he must have been a good-looking guy when he was younger, with his long, chestnut-colored hair and Arrow-collar features; but by the time Floyd came into their lives, the world had whipped him pretty hard.

There seemed, Val thought, a lot of grim history of ruined relationships in Floyd's watery brown eyes and wary manner; as if the best friend he'd ever found was a bottle of bourbon.

Val had tried a few times, mainly out of sheer boredom, to piece together Floyd's ill-fated past; but to coin a phrase, he never disclosed much more than his name, rank, and serial number. Val had, however, once heard his mother tell one of her Mexican friends that Floyd had been seriously wounded in the Second World War. Then he had come home from the army only to suffer a more grievous injury. His wife soon left him for another man, and took Floyd's young daughter along for the ride. He never saw them again.

Yet little as Val had ever learned about Floyd, he knew even less about his real father. He'd been killed, Lupe said, right after Val was born, trying to save the lives of some men trapped in an oil field fire. Val's mother, like Floyd, never talked much about the past. Yet she had told Val enough about his old man to convince him that Frank Cooper was just about the greatest guy he was never going to meet.

The loss of his father had made a huge hole in Val's life, and he had spent much of the last eighteen years trying to fill the depression with whatever material he could find; mainly the stories Lupe had told him, and his own wild imaginings, which finally created a character more noble and fascinating than anyone else Val had ever met.

His impression of Frank Cooper grew so vivid that later, when Floyd first walked into the diner, he seemed more like a ghost than Val's father might have been, after returning from an oil-drenched coffin.

In the years that followed, Val never gave Floyd much thought or affection. Nor did his mother. Floyd seemed to exist on the outer edges of Lupe's heart, getting by on the leftovers of her love for Val's father. Yet Val thought the main reason his mother married Floyd might have been his willingness to settle for so little.

Walking away from the partition, Val balanced the three heaping plates of food in his hands, and somehow made it safely through the crowd to a table by the front window. Two burly truck drivers sat awaiting their food, grumbling as if they hadn't eaten in more than a month.

"Damn, Pancho, about time you got here with the feedbag," the older trucker groused, tucking a napkin around his bulging neck. "But say, boy, oughta think about becoming one of them there circus jugglers. Make yourself a fortune."

"Oh, this dark-skinned buck gonna make hisself a fortune, for sure," the younger man sneered. "Hear tell his girlfriend's father owns the only tractor franchise in town."

Val's girlfriend was named Bonnie Gortner; if his mother comprised half the problem in escaping from Big Bend, Bonnie constituted the other half.

For a moment, Val thought about giving the truckers a long monologue on the nature of insurmountable odds; but he simply smiled grimly and drifted over to the window. The truckers' tractor-trailer rig sat parked just outside. Whenever Val saw such machines, he always wondered where they were headed.

"Where you hauling to this time?" he asked, trying to sound bored by his own question.

"Headed west, Pancho. All the way out to that so-called City of the Angels... or 'Angles,' I should say," the older man grumbled, between mouthfuls of grits and gravy.

Val looked a bit wistful. Los Angeles had long been his favorite place, though he'd never even been there. Yet in his mind, it seemed a paradise filled with palm trees, swimming pools and best of all, the fantasy factories whose films filled the movie theatres of the entire world.

Climbing out of his daydream, Val took up a pile of dishes from another table and carted it over to the sink, where a large stack of dirty dishes already awaited his attention. He whacked away at them, as the breakfast trade began to wind down.

His mother was watching him with an approving eye, and when she called Val over to the cash register, she was grinning. Her smile troubled him; she usually saved it for the customers.

Something was definitely up; Val noticed that even the jukebox had gone mute, as if in respectful observation of whatever was coming next.

Then Lupe reached into the register and took out a small, gift-wrapped box. Handing it to Val, she gave him a hurried hug. The gesture surprised him. Open displays of affection were not part of his mother's emotional repertoire.

"*Feliz cumpleaños, hijo,*" she said quietly. "And now you hurry to Noah Carson's office. He have a special birthday gift waiting for you. I already make appointment for you."

This struck Val as a happy coincidence. He had hoped to see the lawyer that very day, anyway.

"What about the dirty dishes?" Val asked, pushing his luck.

"Oh, Juana do them when she finish to clean the cabins," Lupe casually replied.

Now Val knew something serious was in the wind; laying off work on old Juana was usually his trick, not his mother's.

The gift-wrapped box contained a slide rule. Val frowned. He had been hoping for a wristwatch, though he was aware that always knowing the exact time of day in Big Bend could only make the hours pass even slower.

Val tried an appreciative smile, but made a mess of it. His mother's eyes went cold. She seemed disappointed that he was so obviously dissatisfied.

"You use this when you start the junior college here this September that is coming... and meantime it help you add up the customer checks for a change correct."

Val frowned. For the past few months he hadn't made any mistakes, least none he hadn't caught before his mother did. But he was in no mood to trip her up on a technicality. Already he was mentally making tracks toward Noah Carson's office. Val was counting on the lawyer to help him persuade Lupe to allow him to leave Big Bend.

"*Valentín, el regalo es de Floyd, también,*" Lupe said, stiffly underlining the conjunction. Val got the message.

Floyd still stood over his griddle, flipping flapjacks in his usual expert manner.

"Hey, thanks a lot for the slide rule," Val said, flushing up an anemic display of gratitude. "Sure seems like a good one."

Floyd emitted a loud snort, which was about as close as he ever came to laughing. "Well, cost better'n six dollars... but the way you add up your checks, it could end up saving us a lot more'n that."

Val's grin melted into a grimace. "Yeah, well, it's the gift that counts, right?"

Floyd turned and grunted something to his flapjacks. Once again the conversation had run off the road before it could pick up any speed. Val started for the front door, on his way to his cabin to change into his best clothes. A formal appointment with Noah Carson was not an everyday event in Val's life.

"*¿Le dijiste gracias a Floyd?*" his mother asked as he strode past the register.

"Thank him for what?" Val mumbled. "Far as he's concerned, that slide rule is just another business investment."

Lupe's smile crumpled so quickly, Val suddenly felt sorry for her. For the past eight years, she'd been caught in a vise of sorts: crushed in on one side by her obligations as his mother, pressed on the other edge by her duties as Floyd's wife. A no-win situation for all three parties, and one more reason why Val was so desperate to get out of Big Bend.

As Val moved toward the front door, a customer rose from his table, and laid out a coin. The middle-aged, craggy-faced rancher had been coming into the cafe for breakfast every morning since his wife had died a few months earlier. Yet he had kept his grief to himself, never once playing for sympathy. Val admired him for that, and suddenly decided to terminate the rancher's long spell of self-imposed silence. To Val, total quiet seemed almost as sad as death itself.

"Sorry about your wife, Mister Rawlins. Everybody thought she was a fine lady."

The lanky rancher seemed grateful that somebody had finally dared to mention the demise of his wife. But Val's interest had already shifted to the coin Rawlins had left on the table.

"You left a quarter on the table, sir."

Rawlins decided to smile. "Well, Val, beginning to think you'd plumb lost the trick of talking. But now if you're too proud to pocket that two-bit piece, I sure ain't too proud to take it back."

"Oh no, sir," Val stammered, somewhat startled by the sound of the rancher's newfound voice. Then, glancing back toward the kitchen, Val quietly added, "But can you do me another favor? Just drop this quarter into the jukebox. Selection number nine. All three times. Okay?" Rawlins had some idea of the little game Val wanted to play on Floyd. Chuckling, the rancher took the coin and ambled toward the jukebox.

Val was already outside the door when the loud wail of the "Wild Goose" came swooping through the cafe. Peeking back in through the dusty window, he saw Floyd's head pop out from the partition. Predictably enough, his stepfather looked fried to a crisp. Val had pulled this same stunt a few times before, always to less than rave reviews.

Yet this time, his mother, hiding off to one side of the cash register, was struggling to squelch a smile. Val figured she was cutting him some slack because it was his birthday. He hoped she would be in a similar mood when he told her about his plans to claim his legal rights and finally leave Big Bend.

Striding up to his cabin out behind the diner, Val walked into its twelve-by-sixteen-foot living space, where he put on his least-worn pair of Levis and best cowboy shirt, brushed down his hair, and wiped the dust off his bike; then, emerging into the broiling sun again, he began to pedal toward the downtown area.

His declaration of independence, he had decided, could come a little later, when his mother was less busy, and after he had enlisted Noah Carson to his cause. If all went well, this might be his last day at the diner.

Chapter 2

Val had built a bracket on his bike for his transistor radio, and riding through town he'd always turn it full blast. Some of the local merchants found this deeply annoying—especially since the disturbance was caused by a Mexican. But Val didn't care. For the past few years, he had been so anxious to escape from Big Bend, he hoped its noise-crazed citizens might eventually have him thrown out of town.

His recurring vision was of hundreds of people marching up to his cabin some dark, windy night, carrying blazing torches and an expulsion order signed by the mayor himself. The shame of such a banishment would not have bothered Val in the least. He had decided a notorious reputation was better than none at all.

But on this particular morning, nobody seemed to even notice the noise. This depressed Val; being ignored rated lower than being disliked. But as he pedaled along the elevated wooden sidewalk that ran the full five blocks of the business section of Big Bend, he spotted something that suddenly lifted his spirits.

The Palace, the only movie house in the downtown area, was advertising an upcoming picture: an auspicious event, as films usually played at the Palace until their prints fell apart. Big Bend, Texas, was Hollywood's last stop.

The upcoming picture was a western starring Randolph Scott, who, along with Humphrey Bogart and Anthony Quinn, was Val's favorite film star. Quinn had made Val's short list because the actor was born of an Irish father and a Mexican mother. That gave Val the same bloodline as the famous actor, though Val often joked that had they both been vehicles, Quinn would have been a Cadillac, and himself a motor scooter.

The western's shiny new poster was fastened in front of the theater. Val, an avid collector of such movie material, got off his bike to more closely inspect it.

When it came to stealing movie posters, Val had no scruples. This lapse of morality he had long-since justified by three reasons: first, he loved movies more than almost anything else; second, Old Man Metcalfe, who owned and operated the theater, had been pocketing most of Val's weekly allowance for as long as he could remember. The third reason was revenge.

Several years earlier, Val had been about the only kid in town ever subjected to the old man's strange spiel. Maybe he figured that Val, being half-Mexican, was just dumb enough to half-believe his stories. Metcalfe would always corner him after the Saturday matinee to squawk about how tough it'd been to make the movie Val had just seen.

Grinding what was left of his teeth, and twisting around what remained of his hair, Metcalfe would grumble about the grueling hardships and problems the film company had encountered on the movie's distant and desolate locations: the celebrated director so blind-drunk he could never tell if the camera's lens cap was on; or the movie's famous romantic team, who in reality were "faggots," and could scarcely bear to touch each other.

Val had no idea what "faggots" were, but they seemed like people he should avoid, as Metcalfe usually lumped them into the same category as "anti-Christ Commies."

And always at the end of these tirades, the old man would affect a world-weary attitude, as if providing poor little Mexicans like Val, along with the rest of America, with its best-loved form of entertainment was a soul-searing, dollar-draining job. But somebody had to do it.

Then Old Man Metcalfe would lapse into sullenness and sneak away to finish off his pint of sour mash whiskey. By then, young Val was usually so upset he could have used a drink himself.

Yet Metcalfe was his only connection to the movies, and Val wanted in the worst way to believe that because he owned and operated a theater, the old man must be associated in some way with the films that played there.

Val would stubbornly cling to the notion that Metcalfe was involved in the financing, if not the making, of most of the movies which played in his theater, even after this ridiculous idea had made him the laughingstock of his entire grade school. So when it came to Old Man Metcalfe now, Val figured he had earned more than a few of the theater's posters.

Now, staring at the Randolph Scott poster, he felt the urge to strike once again, unaware that all this while somebody was staring at him.

His friend Clarence Kendall could sometimes sneak up on him as quietly as a Black Foot Indian, a tribe not indigenous to West Texas, but rather one Val had once seen in a movie. Films were not only his favorite form of entertainment, but main source of knowledge, as well.

Val had learned about the Mexican Revolution from watching the movie "Viva Zapata" five times. Zapata himself was one of his heroes. In 1955, there weren't many Mexican role models in West Texas. Val was grateful for those he could find, even if he had to recruit them out of a movie house.

Clarence had eased his battered little Willy's pickup right behind Val. His friend's truck invariably sounded as if half its parts were on vacation, and Val would have heard its arrival even without the louder noise coming from his radio.

Then came a sound that blew everything else away. His friend had rigged the truck's horn to sound like a cavalry charge, and over the blaring bugles Clarence bellowed, "Hey, it's the poster thief—Oh God, folks, stop him before he strikes again!"

Swallowing his surprise, Val ambled over to the cab of the pickup. Clarence was his best friend, though a few folks had always wondered why. He and Val had grown up together, bonded from the beginning because they were both social outcasts.

Val was half-Mexican living in a town where "greasers" were almost as suspect as creatures from outer space. Clarence's reason was a bit more complicated.

First off, he was a little guy living in the Territory of the Tall Texan. This struck some townspeople as being downright un-American. But Clarence's image was further diminished by his greater interest in studies than sports; to some folks, this seemed almost subversive.

However, Clarence had gotten the last laugh. His grades in high school were so good he'd been granted a scholarship to the University of Texas. He planned to earn a degree in pharmacy, just as his dad had done twenty-five years earlier.

Clarence and Val had once shared three mutual interests: the first and most compelling was their fierce desire to someday get out of Big Bend. Come next September, Clarence would finally escape.

That left them with only two interests in common: watching movies and dreaming about girls both knew they would never get to date. Val did better with girls than Clarence. But only slightly, though he was a head taller, and built like a linebacker; which, along with fullback, was the position Val had played on Big Bend's perennially winless high school football team.

Val also had his mother's green eyes and wavy black hair; except for one presumed handicap, he was considered a good-looking kid. That impairment, however, created many a drawbridge that had been abruptly pulled back by the parents of almost every girl Val ever tried to date.

Though he was only half-Mexican, Val was even darker-skinned than his mother; and it sometimes seemed to him that in the eyes of the Anglo townsfolk, looking like a Mexican constituted a more serious sin than actually being one.

Clarence did better with films than with females, and had memorized much of the dialogue from John Wayne's most famous movies, even developing a passable imitation of the actor's voice; an impersonation Val usually found hilarious, as Clarence wore horned-rimmed glasses, possessed a mouthful of tiny pointed teeth, and couldn't have stood much higher than the midsection of John Wayne's stomach.

But on this particular morning, Val didn't find Clarence so funny. "Hey, one of these days I'm gonna bust your lights out, and I'm not talking about the ones on your pickup truck."

"Not if you get busted first for stealing movie posters," his little friend exclaimed, flashing a sharply chiseled smile.

Val bared his own teeth, in what he hoped was a facsimile of Humphrey Bogart. "Yeah, and I also plan to swipe that one," he growled, glancing back toward the theater. "And if anybody finds out, I'll know the name of the rat who squealed."

Clarence snickered. Val's Bogart was no better than his friend's John Wayne. Then, peering toward the poster, Clarence abruptly changed the subject. "So you still think your father used to look a little like Old Randy Scott, huh?"

"And you're gonna tell me different, even if you never even saw my dad, huh?" Val muttered, already on the defensive.

"Hey, Val, I believe you," Clarence chortled. "Just like I believe my dad looks a little like Clark Gable."

"Yeah, around the elbows, maybe," Val shot back, and was instantly sorry he had made the remark. Val liked Clarence's dad, and it was not his fault he didn't resemble the film star.

"Well, Val, you're luckier than I am," Clarence muttered, slowly reeling in his saw-toothed smile. "Having your old man dead and gone, you can make up anything about him you like, huh?"

Val held up his hands to indicate total surrender. His pal was no fun to argue with, though many a time Clarence had gone along like a good soldier on one of Val's half-baked schemes. Their misadventures had begun when he and Clarence were only in the third grade. Imagining himself a budding entrepreneur, Val had decided to go into the donut business. Having discovered that a box of six glazed donuts could be bought at the local bakery for twenty-five cents, he quickly hatched what he thought was a fool-proof scheme. If he later sold each donut for five cents, his profit margin would amount to a nickel per box. The problem, however, was his lack of capital. That's where Clarence came in.

They launched their business one wintry weekend. Stationed near the corner of the only busy intersection in Big

Bend, they began to hawk their wares. For the next few week-ends, business was brisk. They sold many donuts. Yet they failed to move into a profit position because either Clarence or Val invariably ate the last donut out of every box. Even worse, they both came down with severe colds and developed a premature case of acne.

But the donut business ranked as only a regrettable dud. Some years later Val talked his friend into a venture that proved far worse than a failure. They both had just started high school when one Saturday night, watching a newsreel at Metcalfe's movie house, Val convinced Clarence that they should hop a westbound freight train that very night. The newsreel featured a golf match out in "sunny, sultry Southern California." It was snowing hard that night in Big Bend, and they opted for an immediate change in climate.

Managing to hop the freight without killing themselves, they soon discovered that all the boxcars were locked tight. Huddled together on an open flat car, they lasted only a half-hour before the freezing wind and driving snow caused them to cancel their travel plans.

But outside a little town about twenty miles west of Big Bend, they had no sooner jumped from the train—nearly break-ing their frozen ankles—when they were grabbed by the cops. They were taken, limping, into the police station, where the cops called Val's mother to come get the humbled travelers.

The highway was snowed in, however. Clarence and Val had to spend the night in jail. Worse yet, the men's jail was filled with the usual Saturday night rowdies and drunks, so they were left to languish the entire evening in the women's cell.

There were just three women in the cell, but they were all drunk and for the rest of the night, they sat singing the same song, over and over again. "Good night, Irene, good night."

He also hated what followed that twenty-mile trip. He and Clarence were grounded for the next two months. Yet never after this, nor in the wake of any of Val's other disastrous schemes, had Clarence said, Well, I told you so, Val. Of all the jerks who gave Val the jaws, the I-told-you-so types were the hardest to swallow. He would sooner have been best pals with a convicted bank robber. Clarence, Val thought, had real character.

Now, as they stood outside Old Man Metcalfe's movie house, Clarence knew he had just won the argument about Val's father. Trying to lift Val's morale, Clarence buckled on his impression of the man he called "The Duke."

"So where you headed this morning, pilgrim?"

"Over to see Mister Carson," Val said, grateful to be off the subject of his deceased father.

Clarence tried to appear unimpressed. But his friend's curiosity had been piqued. It seemed stupid not to stretch out the suspense.

"And just what might your business be with this illustrious personage?"

"No special reason. Just smart to check every now and then with your legal counsel, that's all."

"Play your cards close to the vest, don't you, pilgrim?"

Clarence was still trying to talk like John Wayne, but his curiosity had eroded the imitation. He sounded more like an old man who had just dropped his dentures.

"Well, come on, Val," he finally grumbled. "Hop aboard, I'll get you over to Carson's office in style." Val swung his bike into the back of the pickup, then climbed in after it.

But no sooner did his feet find the floor when Clarence went wheeling into a tight turn that almost sent Val flying off into space. A few hair-raising seconds later, they slammed to a stop in front of a two-story brick building that sat almost directly across the street from the theater. They had travelled less than a hundred feet, yet it felt to Val more like a mile over a deeply rutted road.

Climbing down from the truck, Val nodded to a group of old, frozen-faced men, and started up the flight of steps that led to Noah Carson's office. Always when Val came to Carson's office, he saw that same group of men, leaning back in their rickety chairs, silently chewing their tobacco, grimly staring off at nothing in particular.

The sight invariably made Val's blood run cold. Unless he could someday escape from Big Bend, Val was sure he'd eventually become part of another such group of empty-eyed old men, wondering how the bus out of town could have left him behind.

A welcome scene suddenly flashed through Val's mind: though he had neared the top of the steps, he saw himself standing back down on the ground. Another guy about his same age and size had started up the stairs: an Anglo, dressed in old frontier clothes, with a brace of six-shooters strapped across his chest.

Then, just as this young man reached the top of the steps, several shots rang out. Val saw him wheel around, grasp his side, and stumble dangerously close to the wooden guardrail.

Suddenly a dyspeptic-looking movie director screamed, "Cut!" Everything froze as still as a photograph. "Okay, get the Mexican stuntman in there," the director snarled. Several people in the cast and crew glanced at Val with pity. Good luck, kid, they seemed to say. Hope you got your insurance paid up.

Hurrying to the top of the stairs, Val moved next to the young actor, and assumed his exact position. When he had done so, the actor clapped him on the shoulder and said, "Better make me look good, Pancho."

Glancing down to make sure the air mattresses were properly placed, Val girded himself for the long fall to the ground. But at that point in his daydream, the lawyer Noah Carson broke through the crowd and yelled, "Hey, stop that Mexican kid. He's going to get himself killed!"

Chapter 3

Noah Carson was the most mysterious man Val had ever known. Five times Carson had argued cases before the Texas Supreme Court and whipped the high-powered, big-city attorneys opposing him. Yet for reasons no one could understand, Carson had chosen to practice law in a town which didn't deserve his talent. Moreover, Carson's integrity wasn't for sale—and God help the poor fool who ever thought otherwise.

Carson's face perfectly matched his character. Val thought his features could have come right off Mount Rushmore: long jaw, a flowing frontier mustache and a forehead that went on forever. His dark blue eyes were kind, resigned and knowing, the eyes of a poet; and not at all similar to the cold, shifty eyes of other attorneys Val had seen around town.

Carson had taught Val how to play an expert game of poker and blackjack, skills the lawyer considered indispensable. Carson was also a master at another game: staying single. As far as Val knew, Carson had never married, though he did occasionally go out with a few of the local ladies, all of whom seemed obsessed with changing his marital status. They would have better luck, Val thought, trying to best him in a court of law.

Val's mother also was fond of Carson. He had once nicknamed her "*Señora* Spitfire" and often joked that he was going to get her elected sheriff—so together they could clean the varmints out of City Hall.

But after Lupe married Floyd, Carson didn't come around anymore. Yet that didn't alter Lupe's opinion of him, nor keep her from continuing to quote him as if he were some sort of walking encyclopedia. Even Val's stepfather, who usually ladled out compliments with a very small spoon, often said that Carson was shrewder than any three men he had ever met.

Yet Floyd, along with a lot of other people, could never figure out why Carson had chosen to bury himself in Big Bend. Often Val had amused himself by dreaming up scenarios about why Carson never saw fit to live in a much bigger, more interesting place. Maybe he was hiding out from somebody or running away from an unspeakable scandal. But whatever his reason for staying in the arid wasteland of West Texas, it made for an intriguing mystery in a town where the lives of almost everyone else read like the pages of a third-grade primer.

That morning, Val and Clarence had been ushered into Carson's private office by his secretary and only employee. Miss Violet was a cranky old lady, with hair the texture of a steel brush, and a badly painted mouth that almost always had a cigarette dangling from its left edge. Miss Violet had worked for Carson since almost the first day he came to town.

Before that, she'd been a court reporter, and before that, well, one could use up an awful lot of prepositions in reviewing her long career. Some joker around the courthouse liked to say that she once belonged to the Lost Tribe of Israel, and had finally chosen to live out her later years in rocky terrain much like that of her original homeland.

Carson's office sat at the back of the building. From there one had a better view of the surrounding countryside, such as it was. A trillion tons of sand, framed by barren plains and purple-hued mountains that resembled monstrously large mice.

The office was cluttered with memorabilia of the Old West, including dozens of grainy photographs taken back before the turn of the century. Carson often joked that he'd been born into the wrong century. That gave him and Val something almost in common. Sometimes Val felt he'd been born in the wrong country.

"Grab yourself a seat, Val," Carson called over from the small adjoining bathroom that also served as his kitchen. "Been expecting you all morning."

Carson came in carrying a steaming cup of coffee, which he laid down between his small marble statuettes of Abraham Lincoln and Clarence Darrow. They were the two big heroes in his life, and he had told Val dozens of stories about them. Val admired these legendary men for many reasons; partly because, as he had joked to Carson, they'd once had guts enough to leave their own hometowns.

"Thank you kindly, Miss Violet," Carson said sweetly to the old woman, indicating she could return to whatever she'd been doing. But Miss Violet didn't receive the signal. She kept fluttering around the cramped little room like a caged canary. Then she suddenly snapped her head back as if she'd just remembered something.

Muttering to herself, she charged off into an adjoining room which Carson laughingly referred to as his "waiting area," though usually the only person who ever did any waiting there was Miss Violet. Despite his reputation, Carson had a less than flourishing practice. He only took cases that interested him, and most of those involved clients with little or no money. Every Mexican in town carried Carson's card in his pocket.

After the old lady closed the door behind her, Val turned and shook hands with Carson.

"Oh, and this here, sir, is my friend Clarence Kendall. He drove me over this morning," Val muttered, trying to justify the presence of his pal.

"Nice to meet you, Clarence," Carson said, smiling as he leaned across the desk to shake hands. "I know your daddy real well. He's my local cough medicine connection."

Clarence nodded politely, then shot Val a nervous glance.

Carson chuckled. "Well, sit down, boys. Stop acting as if you're here to get your teeth drilled."

They sat down. But the move didn't seem to make Clarence any more comfortable. Probably because of Carson's teeth-drilling remark. Val's best friend was as sensitive about his pointed incisors as Val was about his long-lost father.

As Carson began to thumb through the small stack of files on his desk, Val made a feeble attempt to break the ice. "Clarence thinks his father looks like that movie star, Clark Gable."

26

Carson, managing to grin, said, "Well, Val, everybody's got the right to think what they want about their old man... which gets me around to why I asked you to come see me today."

Finding the file he wanted, Carson took from it a piece of paper. Handing it to Val, he turned to sweeten his coffee with a shot of brandy.

He had given Val a cashier's check, and what immediately nailed his eye were the numbers on it. "Two thousand and eight hundred dollars and fifteen cents, huh?" Val muttered, acting as if he dealt with such lofty figures every day of the week.

Carson grinned. "Read the rest of it, son. It gets better."

Val started to stammer. "Hey, this thing is made out to me! What's the catch, Mister Carson?"

Rising from his tattered leather chair, Carson turned to stare out the window. His words, when they finally came, seemed chosen with great care.

"Well, Val, your father, just before he... died, set up a little trust fund for you. Originally, it was a thousand dollars. What you're holding in your hand there is what it's matured to over the course of your first eighteen years."

Suddenly Val felt a little giddy; and unable to think of a single thing to say, he handed the check to Clarence, who gawked at him as if he'd just become a movie star himself.

"You never knew my father real well, did you, sir?" Val asked.

Carson frowned and added another slug of brandy to his coffee. Taking a sip, he started to straighten out the mess on top of his desk, something Val had never seen him do before. The cluttered old maple desk was one of the many things Miss Violet was always muttering about, but rarely did anything to fix. Probably afraid, Val figured, something might reach out and bite her.

"No, Val, I scarcely knew your father," he murmured. "He came into my office just that one time to set up your trust fund, and then, couple of weeks later... there was that oil field explosion out around Pampa, which—"

"I thought he was killed in Midland," Val said, eyeing him suspiciously.

Carson winced. "Oh, yeah, that's right. But it was a long time ago, and I'm a little hazy on the details now." Then, with a sheepish smile, he added, "Or maybe just getting a mite sluggish between the ears. This town'll do that to you."

Carson's voice trailed off. For a long moment the office went completely quiet, except for the soft sound of coughing coming from the other room. Everybody knew that Miss Violet smoked too much. But Carson never said anything to her about it. He once told Val that most people usually find a way to punish themselves, and almost always for the wrong reasons.

Occasionally, Carson had implied that Val suffered from a similar malady. He thought Val was embarrassed about being a Mexican. But Carson had said that with luck Val might someday realize that his heritage was an honorable one, a source of strength, not shame. This was, however, a subject Val never cared to discuss at any length.

"Well, Val, guess you hit the jackpot," Clarence finally declared, handing him back the cashier's check. "You been yapping for years about someday deserting this dump. Now you have the price of the ticket."

That was Val's cue to open up a discussion about his travel plans with hopes of enlisting Carson's aid in convincing his mother to let him go. He creased the check and put it into his shirt pocket.

"Don't hurt to fold it, does it, sir?"

Carson laughed and shook his head. "No, boy, the numbers on it stay the same. But just to see that they do, let's go set up a bank account for you. Then rather than your paying me my standard fee, you can buy me a cup of coffee somewhere, huh?"

"Yessir," Val exclaimed, relieved that Carson seemed himself again. "But I sure owe you a lot more'n a cup of coffee."

Carson's expression grew wistful. Coming from around his desk, he started toward Val. Some instinct told Val to stand up.

"All right, son, I'll tell you what else you can do for me," Carson quietly declared, his blue eyes snaring Val's undivided attention. "Use some of this money to enroll in our local junior college this coming fall semester. A good education could be your real ticket out of this town."

Earlier that morning, Val's mother had said much the same thing. But coming from Carson, the suggestion posed a double dilemma. Of the few people Val hated to disappoint, Carson topped his short list. But Val had barely managed to graduate from high school, and was not anxious to prolong the agony by pursuing a higher education.

Besides, what he thought important to learn was not taught in the local junior college; and what he hoped to experience could only be done many miles west of Big Bend.

"Well, I'm thinking about going out to California, get me a job—"

"Doing what?" Carson snapped. "Waiting on tables? Hell, you can do that right here in Big Bend!"

"Geez, Mister Carson, I was sorta hoping you might help me talk my mother into—"

"Forget it, Val," Carson said. "I only take cases whose causes I believe in. You get a good education first, then I'll help you go to Mars, if that's where you think you want to work."

Val stood pawing at the worn carpet. Carson's expression turned solemn. He had offered what he thought was good advice. But Carson was not the type to push his opinion on anyone. Either you were smart enough to heed it, or you weren't. Val knew that he fell into the latter category.

Then Carson, putting his arm around Val, gently steered him toward the door. They had just about passed through Miss Violet's cubicle when she indicated with a grunt that they had forgotten something.

Clarence was still sitting in Carson's office. He looked rather dazed by the dazzling change in Val's financial status. Noting his muddled condition, Val laughed. But he soon lost his smile. The best lawyer in West Texas had refused to take his case. Val would have to make the plea to his mother alone.

Chapter 4

By eleven o'clock that morning, Val had deposited his check, opened up his first bank account, and coffeed Noah Carson to capacity. All three occasions, however, failed to cheer Val up. He still worried that his financial windfall might prove the beginning of an emotional hurricane.

After saying goodbye to Noah Carson, he hitched a ride with Clarence back to the cafe. But when they got there, Val was in no hurry to get out of the truck. He dreaded what his mother would say and do when he announced his plans to leave Big Bend.

Over the past two years, Val had saved up almost a hundred dollars; enough, he thought, to get him to California, though probably not sufficient to keep him housed and fed until he could nail down a job. But now money was no longer a problem. If he had ever been looking for a good reason to back out, he had lost his last excuse.

Val sat staring at the diner. Clarence was quick to pick up on his wary mood. "You know, Val, they say when you leave your hometown and then come back, everything seems a lot smaller," Clarence quietly observed. "But what about after coming into a big pile of money?"

"No, diner still looks like the same old dump. But I'd sure like to test out that first theory of yours," Val said, climbing out of the pickup. "How'd you like to come along, all expenses paid, when I do?"

Clarence smacked his horn. "Yahoo," he exclaimed, over the bugle call of the Seventh Cavalry. "Hey, like the song says: 'If you got the money, honey, I got the time!'"

Feigning a smile, Val reached into the bed of the truck to lift out his bike. But when he turned back to the diner, it did indeed suddenly look a little different to him. Not any smaller, but now rather mysterious in a way he'd never noticed before; like a tomb of sorts, only where secrets, rather than bodies, might be buried.

"Hey, what's the biggest lie anybody ever told you?"

The question just popped out of Val's mouth. He knew it had also surprised Clarence; for a change his friend had to think before answering.

"Biggest lie? Oh, some silly little twit in my science class once told me I was kinda homely. Of course, I suggested she buy herself a new pair of glasses."

Val snorted something in Spanish. There seemed little sense in trying to make serious conversation with Clarence when he was in one of his self-satisfied moods. Instead, Val thanked him for the ride, and trudged off toward the diner. Clarence called in the cavalry for one final charge, then went spraying gravel back toward the highway.

Inside the L-shaped, red, white, and green diner, the late-morning lull that always preceded the noontime rush was in full slumber. An old Mexican man was sitting off in one corner, solemnly nursing a cup of coffee.

Val called over to him. "*¡Hola, Señor Salazar! ¿Como va la lucha?*"

"*Aiii, Val, todavía hablas español como un gringo,*" the man answered, laughing. Val nodded sheepishly. Every time the little Mexican came to the cafe, he teased Val about his Spanish.

For the past five years, Lidio Salazar had been supplying the restaurant with its produce, often trucking it in from as far away as thirty miles. Lupe paid handsomely for this service, but Salazar's fruit and vegetables were always choice. Still, Floyd often grumbled that it was a needless expense. Val, though no expert on arithmetic, had to agree.

Lupe finally admitted her real reason for doing business with the elderly Mexican. Lidio Salazar, it seemed, looked a bit like her father. That didn't seem sufficient cause to Floyd, but at the time Val had understood his mother's attitude.

Val had been named after his grandfather, but never got the chance to meet him. But Lupe had told Val that Valentín Santana was a fine man and a good father. He had died before Val was born.

The truth had come out, however, during one of Lupe's recent bouts with a bottle of wine. Many years earlier, Lupe and her motherless family had migrated from Chihuahua City up to south Texas in search of work. But the Depression had humbled the Rio Grande Valley; what little work that existed paid only fifty cents a day. Lupe's father, hard-pressed for another way to make money, soon realized that his oldest daughter was one of his few assets. Lupe was only fifteen, but already her face and figure were drawing admiring attention.

Valentín, desperate to keep his younger children clothed and fed, put Lupe up for marriage. But her prospective husband, a well-to-do widower, was old enough to be her grandfather. When Lupe balked at the arrangement, her father threw her out of the cardboard shack they were living in.

Soon after that scarring event, her father heard that there was still fruit-picking work available in California. When he and his other children migrated westward, he left Lupe behind like an abandoned dog. Telling Val this part of her story, Lupe's voice had choked with shame.

For the next few years, she remained in south Texas, working at whatever job she could scrounge. Finally, saving what she hoped was enough to get her to California, Lupe set off to rejoin her family, though she had no exact idea where they were living.

But Lupe had miscalculated. She only made it to West Texas before her money ran out. Big Bend was as close to California as she ever got. Lupe never saw any of her family members again, though she later learned that her father died a few years after the family had settled somewhere in the San Joaquin Valley.

Yet until very recently, Lupe had always bragged that her father was a wise, warm-hearted man; the Mexican equivalent, Val supposed, of the hero of the popular TV series, "Father Knows Best." When Val learned the truth, he could not understand why she had named him after a man who left her behind like a sack of discarded clothing.

Val nodded at Lidio Salazar and took a seat at the counter. His mother had heard the bell over the front door, and as she came out of the kitchen, he quickly propped a menu card up in front of his face.

"Good morning, *Señora*," Val muttered, from behind the card. "What do you recommend today?"

He knew the question was one his mother loved to hear. It always gave her the chance to proudly reply, Everything! But on this particular morning, Lupe didn't seem in the mood to go along with his little game.

"What I recommending," she said, lifting away his makeshift mask, "is you to tell me *exactamente* what can you now afford."

Frowning, Val reached into his pocket for the bank deposit slip. Whenever his mother used the word 'exactly,' that was precisely what she meant. Handing her the bank slip, Val slid down a couple of seats to check out the cherry pie cooling on the counter. As he cut off a piece, Lupe stared at the deposit slip. When she finally looked up, she had tears in her eyes.

Val thought the emotion must have surprised her, for she suddenly seemed annoyed with herself. Turning away, Lupe walked over to the sink where she began to scrub some skillets he had already cleaned earlier that morning.

Now that her back was turned, Val quickly sliced off another piece of pie. After wolfing down half of it with only a couple of bites, he felt a little better. It was finally time to announce his immediate plans.

"Gonna use some of that money to take a little trip."

"Oh, yes?" Lupe quietly said. He could almost feel the frost in her voice.

"Los Angeles, probably. Gonna try and get a job out there."

His pronouncement carried over to the kitchen. Out of the corner of his eye, Val saw Floyd come up to the partition. But from where Lupe stood, she couldn't see him. She would have been surprised to see him smiling. On Floyd's face, a smile was nearly as rare a sight as a Mexican in Big Bend. Val assumed that

Floyd approved of his travel plans, and couldn't wait to unplug the jukebox.

Lupe, however, was nursing another notion. *"No, Val, tu padre te dejo ese dinero para que podrias entrar al colegio aquí en Big Bend."*

Val tried not to groan. It seemed everybody wanted him to go to the local junior college; yet no one had ever offered a single suggestion as to what he ought to major in, once he got there. His grades in high school had stunk in every subject but physical education; such a major, however, could only lead to a career in coaching, and forever doom him, he thought, to the sidelines as his life went whizzing toward its eventual demise.

"Yeah, this local junior college idea is like a virus that's going around," he grumbled. "But I'm not catching it myself. I'm going to California, Mom. Maybe I shoulda given you more advance notice, but now you gotta find yourself another waiter."

Lupe turned to glower at him. "You going nowhere but to the college here—unless you want to be a waiter for the rest of your life!"

Val sighed. Then, hoping to put his mother on the defensive, he said, "And hey, didn't you tell me my father was killed up in Midland?"

"Fue precisamente donde paso," Lupe growled. *"¡Y te he dicho eso mil veces!* Your father was killed to save the life of some other men... and you hear something else, you talking to the wrong people!"

The harshness in her voice startled Val. Glancing over at Floyd, he saw his stepfather's smile erode into a frown. Val knew Floyd was awfully tired of hearing about Frank Cooper's heroic death, and couldn't care less where it had happened.

Val turned back to his mother. "Then why did Mister Carson say Dad was killed in Pampa? Old Noah doesn't make mistakes—"

Lupe wheeled around so fast, some of the water in the sink sloshed out. *"Y piensas, Valentín, que te he dicho mentiras por todo este tiempo?"*

Whether she'd been lying to him for all these years seemed a fair question. But one Lupe apparently didn't want Val to answer. Throwing her sponge into the sink water, she stomped off toward the kitchen, her parting words trailing behind her like an echo.

"Damn you, *hijo*, just because it your birthday, you think now you say and do what you want? What getting into you today?"

Whatever it was, the thing was suddenly chewing away at Val like an ulcer. He sat glumly eating his pie. Maybe a little more food would settle his stomach. Then, looking up, he saw Floyd still standing just beyond the partition. He stared at Val for a few seconds, then slowly shook his head.

➤➤ ◄◄

About five o'clock that afternoon, after Val had finished his chores for the day, a windstorm came howling down from the north. Whenever the wind really began to whine, people always rushed inside to escape its snarling path. During a sandstorm, Big Bend looked like a ghost town, as tumbleweeds tall as full-grown men came darting across the desert. Val thought they looked like creatures from another planet, though why they would choose to settle in such a lousy locale was something out of a scenario even he couldn't envision.

Now he imagined the tumbleweeds trundling through the center of town, whirling toward Old Man Metcalfe's theater, where a few of them finally nestled right next to the new movie poster. Val hoped they wouldn't scratch the poster too badly before he had the chance to steal it.

Thinking about movies usually helped Val relax. He needed a little relaxation now. He had spent the past few hours cleaning up the restrooms in the other cabins, and still awaiting him was his job at a drive-in theater; a job that already had begun to seem crummier. Clarence was right. Things were looking different since he'd come into money.

The sun had slid off behind the mountains, its reddish light hanging over the horizon like a strip of neon. When Val finally tired of staring at it, he drifted over to his cabin, planning to grab a little nap.

But instead, he lay on his bed, peering at all the movie posters he had swiped from Metcalfe's theater. Val's favorites were from "The Treasure of the Sierra Madre" and "Viva Zapata." He had never been able to steal a poster, however, from the movie he loved best of all, a Humphrey Bogart picture called "Sahara." Val had seen the film seven times and had memorized every line of dialogue.

In the movie, Bogart played a tank sergeant who along with a handful of other men holds off a large group of Germans from getting to a water well. The scene Val liked best came when an American soldier, whom Bogart sends for help, finally loses his way in the desert. Out of food, fuel, and water, he begins to crawl up a huge dune, as the sand comes spilling down past his face.

Val admired this scene so much that whenever he and his girlfriend Bonnie went out on picnics, he often re-enacted it for her. But his performance never impressed Bonnie, and she was always annoyed that he'd gotten so much sand in his mouth.

Now, Val lay wondering why it was that he so yearned to someday become part of the world of movie-making, even if he never became anything more than the guy who carried around the coffee tray.

It seemed simple now. Movies were less complicated than real life. They had a beginning, middle, and an end; and at the finale all three parts fulfilled a dramatic purpose. Better yet, the good guys usually won—and sometimes they were even Mexicans.

Beyond that, however, movies possessed a pull so strong and personal, Val had never discussed it with anyone. Not even with Clarence. Already Val had sensed that he would probably never get married, what with traveling to distant film locations, and all; he might never have children either. The responsibility of having a wife and children could only slow him down.

There would be no one he could leave behind; little or no human trace that he had ever lived. Yet if he was involved in the making of just one movie, and had done his own small job well, there would always be that film showing somewhere in the world. Perennial proof he had once existed.

His first eighteen years would certainly leave behind no lasting legacy. All he could claim with any pride was that he had played first-string fullback for two years on his high school football team. But the achievement was badly marred by the team's record over those two years: two wins, sixteen losses.

During that same period, Val's girlfriend, Bonnie, had been the captain of the cheerleading squad, though many people thought, since she was the least comely of the cheerleaders, that she had won the position only because of her family's influence.

Thinking about Bonnie made Val dwell again on the family he probably would never have. Sometimes it saddened him that he might never have children.

He turned to stare at the little photograph on the stand next to his bed. The picture was of his father, holding him in his arms: the only photo of him Val had ever seen. Lupe had taken it just a few weeks after he'd been born. His father, standing out in front of the diner, wore a dazed look on his handsome face. The picture had blurred over the years; yet it was Val's most prized possession, and about the only proof he had that there had ever really existed a man named Frank Cooper.

» PART TWO «

Chapter 5

Frank Cooper's Cadillac convertible streaked through the barren foothills along the western edge of the state of Nevada. With the dying sun in his face, Cooper was squinting, his features set like granite.

The convertible was painted sky-blue, and its top was down, as Cooper hardly ever put it up. He was a man people liked to look at, and he liked for them to look. Cooper prided himself on being so well preserved. He stood a ramrod-straight six feet, and was still swift for his age, which was fifty-five.

That afternoon, he was wearing one of his expensive custom-cut western suits, with a coffee-colored, fifty-dollar Stetson sitting on the back of his head, tucked tight around his short-cropped graying hair.

But there was more to his appearance than just handsome features, a lithe build, and fancy clothes. Something in his dusky blue eyes and caramel-coated voice fascinated both men and women. Cooper wore the enigmatic look of a man who had won just about every game he'd ever played, yet in the process had somehow lost something precious.

Back in that summer of 1955, Reno, Nevada looked like a movie set. Coming into the town under a sign that read: "RENO—The Biggest Little City in the World," Cooper pulled his Cadillac to a stop under the portico of the glitziest gambling casinos in the downtown section of Reno. A young valet hurried toward him. Cooper was always good for a sizable tip.

"Hey, how goes the battle, Mr. Cooper?" the slick-haired parking valet inquired, opening the door of the convertible.

"Too early to tell, Billy," Cooper drawled, climbing out of the car. "First, let's see if I can sneak past that orangutan they got guarding the front gate."

The young valet smiled. Cooper's reputation was well-known in Reno. Handing the valet a five-dollar bill, he started for the casino's main door. "Get George spruced up, will ya, Billy?"

Nodding, the valet patted the hood of the car. 'George' was Cooper's pet name for his convertible.

The burly doorman saw Cooper coming, and quickly positioned his ape-like bulk directly in his path. "Now Mr. Cooper, you know I got orders to keep you outta here," the large man grunted.

Cooper reached toward the breast pocket of his coat. "Hey, King Kong, you saying I can't give your clip joint here first crack at all the horse-racing money I just made?" he asked with a careful smile.

The smile was too small to register. The doorman's eyes were riveted on whatever Cooper was slowly pulling out of his pocket. The doorman looked sheepish when he saw it was only a pack of Spearmint chewing gum. Then he saw the fifty-dollar bill tucked inside the pack.

"Hey, Kong, I hear gorillas like chewing gum. Here, keep the pack," Cooper said, holding the package of gum just out of the doorman's sizable reach. Finally, flashing a gap-toothed grin, the big man mumbled, "Well, just steer clear of the blackjack tables, okay?"

"Same old story," Cooper drawled, between chomps of chewing gum. "Casino don't mind me gambling, just so long as it ain't at any game I can win, huh?"

The doorman bared a shameless smile. Cooper had correctly called the situation. For years, he had been barred from playing blackjack in every gambling establishment in the entire state of Nevada. The casinos would have rather seen an outbreak of the bubonic plague than allow onto their premises a "counter," that being anyone who could count cards so fast that the odds usually tilted slightly in their favor.

Cooper considered this policy an illegal restraint of free trade, as well as a clear-cut violation of his constitutional rights. But by now he had made his peace with the restriction; besides, he had long ago discovered various ways of worming around it.

But a few of his methods were well-known around Reno, and no sooner had Cooper walked into the casino when the doorman walked over to an extension phone. He had standing orders to alert his bosses whenever Cooper came within so much as fifty yards of one of the blackjack tables.

Cooper knew this, and now decided to have himself a little fun. Striding past the blackjack tables, each stacked high with hundred-dollar chips, Cooper gave the dealers a curt nod and a steely smile. Then he took in a deep breath of the cigarette and sweat-fouled atmosphere. The stale air and the raucous ambience was like pure oxygen to him.

A few hours later, the casino was really humming, and so was Cooper. He was on a hot streak at a crap table, and whenever he really ignited—especially with a few bourbons under his belt— he could put on a show better than the one billed out on the marquee. But more than anything else, it was his winning streak that had drawn the crowd toward his table; the more he won, the closer they came.

One of the many people watching him that night was Blue Morgan. For years, Blue had been hearing stories about Cooper, but prior to that evening she had never seen him in action. Blue had lived in Reno for almost twenty years; what little she didn't know about gamblers, she probably had once known but elected to forget.

That evening she stood in the mob packed around Cooper for better than an hour, but was unable to catch his attention. Blue was not that easy to overlook, with her honey-blonde hair, light green eyes, perfect features, and a voluptuous figure that could have slowed down a troop train. Her addiction to milk, however, had added a few unwanted pounds to the wrong places.

But whenever Cooper gambled, he rarely had eyes for anyone but Lady Luck. That particular evening his good fortune stuck with him for several hours. When it finally dumped him, however, it came about in a way that seemed to signify, to Blue at least, more than simply a reversal of fortune.

Blue was watching the action from a little balcony nearby, relaxing "between engagements," as she coyly termed it, when she noticed the ominous early-warning signals of Cooper's eventual fall. He was still winning, but didn't look to be enjoying it anymore. Then Cooper began to lose; first a little, then a lot. And the more he lost, the more feverish he seemed to become. Blue had seen that frenzied look before on the faces of many other compulsive gamblers.

A good gambler, once his luck sours, will usually cut short his play, or move to another table. Sometimes even switch to a different game. Yet Cooper went on playing the same game at the same table, hour after hour; and the more he lost, the bigger he bet.

Blue noticed another thing that night. There was something ineffably sad about Cooper, a melancholic air his free-wheeling style could not completely mask; he looked like a man who had paid for his independence with something he knew he could never replace. This made him all the more attractive to her.

Then a very tall, bearded man strolled over to invite Blue up to his room for a drink. She was well-known in Reno as a "paid companion," but she had honed her services into an art form that rarely if ever involved sex.

Instead, Blue's stock in trade was a beautiful face and body, a bouyant personality, a profound understanding of gamblers, and a reputation for bringing them luck. Men liked to be seen in her company, and paid well for the privilege.

By now, Blue had given up trying to attract Cooper's attention, so she went with the stern-looking stranger, lugging along the glass of milk she'd been sipping for the past hour. For years Blue had been nursing an ulcer.

As she left the gaming room that night, all that really troubled her was that she'd lost an opportunity to finally meet the man most of the gambling crowd considered a legend, as well as a bastard.

≫ ≪

The modest morning light was just creeping through the lobby of the casino's hotel when Blue stepped out of the elevator. She stopped the moment she saw Cooper. He was coming from the main desk, walking toward her. Blue eased back into the elevator, and hurriedly decided on a plan of attack. She was freshening up her lipstick when Cooper strode into the elevator.

He nodded politely, then turned away. Blue frowned, figuring she hadn't made much of a dent in his defenses. There was only one other person in the elevator, a mousy little man with no more hair on his head than Cooper had in his mustache.

The man had come down in the elevator. But when the door opened onto the lobby, he suddenly appeared to have decided it might be safer to stay inside. Blue flashed him a reassuring smile, figuring he'd been dazed by drink or disaster.

Cooper, standing near the selection panel, politely asked the man what floor he wanted. The mousy guy's face shrunk with a worried frown. He hesitated, as if wanting to weigh the question more carefully before committing himself.

"I think he's just along for the ride," Blue whispered. "But if you'd be so kind, my floor number is eleven."

"Lucky number," Cooper chuckled. "The first roll, anyway."

Blue gave Cooper's line a larger laugh than it deserved. She had only eleven floors to make her pitch. But elevators usually gave Blue a case of lockjaw. She had seen this happen to other people, as well. They sometimes grew as quiet as if they were strapped inside a gas chamber, just waiting for the first deadly pellet to drop. Maybe, like Blue, they were simply waiting for the elevator itself to fall.

It took Blue a couple of floors before she finally turned to face Cooper. Looking over the head of the dazed little gent standing between them, she playfully chirped, "So how'd you do last night, Mr. Cooper?"

Cooper was thinking about the same thing himself. Turning toward her, he peered past the glistening head between him and Blue, and studied her for a few seconds. Cooper often peered at people as if they were a painting he was thinking of buying.

"I'm sorry, ma'am. Have we met before?" he politely asked.

"No, not yet, not formally at least," Blue said. "Well, we coulda met last night at the crap table, but you was courting old Lady Luck something fierce, and I didn't wanna confuse the issue—which is, uh, usually my speciality." Over the years, Blue had learned how to play dumber than she actually was. Smart women made most gamblers uncomfortable.

Cooper grinned, but his eyes made obvious that Blue's market value was not rising with each passing floor. His frigid expression made her uneasy.

"Anyway, you was sure winning big when I left your table," she gushed. This was a smart fib. She knew gamblers didn't like to be reminded of their bad luck. Blue also knew that the stock answer which might come next would give her a natural opening.

"Oh, hell, honey, why didn't you take me with you when you left?" Cooper muttered. "Coulda saved me a mountain of money."

Blue had been given her opening, and she was about as shy as a fullback in taking advantage of it. "Hey, cowboy, 'better late than never' is my motto... That is, if you still have any pocket change left over from last night. My conversation and company don't come cheap."

Cooper still had plenty of money left. Only he didn't seem crazy about spending any on something that ordinarily cost him no more than the price of a drink.

"Yeah, still got a bit of loose change," he grumbled. "But not near enough, I'm afraid, to afford a top-of-the-line model like yourself."

Blue glanced at the elevator's indicator. They were coming up to the eleventh floor. Time to fire off her best shot. Giving Cooper a mock-seductive stare, she fell back on what she hoped sounded like an imitation of Mae West.

"Yeah, cowboy, but if you was to smile a little more, might qualify for my early-bird discount."

Cooper looked as if he thought she sounded more like Groucho Marx than Mae West. In any case, he didn't seem interested in just a discount. Anything less than what the casinos called a "full comp" was apparently not his idea of a bargain.

The elevator stopped at the eleventh floor. Coming forward, Blue glanced at Cooper. It didn't appear as if he would change his mind. Masking her frustration, Blue smiled, shrugged her well-tanned shoulders, and started out the door. But she had sashayed no more than ten feet out of the elevator when she heard a voice.

"But say, you take personal checks?" Cooper asked.

Stifling a smile, Blue wheeled around, expecting to see him coming out after her. But from her angle, all she could see was the little guy. He had a silly smirk plastered across his perspiring face, as if he was longing for a breakthrough in the negotiations. Blue hoped his attitude was contagious.

"And would this here personal check be worth any more than the paper it's written on?" Blue sweetly inquired, trying hard not to sound like a banker; but she had heard stories about ladies so dumb they had amassed enough worthless checks to wallpaper the bathroom of their apartments in a furnishing style that could have been called "Early Insufficient Funds."

"Would my check be bankable, you mean?"

"That's exactly what I mean, cowboy," Blue retorted.

"Well... before last night, it woulda been. But now, I ain't so sure."

Blue chuckled. She was a sucker for an honest answer, and Cooper's forthright reply had seemingly turned up his cards. "Well, do you at least have a room? You know, something with the standard number of walls around it?" she asked, thinking again how close her calling sometimes came to social work.

Blue saw a large room key dangling from its holder come into view. Smiling, she started back toward the elevator. "Well, okay. Maybe we'll change each other's luck, huh?"

"Honey, I think mine just did," Cooper drawled, chuckling.

Then Blue noticed something down the hall that made her hurry her step. A few doors away from the elevator, a man had lurched out of a room. His black suit looked as if he'd slept in it. He saw Blue, which did not seem to delight him. He was the same man who hours earlier had invited her up to his room for a drink and whatever else he hoped went with it.

The elevator was just closing when his voice boomed out: "Hey, hold that thing!"

Cooper obligingly caught the door with his hand. Blue shrunk back and tried to position herself behind the bald-headed little man, who was now avidly following the situation.

A moment later, the tall man in the rumpled black suit came into view. He had a thick, gray-flecked beard and an air of self-righteousness so strong it almost stank. When Blue had first met him that night, she thought he might have once been a preacher from the Bible belt.

Blue stared down at her fingernails. "Hey, mister, you got drunk and passed out," she murmured in the direction of her fingers. "What was I supposed to do, sit around till you sobered up, just so's you could get your nickle's worth?"

"That's exactly what you shoulda done," the man sneered. "Anyway I'm wide awake now... And I bought your company for the entire evening, remember?"

Blue remembered all right, but she wasn't that keen on reviewing the arrangement in front of Cooper, who was watching intently as the little drama unfolded. He appeared undecided as to who was the antagonist in the piece. Only when the bearded man moved menacingly into the elevator did Cooper come off the fence.

"Say, now hold on there, mister," Cooper said, tapping the preacher on the shoulder. But the man kept coming, his bloodshot eyes fastened on Blue like grappling hooks.

"Butt outta this, pig farmer," he growled to Cooper. "This is just between me and the little hustler."

Cooper tapped the tall man on the shoulder again. "You're wrong about that, mister. You see, this little gal you called a hustler happens to be my wife."

The preacher took only a moment to recover. "Hey, I don't give a damn if she's your mother! She's gonna give me what I paid for. Or else..."

At this point, the bald-headed little man, apparently having decided that the elevator was too crowded, made a speedy exit.

Then the tall man in the wrinkled serge suit grabbed hold of Blue's blonde hair and tugged her toward the exit. Cooper quickly punched the button to close the door.

Moments later, the elevator arrived at Cooper's floor. But when the door opened, the preacher seemed nowhere in sight. Blue was leaning against Cooper.

The tears in her eyes had smeared her mascara. She looked as if she'd just witnessed a near-fatal car crash. "Geez, Mister Cooper, sorry you had to get involved in all this... Don't know how I'm gonna make it up to you."

"Oh, I got an idea or two about that," Cooper said, gently wiping Blue's mascara with his hankerchief. "Besides, once I told the bastard you was my wife, I had to defend both your honor as well as mine. Right?" Blue smiled and blew her nose with the hankerchief. After she had done so, Cooper led her out of the elevator. The man in the black rumpled suit was asleep again, this time down on the floor in the far corner of the elevator.

Chapter 6

Blue Morgan grew up in the small town of Hutchinson, Kansas. She lost her father at an early age. He had driven to Topeka one day to try and find work. But whatever he finally found, it was enough to keep him there. He never came home.

A while later, Blue's mother seemed to leave home as well. She dropped into a deep depression that lasted for a couple of years. Then came a startling change that seemed to Blue almost as frightening as what it had replaced.

Back in the 1920s, Hutchinson sat right in the middle of the religious revival belt. When the show hit town one summer, Blue's mother was revived with a vengeance. She began to memorize entire passages from the New Testament. Before the long summer was over, almost everything that came out of her mouth was a quote lifted from either Matthew, Mark, Luke, or John.

Then she started to hear voices; one was that of her not-so-dearly departed husband. Blue's mother would hear him at all hours of the night, and whenever she did, she would piously declare the fiery fate that awaited his soul.

Needless to say, little Blue never got much sleep. She was always nervous, waiting for the next "conversation" to begin. Then Blue had begun to hear voices herself; having no other place to turn to for consolation, she took refuge in movie houses.

There, in those dark, comforting cocoons, the voices would sometimes sing. The more Blue heard them, the more convinced she became that God was speaking to her, as surely as He had to her mother.

For the next seven years, Blue worked at whatever job she could find, saving her money to pay for singing lessons. She struggled, but kept improving, finally getting good enough to win amateur talent contests all over the state of Kansas.

Then, on the day Blue turned eighteen, she kissed her mother and her home-state goodbye, and headed for the recording studios in California. But she never made it any farther west than Reno.

Twenty years cruelly crept by, leaving her aspirations battered. Yet a small spark of Blue's dream refused to die.

The nightclub sat a few blocks off Reno's main strip, wedged in between a couple of pawnshops. Inside the club, all the house-lights were on. In the harsh glare, very little was left to the imagination—especially the age and general condition of the half-dozen singers who had come to audition their wares.

Blue and Cooper were sitting at a cocktail table near the entrance. After their encounter in the hotel elevator several hours earlier, they had slept most of the afternoon, then eaten breakfast at a time of day when normal people were thinking about supper. By now, Blue was somewhat stuck on Cooper.

On those rare occasions when she met a man with any style, she'd been inclined to make hurried, rose-colored appraisals. Cooper was, Blue thought, the classiest gentleman she'd met in ages, though given her line of work, she knew that wasn't saying much.

Cooper had come along with Blue to the audition just to kill a little time, not yet having decided what to do over the course of the next week; but whatever that was, it would have to fit into his overall strategy. In his mind, he was already moving people and places around like pieces on a life-sized Monopoly board.

Down near the piano, a busty blonde stood belting out a raunchy rendition of "Right In Your Own Backyard." She was accompanied by a bored-looking, bald-headed pianist. Off to one side, crouched over one of the tiny tables, sat the club's owner, a stout-chested, dwarfish man. Dressed in a checkered suit whose coat barely covered his ample stomach, he was shelling and eating peanuts with such persistence, Blue wondered if he even knew the audition had begun.

Sizing up the assemblage, Blue announced to no one in particular: "All the folks in this joint have got a problem, huh? Including me."

Cooper didn't say anything. His moody silence made Blue more nervous. Thinking his attitude was related to her quickly applied makeup, she fished a compact from her purse.

"Well now, my problem, since you ain't been kind enough to ask, is this," Blue quietly declared, glumly studying herself in a little mirror. "I need to get together enough money to buy my own nightspot."

"My problem is," Cooper finally replied, "I got little more'n a week to rustle me up a 25,000 dollar stake for a poker game here in town. Might have to find my way down to El Paso to get me the money."

"Hey, Frank, I'd love to tag along," Blue chirped, suddenly cheerful again. "I been known to bring a fella a lot of luck."

Blue's previous experience with professional gamblers had been vaguely enjoyable. When they won, the men always tipped her big. They also were usually more interested in cards than sex, which suited Blue fine. It gave her a chance to catch up on her sleep.

Cooper continued to chomp peanuts. "Naw, but thanks, anyway. See, I been flying solo for so long, afraid I'd make for mighty miserable company," he muttered, as if reluctant to reveal such a personal failing. "Can you understand that, Miss, uh..."

"Morgan, Miss Blue Morgan!" she interjected. "Geez, don't even remember the name of folks you share a bed with!"

A cruel expression cracked across Cooper's features. It looked to Blue like the fissure of an earthquake. He took a long sip of beer before finally rendering a response. "'Blue Morgan', huh? That really your name, or just your state of mind?"

Cooper's sudden show of contempt stunned Blue. "Look here, cowboy," Blue sputtered, "I'll have you know that's the name I been trying to sing under for the past twenty years—professionally, I might modestly add. Oh, not that anything about me matters to you more'n a bowl of hot spit!"

Blue's outburst embarrassed Cooper. He disliked emotional displays in public unless, of course, he instigated them himself.

"Okay, Miss Blue Morgan," he murmured with a queasy smile. "But can you lighten up a little? I'm just a guy you met in an elevator, remember?"

Then Cooper smiled gently and took Blue's hand in his. She promptly melted right down to the stump. "Yeah, and thank God you came along when you did, because otherwise mighta been me instead of that black-bearded bastard curled up in the corner of that damned elevator."

Cooper shrugged off the compliment. Then Blue went on as if her original train of thought had never been derailed. "Anyway, that's the story of my pipe dream. Way I figure, I could always count on a steady singing job if I owned part of the joint. See?"

But all Cooper saw was the hunger in Blue's green eyes. Her look of subtle desperation made him even more uneasy.

"Okay, that's enough," the club owner was yelling over to the busty singer, brushing the peanut shells off his plaid suit. "You did just fine, honey. Now next up is who...?"

"Right here, sir," Blue called out, and went wobbling on her stiletto heels down toward the small stage. The hefty-chested blonde reluctantly backed away from the microphone.

Climbing onto the stage, Blue blinked into a bank of lights. "Well, uh, thank you all here at the famous Kit-Cat Club for this wonderful opportunity. My name is Blue Morgan." Turning to the piano player, she said, "I'm gonna try 'Frenesi,' okay?"

The piano player shrugged, took a drag on his cigarette, then asked in a voice so sweet it sounded sarcastic, "Any idea what key you gonna try it in?"

The question caught Blue by surprise. It had been a long time since her last audition. She quietly hummed a few bars to herself, then whispered, "Think I'll try F, okay?"

The piano player muttered something and started his musical introduction. But Blue missed the first cue, which made her all the more jittery. Peering out past the stage lights, she couldn't see the owner too well, yet sensed he was already getting set to "next" her. The piano music started off again, and this time Blue managed to climb onboard.

'Once long ago, I found my love down in old Mexico—'

The piano player stopped abruptly. Taking another drag, he quietly said in the direction of his cigarette, "Well, maybe so, honey. But you musta also lost the key of F down there. Let's make it easy on everybody. Try G, huh?"

Whether he knew it or not, the pianist had just rendered an expert judgement on Blue's singing abilities. Years before, she had sung easily in the higher key; but time, trouble, and neglect had taken a toll on her range.

When Blue started to sing again, everybody in the room seemed to sense how good she must have once been. Her voice had a husky, sultry quality, though she was now more of a performer than a singer. She felt and acted the song better than she sang it. Even Cooper was impressed.

While Blue was singing down on the stage, Cooper had seen the edge of her bankbook sticking out of her purse, and he now took a hurried look at its numbers.

She always carried her bankbook in her purse. It was proof that her twenty years in the desert had not been totally barren. She had saved up a sizable amount of money, and whenever she felt discouraged, she would thumb through her bankbook as intently as her mother had once done with the Bible. Blue never left home without her savings deposit book.

Then came the little man's voice again.

"Okay, that's enough," the club owner exclaimed, after Blue stumbled off-key for the first time. "But you did fine, honey. Now next up is who...?"

Blue took in a deep gulp of stale air, clenched her fists, and started off the stage. But nearing the owner's table, she stopped.

"Hey, Fats," Blue barked to the owner. "Don't they teach politeness on the planet you come from?"

The owner squirmed but said nothing. This suited Blue fine. She didn't want to share center stage with anybody. "But see, this here, Peanuts, is the planet Earth. You know, human beings and all that. So maybe you could expand your vocabulary enough to give folks the idea that you're auditioning talent up here, and not just reviewing robots!"

There were several seconds of complete silence. The singers who had already been turned down were smiling; but the ones yet to audition wisely maintained their neutrality. The owner wasn't smiling either, though after he'd calmed down a bit, a look of guilt snuck across his flushed face.

"Sorry, lady," he finally muttered, his gravel voice now as smooth as concrete. "Just the less I say, easier it seems to be on everybody. But for what it's worth, I woulda loved to heard that voice of yours five years ago, though you're still a damn fine performer. Now, please, next..."

Blue had won the battle, yet lost the war, and the tears came. It was only a one-week gig in a dirty little dive where the audience never listened to the music, anyway. But Blue wasn't crying about losing the job; she'd had plenty of experience at that, and with each rejection, her protective shell had grown thicker.

What had reduced her to tears was the owner's compliment, left-handed though it seemed. His remark cut to the core of what Blue knew was her real problem. Through long neglect of her God-given talent, she was now no better than an amateur trying to compete at a professional level.

Another singer was cooing into the microphone when Blue got back to the table. Cooper came to his feet. Taking out his silk hankerchief, he gently dabbed her eyes dry.

"Don't let that bastard get you down, honey," he murmured. "Ain't nothing wrong with your voice that a hearing aid for that dwarf wouldn't fix."

Blue started to cry again. Two compliments in as many minutes had overloaded her circuits. Fishing out a little mirror from her purse, she glumly assessed the damage to her mascara.

"Bull-a-shit," Blue muttered. "I stunk—but there ain't nothing wrong with my voice that a lot of practice won't fix."

Then she sat down to repair her makeup. Cooper stayed on his feet, figuring that what he wanted to say would play better with him standing up.

"Well, old Doc Cooper's prescription would be both a lot of practice and a little vacation. Down to El Paso, maybe... with all expenses paid by the management."

A surprised stutter came from behind Blue's compact-mirror.

"Yeah, but I thought you liked flying solo so—?"

"Only, but that was before I heard that fine little voice of yours, and then remembered my car radio's on the blink," he said, smiling. "Besides, I ain't never been fond of bunking in at night with nothing more'n a cold deck of cards."

Blue trained her mascara-stained eyes on Cooper. Earlier that day, back in his suite at the hotel, he hadn't seemed too interested in anything but getting some sleep. Blue had curled up on the same bed, feeling both grateful, as well as insulted. But now Cooper was coming on like a smitten schoolboy.

"Now you wouldn't kid somebody who's already a little down on her luck, would you, cowboy?"

Cooper looked offended. "Hey, lady," he drawled, "I don't say nothing I don't mean."

Blue finally smiled and slowly floated into his arms. He was probably lying through his teeth, Blue thought, but she liked to believe the best about everybody.

Yet Cooper had told her the truth. His car radio was indeed on the blink, and he certainly didn't enjoy going to bed with nothing more than a deck of cards. Whatever else Blue read into his words, though, was from her script, not his. Cooper hardly ever said what he really thought, yet rarely told a bald-faced lie.

Chapter 7

The Good Times Drive-In Theater sat some three miles west of the diner, out on the old highway toward El Paso: a long haul for Val to make on his bike, especially in the wintertime. For the past two years he had worked there six nights a week, lugging popcorn, sodas, and candy around from car to car. Business wasn't bad in the summer; but in the colder months what Val cleared on commissions often barely covered the cost of his cough medicine, and extra sets of long-john underwear.

There were, however, two major benefits: Val got to see an awful lot of movies, and more of his girlfriend, Bonnie Gortner, who usually came out to the drive-in every Sunday night, always piloting her mother's fancy Ford convertible.

No matter what the weather, Bonnie kept the top up so that Val could hide out inside the car whenever business grew slow. Sometimes even when it didn't.

Bonnie was from one of the few wealthy families in Big Bend. Her mother Mildred was the Queen Bee of the town's social set, a group Val's mother often compared to a nest of hornets. More than once Val had felt their sting. Mildred Gortner had convinced most of her friends that he was a half-crazed Mexican going nowhere at an alarming rate of speed. Val agreed with her, as long as he stayed in Big Bend.

But Bonnie's mother didn't know that for the past several months, Val had greatly increased his speed. He and Bonnie had finally worked up the courage to make love, an event that took place in the backseat of her mother's convertible; poetic justice, Val had thought at the time.

He still remembered every detail of that fateful evening; could even recall the name of the monster movie playing that night. Afterwards, Val and Bonnie saw many monster movies from the backseat of her mother's convertible.

They had talked a few times about getting married; or rather Bonnie had talked, Val had listened. Still, Val liked her a lot. She was the smartest girl in her graduating class, and when she smiled, she came close to being pretty. Val also admired the way she stood up to her mother.

If he had ever stood up to his own mother in such fashion, he knew she would have served him up the very next day with the diner's cold cuts. But Bonnie didn't care what anyone thought, including her girlfriends, who could never understand why she was going steady with a Mexican. Especially a poor Mexican.

Val couldn't understand it, either. But Bonnie could. From the beginning, their affair had been another way of declaring her independence from her mother; besides, Bonnie thought Val was handsomer than most of the boys in her class, and a smoother lover than any of the bumblers she had dated before.

That night, Val had just climbed into the convertible when Bonnie greeted him with a kiss that felt as if she wanted to reach his brain through his mouth. The movie that evening was called "The Brain Suckers."

But when he failed to respond fast enough, Bonnie gave him that piercing look she always used when she thought his passion not quite up to par. Often, after they'd had sex, Val felt as if he'd just fought a wrestling match, and lost.

"Wow, Val," Bonnie quietly complained. "About as romantic tonight as some underpowered robot."

"I'm not a sprinkler you just turn on when the grass gets dry," Val said, turning away from her. "Besides, I got other things on my mind. Didn't tell you yet, but—"

"Tell me what, Val?" Bonnie asked. The enthusiasm in his voice seemed to scare her.

"Well, see, I found out today that my father left me some money. What they call a trust fund, I guess—"

"I already know about it."

Cabrón, Val thought. Just one more reason to hate Big Bend! Everybody knew everything that happened in town, sometimes even before the involved parties themselves.

"So how'd you find out?" he asked. Then he remembered. The teller at the bank that morning was one of Bonnie's best friends.

"Well, Val, it's just great your daddy left you a little money," she exclaimed.

But Bonnie was worried. Money usually made people feel much more independent, and since learning of Val's windfall, she had wondered how it might affect him. "But don't you think it's time you talked to my own daddy about getting a good job?"

Val's interest in "The Brain Suckers" faded instantly.

"What are you telling me, Bonnie?" he mumbled, still staring at the screen but no longer seeing the movie.

"Oh, nothing. Just wish you'd start sweet-talking my daddy into giving you a real job, so we could make some marriage plans and all..."

Marriage, along with college, was not one of his favorite topics. Bonnie knew this, yet every time they'd seen each other over the past week, she had talked about it. He had managed to change the subject, but now he got mad.

"Geez, some chance we got to live happily ever after! You think I act like a robot—and you sound like a broken record."

Val turned up the volume on the car speaker. The slurping sounds blaring from the screen sounded like the roar of a tidal wave. Broken brains were everywhere. Val felt as if one of them was his.

When he looked back at Bonnie, she had tears in her eyes. The sight unnerved him. In the two years they had gone steady, Val had never seen her cry.

Not quite sure how to respond, Val did think to turn down the volume on the speaker. "I'm sorry," he finally managed to mutter, not sure if he was really sorry, or just sad. "Just that, well,

I been thinking there's something bigger waiting for me outside this town—and until I find it, or at least discover that it's not there, I'm not gonna be worth shooting, much less marrying."

Val had never told Bonnie about his dream of someday getting involved with the movies, though Bonnie loved them almost as much as he did; yet to her they seemed only a diversion, certainly not a potential profession. Val figured it would be easier to say he planned to make a career out of climbing Mount Everest, barefooted.

"Anyway, Bonnie, see what I'm saying about hoping to find something bigger in my life?"

Bonnie understood better than Val hoped she would.

"Are you searching for something bigger—or just anything that's a little different?" Her soft blue eyes looked frightened.

Val worked at clearing his throat. "Well, guess that's part of what I have to find out..."

Judging from her crushed expression, his explanation needed work. Val hurriedly amended his statement. "But hey, maybe things can get better for both of us, huh?"

He had implied they still might have a future together. Val craved the adventure of movies, and the travel that usually went with it; yet he also wanted a return-trip ticket back to Big Bend safely tucked away in his pocket, just in case. But he had seen enough movies to know that such spineless characters usually dropped out of the picture by the third reel.

"Well, Val," Bonnie whispered, wiping her eyes as she slid closer to him. "Whatever you're searching for, I just know that together we can find it. I bet four eyes can find something twice as fast as just two, huh?"

When Val hesitated, Bonnie suddenly clamped her lips on his, and twisted one arm around to unhook her brassiere. Val often teased her that she used sex like most people take medicine, considering it a cure-all for everything from frustration to a three-day case of the flu.

The kiss went deeper and deeper. Finally, all Val could think about was that brassiere. Why the hell was it taking so long to come unhitched?

"Honey, let's get into the back before we both end up look-ing like pretzels," Bonnie murmured in an emotionless voice. Val sensed that despite what she was saying and doing, her mind was far removed from sex that night.

He was following her into the backseat when he heard what sounded like the clanging of bells. Then he realized that the bells were car horns, loud ones, and all belonging to movie patrons wondering what had happened to their refreshments.

The brain-sucking sounds from the screen abruptly went dead. An annoyed voice came over the speaker.

"Please pardon the interruption, folks—but if the Mexican kid don't get back to work mighty pronto, he's fired—thank you, folks, and enjoy the picture!"

The sucking sounds came back on. Staring at the speaker, Val felt as if mice were racing around all over his body. Vaulting from the car, he hoisted up the refreshment container he had left hidden under the car and strapped it over his shoulder.

Bonnie quickly moved toward the window. "Val, can I tell Daddy that you'll go see him about a job tomorrow morning?"

"Forget it!" Val exclaimed. "In another five minutes, I'll be unemployed, and I plan to stay that way till I get where I'm going!"

Tears welled up in Bonnie's eyes again. Val wondered why she was taking it all so seriously. She had never before men-tioned that he work for her father; indeed, she often joked that her father's tractor dealership was the most boring place in the entire world.

"Okay, Bonnie," Val muttered. "Hell, if it means that much to you, I'll go see him in the morning. But don't expect to see me herding around tractors anytime in the near future, okay?"

"Okay," Bonnie murmured, trying to smile.

Val started off toward the concession stand. Several patrons spotted him, and began to fire a verbal barrage in his direction.

"Hey, Pancho, where you been—taking a siesta?"

Amidst insults, Val let his imagination run wild. He saw himself in a World War II movie, maneuvering his battered B-17 bomber through ferocious enemy flak. The fusillade became more brutal, but Val stayed on course until he reached the concession stand. His boss, Wilber Haynes, saw him come in.

Haynes was dashing around behind the counter, trying to serve all the customers who apparently had grown tired of waiting for Val to come to their car.

Glancing at Haynes, Val had to grin. All two hundred and fifty pounds of his boss were bouncing around as if a blowtorch was being held too close to his widest part.

Setting aside his container, Val took in a large gulp of popcorn-flavored air, then strode over to a microphone hooked up to the theater's main sound system. Grabbing the mike, he felt himself swell with anticipation. Few moments in his life had ever seemed so fraught with dramatic potential.

"Hi, Mister Haynes, this is the 'Mexican kid' speaking. I heard your announcement. But you can't fire me, sir, because I just quit! But I cannot leave without thanking you for the three halfway decent movies you've shown here these past two crummy years. So thank you, sir, and good night."

A few hundred feet away, this announcement had come over the speaker in Bonnie's car. Staring blankly up at the movie screen, she felt the tears rolling down her cheeks. Val's declaration of independence had confirmed her worst fears. Yet she hated herself for not being able to celebrate his good luck. Curling up in the backseat, she quietly continued to cry.

Val had clicked "The Brain Suckers" back on, and then strode out of the refreshment stand. Once outside, he could not resist peering through the window. What he saw gave him his first laugh of the night. Several customers, looking like figures in a wax museum, were staring at him with unblinking eyes.

There was nothing frozen about Wilber Haynes, however. He was bellowing like a wounded water buffalo. Val couldn't hear much of what Haynes was saying, but he doubted it would look very good on a letter of recommendation to any future employer.

Chapter 8

Bonnie's father was the town's official cheerleader, and he never tired of bragging that Big Bend was right on the verge of becoming Boomtown, U.S.A. Runaway optimism was Hubert Gortner's main stock in trade; selling tractors was only what he did for a living.

Hubert was a plump little man with many peculiarities. In a town where the only thing more scarce than a tree was a necktie, Hubert Gortner never left home without one. He was, however, nearly without hair, a defect he tried to conceal by combing what remained of it in several different directions, creating a disheveled appearance that even the most expensive necktie could not correct.

That morning, Val went to see Hubert Gortner about a job he had no intention of taking. Now that he had come into money and had the price of a ticket out of Big Bend, he was simply treading water until he could finally leave home.

But he was vaguely intrigued to find out why Hubert Gortner had even considered the idea of employing him. Ordinarily, Bonnie's parents worked overtime at pretending he didn't exist. He remembered this as he tried to stay awake while Hubert Gortner droned on with his standard civic pep talk.

"—Hell, boy, you know the difference between men like me and the average Joe?"

Val roused himself just long enough to shake his head.

"The regular-routine guy can't see past his nose, and is always complaining and asking why. Me, I dream of stuff that never was, and ask why not."

Trying to keep from smirking, Val nodded. He was sure Gortner had filched the line from required reading at Big Bend High School.

"This town was built by men who, like they say in the Bible, could find water where there was none—and with the Good Lord's help, we're gonna make damned sure it keeps on growing—and you can be part of that dream, boy, if you got the guts to do the right thing..."

Gortner's voice had trailed off into a low growl that was hard to hear over the loud clanking coming from a nearby tractor. Yet Gortner's words seemed to carry an implied threat, as well as a challenge. But before Val could think the matter over, Bonnie's father steered him toward the noise.

Then Gortner coaxed him up onto the old tractor. The machine shook and sputtered as Val warily climbed onto it. Perched some six feet off the ground, he felt like a rodeo rider battling to stay atop a Brahma bull. After stripping half a dozen gears, he got the tractor to move. But it travelled no more than ten feet when Gortner empathetically ran his finger across his throat.

Val assumed that Gortner wanted him to turn the machine off. Even that, however, seemed beyond his aptitude. After managing to coax the tractor into neutral gear, he started down.

But no sooner did Val have his feet firmly planted on the ground when Gortner almost took them out from under him with a rousing clap on the shoulder. "You're a real soldier, boy," he yelled over the rattle of the rumbling tractor.

Val tried to smile. "Well, it was a close battle, sir—but I think the tractor won."

"No, boy, you did just fine," Gortner declared, cupping his hands to his mouth. "And nobody wants a wimp for an employee! Now report for duty at O-eight hundred tomorrow morning, ready to go to war."

Bonnie's father had been in the army during the Second World War, and though he'd never set foot on foreign soil, he usually tried to bark out orders like his hero, General 'Blood and Guts' Patton. Whatever military training Hubert Gortner had received, it was obvious to Val that it had forever mangled his mind.

Giving Gortner a mock salute, Val swiftly walked away. He tried, however, to keep from breaking into a run, knowing that might indicate that already he planned to go AWOL.

As Val strode away, he still wondered why in the world he had been offered the job. Gortner had never before hired a Mexican. Bonnie must have been awfully persuasive.

Jumping on his bike, Val bolted off and didn't slow down until he was a full two blocks away. What, he wondered, were his chances of making it all the way to Los Angeles on his bicycle? Then a familiar-looking convertible pulled up alongside him. Val pedaled faster.

"Well, did you and Daddy have a nice talk?" Bonnie asked, scrunching her features into a tight smile. She had been watching his audition with her father from across the street.

"Don't know, couldn't hear most of it," Val exclaimed, still toying with the idea of making a run for it. Yet knowing he could never outpedal the convertible, Val grabbed one of its door handles and began to coast alongside the car.

"Yeah, it's always so goddamned noisy over there," Bonnie chirped. "But tell me about the part you could hear!"

"He wants me to start work tomorrow morning," Val muttered, sounding like a convicted felon who has just barely escaped a sentence of fifty years at rock-breaking labor.

"Oh, that's wonderful, honey," Bonnie said, choosing to ignore his gloomy inflection. "And what else did you and Daddy discuss?"

"Tractors," Val said, somehow making the word sound obscene.

"Yeah, sure sounds like Daddy alright," Bonnie exclaimed. Her smile stiffened. "But what did you talk about, honey?"

"Hey, I didn't get a chance to do more than grunt—but I wanted to talk to you about us waiting for a while before we even think about getting married...."

"Wait...?" Bonnie fell silent for a moment. "But Val, why wait? For what, honey?"

"I don't know, till I get back from wherever I'm going," Val mumbled, gliding along beside the car. "Or maybe I'm waiting for a miracle."

"But Val, they stopped making miracles about two thousand years ago," Bonnie said listlessly. She couldn't blame him for wanting to find some sort of life outside of Big Bend. Yet it seemed forces beyond her control were impelling her forward. "And besides, waiting is the one thing we can't do anymore, not even—"

"Oh, come on, Bonnie, maybe just for a couple of months," Val shot back. He wondered if the green light up ahead would last long enough for them to make it through the intersection.

"No, we can't wait, not even for a couple of weeks!" Bonnie stammered, her eyes fast filling with tears.

"Hell, why not, we've waited this long for—"

"Because I'm a couple of months pregnant right now!"

In the next few seconds, Bonnie slammed to a stop at the red light. But Val sailed right through the intersection.

Ordinarily, there was never much traffic and only three policemen in all of Big Bend. But this time, off to one side of the junction was a police car.

Afterwards, the traffic citation in his pocket and his bike stowed in the trunk of the convertible, Val and Bonnie drove up to the small bluff that overlooked the town.

It was one of Val's favorite places, mainly because it had a couple of full-grown trees, and sometimes even a little trickle of water running down from the Apache Mountains; a good place to think, or better yet, sometimes not think at all.

On the drive up to the bluff, Val and Bonnie didn't say much. She asked what the traffic ticket would cost, and how he could pay for it without his mother wondering where the money had gone; all stuff Val could answer without further straining the mood between them. The big question, the one he was afraid to ask, politely disappeared.

After they sat down under one of the swaying cottonwood trees, Val finally found what remained of his courage.

"How come you didn't tell me all this before?" he quietly asked, peering down toward the old highway that hooked up to the new road. The road that ran all the way out to Los Angeles.

"Would it have made any difference, Val?"

Bonnie's voice was almost lost in the wind. Turning toward her, Val suddenly felt terribly lonely. He and Bonnie seemed the last two people on the face of the Earth.

"...And besides, Val, I've wanted to tell you for days now," she murmured. "Guess I was waiting for you to bring up the subject of marriage before... Fat chance, huh?"

Val ignored the question. He was in enough trouble already.

"Are you sure, Bonnie? I mean about the baby and all—"

"Sure as Doctor Dickinson is."

Bonnie stared down at her oxford shoes. "Just my dad knows. It seemed smart to take it one step at a time."

"So that's why he offered me the job, huh?"

Bonnie mumbled something and bent over to tie one of her shoe-laces. A chill came over Val. It seemed a virus had attacked his entire body; his arms and legs suddenly felt like weights he could barely lift.

When he had recovered himself, Val started back toward the car. Then he noticed Bonnie trailing behind him. She looked like a homeless pup following after a friendly stranger.

"Man, just when I was finally gonna bust out of this town," he barked, jerking his bike out from the trunk of the car. "I been thinking about going out to California—."

"And you were going to leave without even telling me?"

"No, sure I was going to tell you... But, damn, think I'd blow my brains out right now—if I just could figure out where the hell to aim!"

Bonnie took his hand in hers, and she softly said, "There, you see? Has to be a humorous side to all this, if we just look hard enough."

"My eyes aren't that good," Val mumbled.

"Val, why are you making all this sound so tragic? Hey, I know you want to travel, but we can still take nice long trips—

only with enough money to do it right... And besides, Daddy can't run that dealership forever. It'll be ours someday, honey."

"Oh, great," Val muttered.

"Listen, I'm not crazy about that joint, myself. But if you wanted, we could sell it and then—"

Val had slammed shut the trunk, and now wheeled his bike to one side. He paused to stare off toward the west. "That what you really want, Bonnie, to stay in this dump for the rest of your life?"

Bonnie wiped her eyes with the sleeve of her T-shirt. "No, not really... You're not the only one with dreams, you know. But like I told you last night, whatever it is you're looking for, maybe together we can find it, huh?"

Val was afraid to turn back toward her, knowing the hurt in her eyes would surely bring tears to his own. Suddenly, he felt almost as sorry for Bonnie as he did for himself. Both of them seemed caught in a trap they could never escape from without tearing each other to pieces. Val didn't want to take her with him to California; but he certainly cared too much to ever want to hurt her. For the past two years, she had been both his girl, as well as his best pal.

"I don't know, Bonnie," Val said, shrugging. "I don't know anything, anymore... except that you're the bravest and best girl I've ever known." Val felt tears clouding his eyes.

They exchanged a teary smile. They must have looked, Val thought, like two friends who had just been assigned to the same prison cell.

Climbing on his bike, Val waved back at Bonnie, and started down the long dirt road that led to the highway which now ran nowhere but back to Big Bend. Coasting along the narrow dusty path, he let his mind wander westward. Los Angeles now seemed a lost dream.

Yet he couldn't help speculating on how some scriptwriter might improve on the scene he'd just played out with Bonnie.

"Oh, sure, Bonnie, I had a lot of dreams and schemes," Val might have said. "But the important thing is the welfare of you and the baby. That's all that really counts."

"No, Val, you have to follow your dream," Bonnie would emphatically proclaim. "The baby and I will somehow make it safely through life, and maybe someday you'll put us in a movie, and then we'll live forever and ever."

Then he would take Bonnie's hand and gaze tenderly into her blue eyes. "Honey, you got me built up too high. Chances are I'll never be anything more than the first assistant to the second assistant."

"Oh, no, Val, you're wrong. All your dreams will someday come true, and the baby and I shall be proud to have been at least a small part of your life. So go now, darling, and always remember us."

Nearing the highway, Val felt his face flush with shame. It was a silly, selfish daydream. Yet he rather liked it. But already Val knew, as he neared the base of the hill, that his mother would not prove so appreciative an audience.

Chapter 9

The day before, Val had been relieved to catch the cafe during its drowsy mid-morning lull; now, he wished the diner was crammed with customers, so that when he sprang the news about Bonnie to his mother, she might be too busy to immediately wring his neck.

Lupe, however, was nowhere in sight. Playing for time, Val slipped into the restroom. His mother had decorated the men's room with grainy old photographs of the Mexican Revolution, and the pictures were usually a source of inspiration to Val.

But now the ferocious-looking, pistol-packing characters glared accusingly down from the walls at him, as if he was the most chicken-livered punk they'd ever seen. Val turned to the mirror to see if he shared their opinion. They didn't appear to be mistaken.

Slinking back into the diner, Val was nearing the partition when he caught sight of Lupe and Floyd in the kitchen. Floyd was cleaning the griddle, as Lupe lounged off to one side, sipping a cup of coffee. She was gazing at Floyd with what seemed a guilty look in her eyes; maybe she was thinking, Val guessed, of how hard Floyd worked, and how seldom she showed her appreciation.

"We have many compliments on the omelettes this morning," Lupe said softly, with a throwaway smile.

Floyd didn't immediately answer; he too seemed stuck in something serious that morning. "Well... that'll never get my name in the newspapers," he finally drawled. "Truck drivers ain't exactly finicky about much, are they?"

Lupe chuckled. "When it come to pamper their potbellies, yes, and they no keep coming off the main highway just to listen to the music we playing here, eh?"

Floyd smiled sheepishly. "So I added a couple of touches today, just to break the monotony."

"Well, just not put so many of this 'touches' we go out of the business," she replied with an anemic grin.

Floyd grunted and continued to clean the griddle.

Except for the soft scraping sound, it went very quiet. It seemed they had nothing else to say to each other, yet still had a great deal more on their minds.

Val had never overheard any of their private conversations. It made him rather sad. They both seemed to want something from each other that neither had in them to give. It reminded Val of his own predicament with Bonnie.

Then Val tapped the order bell. It didn't make much of a noise, but the sound startled them. For a moment they glowered at him as if he'd just set off the burglar alarm.

"Hi, I'm the headwaiter here, remember?" Val muttered. "Hey, listen, Mom, can we talk outside?"

His mother looked less than dazzled. "*¿Y que quieres decirme que no puedes decir en frente de Floyd?*" she demanded to know.

Val glanced back toward the diner. His mother had spoken loud enough for a few customers to hear. A couple of them looked up from their plates, as if waiting for his answer.

"Listen, no offense, Floyd," Val whispered, peering back into the kitchen. "But Mom, outside would be better."

Floyd turned back to the griddle, the tiniest flicker in his eyes. Lupe noticed it, and her annoyance fast built into something larger.

"Valentín, what is this? We having customers, I cannot go outside for—"

"Bonnie's gonna have a baby," Val quietly interjected.

From Lupe's stricken expression, Val felt as if he'd just set fire to the courthouse. She took a deep breath, then snapped her fingers at him as one would to a disobedient dog. "*¡Valentín, ven conmigo afuera inmediatamente!*"

Trudging into the kitchen, Val followed his mother out the side door. The fenced-in area just past the door was stacked high with dozens of discarded plastic milk crates and wooden produce boxes. Val immediately sought refuge behind them, but after Lupe circled around him a few times, they ended up near the kitchen window. Then Lupe, speaking in rapid-fire Spanish, began using words Val had never heard before.

Even so, he got the message. Val had never seen his mother with angry tears in her eyes. She was even hurling a few choice curses in Bonnie's direction, though she had always liked her.

But when Val meekly mentioned the idea of putting the baby up for adoption, Lupe went blasting over the edge. Spittle formed at the corners of her mouth, as she began to hop from foot to foot in a dance of fury.

Then something strange happened.

She stopped and stormed right up to within a few inches of Val's face. Staring him dead in the eye, she began to loudly weep, her shoulders shaking with anger and grief; yet it seemed she was seeing somebody else, somewhere back in time.

Val felt his own eyes flood with tears. He hated what he had done to his mother, hated what he had done to Bonnie. But what he hated most was what he had done to himself.

Backing away a few feet, he leaned down and took up a few rocks, which he started tossing up toward the hill. He couldn't look at his mother any longer. The anguish in her face cut him like a razor-sharp ax.

Lupe finally calmed down enough to speak again.

"Valentín, I telling you this: you doing right by this girl. You forgetting this travel to California and all this big ideas. You marry, make nice life for Bonnie and the baby right here in Big Bend!"

Then Lupe hauled out what Val had always called "the heavy artillery." In the past, whenever her own arguments had failed to persuade him, she invariably milked the memory of his father. "This what your father would tell you to do! He die hoping his son will be a honorable man. You want him now turning in his grave thinking he is wrong about his own son?"

Val glanced at Lupe to see if her expression had softened. It hadn't. Val went on slinging rocks. The mound above him had taken on a name and a face.

"Yeah, Mom, I read your message loud and clear," Val finally muttered. "But I'm not so sure what my father would want me to do...Heck, I'm not so sure about anything you tell me about him, anymore. Maybe he's always been more myth than man—"

Val never saw it coming, though it didn't hurt that much. Still, it shocked him to the base of his bones. His mother hadn't slapped him since just after she'd married Floyd, and had caught Val pouring hair remover into his stepfather's shampoo bottle.

Yet the blow seemed to stun Lupe even worse. She stood shaking with a half dozen different emotions. Then she stalked back into the kitchen. Val felt like running away himself; but instead he simply leaned back against the wall to cool off in the narrow ribbon of shade that ran alongside the diner. The morning had turned hot. It felt like a hundred and ten degrees, even in the shade.

Several seconds passed. Then Val heard what sounded like somebody opening the big freezer in the kitchen. A moment later, he heard his mother's voice.

"Well, you hear all this, Floyd," she said, in a tremulous voice. "First Valentín tell me he no want to marry this girl. Then he telling to me he no longer believe nothing I say about his father. Someone should take the belt to that boy of mine!"

It went quiet for a long while. Then Val heard Floyd clear his throat, usually a signal of his stepfather's serious intent. Floyd's words, when they came, seemed aimed at Val, as well as Lupe. Val suspected that Floyd knew he was standing just outside the window.

"Lupe, I promised you the day we got married that I'd never lay a hand on that boy, and I ain't about to start now that he's almost full grown. Besides, this thing about his father is your own fault... A kid gets force-fed one fat lie after another, he can sense when he's had enough, even though he still don't know the entire truth."

Outside the window, Val sucked in his breath, and waited for his mother's answer. But he heard only the slap of a piece of meat on the chopping block, then a thumping sound as Floyd began to bang away with his tenderizing hammer.

"Do you say, Floyd, is wrong what I tell Valentín all these years about his father?" Lupe finally asked.

Floyd's voice became softer. "Okay, honey, maybe that was something you felt you had to do for the boy's benefit—but hell, did you have to go on believing it yourself?"

The next thing Val heard was a soft wail, then the creaking of the swinging doors that led back into the cafe. The pounding started again. Bam bam bam bam. Then suddenly Val couldn't hear anything, anymore. There was no sound anywhere, though out of the corner of his eye he could see a large truck laboring along the highway.

Trudging up to his cabin, Val laid down. Never in all his life had he felt so terribly tired. But he couldn't even close his eyes. One question kept beating at his brain, the one he had earlier asked Clarence. What was the biggest lie anybody ever told you?

Val felt a tremor run through his body. He had lost his chance to escape from Big Bend. Moreover, he had deeply hurt his mother and Bonnie, the two people he cared for most.

➤➤ ➤➤

That night, Val sat up watching "Dragnet" on television. A crime show best matched his mood. He felt like a prisoner on death row, awaiting word on the exact date of his execution. Then Val heard a soft knock at the door.

"Who is it?" he asked, half expecting a hooded hangman.

"Floyd," came the voice past the door. Val was only mildly relieved.

Floyd entered and stood in embarrassed silence for a long moment. Then, for lack of something more enlightening to do, he turned on a small lamp. The only other light in the room was the glare coming from the TV set. Val continued to watch the show, as Floyd glanced around the room, casually peering at one thing or another.

Val could count on the fingers of one hand the times Floyd had ever been in his cabin. So maybe his interest was genuine. But Val doubted it; and as idle chit chat was not Floyd's forte, he decided to make it easier for him.

"What's the latest word from the warden?"

Floyd seemed relieved to be asked a direct question.

"Well, your mother went over to see Bonnie's parents tonight. Appears they all agree, the sooner you two get hitched, the less stink there's gonna be..."

"So when's the hanging?" Val asked. Yet he was ashamed that his mother was having to handle all the details. He should have at least gone with her over to see Bonnie's parents. Still, what he could have done or said when he got there, other than throw himself at their mercy and agree to marry Bonnie, was beyond his current powers of imagination.

"Wedding will be soon. But meantime, schedule calls for you and Bonnie to carry out your religious duties tomorrow night," Floyd muttered, studying the posters on the wall. Val could tell Floyd was wondering where they had been stolen from.

"Then after that," Floyd went on, "your mother plans to have a little wedding supper here at the cafe."

"Who's gonna be at the wedding?" Val asked.

"Well, Val, I think the fewer folks allowed to witness this mistake, better it'll be for everybody."

Val turned away from the TV screen, where Sergeant Friday was browbeating a sleazy-looking chiseler. Floyd had finally said something that caught Val's interest.

"Hey, you feel like that, why don't you stop it?"

Floyd had made his way around the room to an orange crate on the far side of the bed. Reaching down, he took up the faded old photograph of Val and his father. Floyd studied it for a moment.

"Val, if I was your real father, think I'd handle this mess a mite different. But as it is, I don't feel rightly entitled to inter-fere."

For a moment Val didn't say anything. For the first time in more than eight years, he suddenly liked Floyd. But it didn't seem smart to tell him so. No sense in becoming friends at this late stage.

"So Mom's gonna have a supper for the Gortners?"

Floyd laid aside the photo and smiled. "Yeah, but we'll try to make it a 'fast supper,' huh?"

"But she's always hated the Gortners," Val protested.

Floyd chuckled and started for the door. "Yeah, I know. But she's still mighty anxious to impress them."

After Floyd softly closed the door behind him, Val turned back to "Dragnet." The show was just ending. The chiseler, an aging three-time loser, had drawn twenty years worth of free room and board at Alcatraz.

"But, Your Honor, I'm too old to do that much time," the man wheezed to the judge.

"Well, just do the most you can," the judge said, smiling.

The ex-con stared glumly down at his feet that were now headed for nowhere but the cold concrete of a maximum-security prison. Val knew exactly how he felt.

Chapter 10

On the afternoon of the following day, the verdict finally came in. Lupe, along with Hubert Gortner and Bonnie, had decided. The wedding would take place at eleven o'clock that next morning. Bonnie's mother, however, had yet to weigh in with an official opinion. Val assumed she was warming very slowly to the idea of getting a poor, dark-skinned Mexican for a son-in-law.

The ceremony would be a closed affair, with few people other than the immediate conspirators allowed to witness what Floyd had so aptly, in Val's opinion, christened a mistake.

Lupe had insisted, however, that some sense of tradition be honored. She planned to host a wedding dinner that night, right after Val and Bonnie fulfilled their religious duty. They would make their confessions to the local priest, Father Donovan, so that the next morning they could get married in a 'state of grace.' But it would require more than a single session in the confessional, Val thought, for him to personally achieve any such lofty state.

The news of his marriage date was delivered while Val lay flat on his back. He had hoped a summer cold might yet develop into pneumonia. But with his luck holding firm, the fever broke late that same afternoon. No sooner did that happen when Lupe insisted he drag himself out of bed. His mother wanted to show him how she and Juana had decorated the diner for what Floyd still was calling "the fast supper."

Before trudging down to the diner, Val grabbed his pump-action .22 rifle, and stuffed his pocket with shells. A little extra protection might come in handy.

Yet when he saw what his mother and old Juana had done to the cafe, the edge came off his anger. The place looked like a banquet hall, with crepe paper hanging everywhere. Right in the middle of the room sat a long table, graced with Lupe's best linen, and ceramic pots filled with store-bought flowers.

Lupe and Juana were fussing around the table when Val walked in from the kitchen. Juana smiled and said something in Spanish. But Val's Spanish was little better than her English, and their conversation ended, as usual, rather quickly.

Floyd, nursing a cup of coffee over at the counter, watched with an amused eye. Then, seeing the rifle in Val's hand, he smiled wryly. "Yeah, I been half expecting this thing to end in a shoot-out."

Lupe made no comment. Val felt insulted by her cold silence. He felt entitled to a little respect. Yet his mother seemed to regard him as little more than a bit player in the production.

"*Floyd, podemos usar un poquito de ayuda aquí con la mesa,*" she abruptly declared.

"Kitchen's my department," Floyd muttered, staring into his coffee cup. "I cook, but I don't decorate."

"Well, at least you have the menu for tonight?" Lupe asked, moving a place setting by no more than an inch.

Floyd smiled at Val. "Oh, I think we oughta serve up just beans and tortillas. Give the Gortners some idea of all the money their daughter's gonna be marrying into, huh?"

The remark struck Val as rather funny. Floyd seemed more humorous since the troubles had started. Obviously, there were some adults, Val thought, who loved to find the mirth in young people's misery.

"Yes, beans and tortillas probably what the Gortners think all we eat here, anyways," Lupe grumbled. "But Floyd, I want them to least like the meal, even if they hating everything else."

Val shook his head with wonder. His poor mother. Part of her hated most of the Anglos in Big Bend, and especially the

Gortners; yet the other part seemed hell-bent on impressing them.

"Okay, Guadalupe," Floyd said reassuringly. "We'll treat the Gortners to roast beef and all the trimmings tonight—but after that they're gonna have to make their way through life without my assistance."

Lupe chuckled approvingly, and as she stood gazing at Floyd, Val slipped out the front door. A few days earlier, he had set up some bottles and cans on a ridge off to one side of the diner, thinking to get in a little target practice. Now seemed a good time to let off some steam.

Val started blasting away. Bottles exploded, cans flew in every direction. Finally, pausing to reload, Val saw Floyd come up to an open window.

"Hey, Val, betcha got a name and face for a lot of them bottles and cans, huh?" Floyd said, smiling. Lupe was not amused. She hated firearms, and had done everything short of getting the Texas gun laws changed to keep Val from buying the rifle.

Chapter 11

Saint Jude's, the only Catholic church in Big Bend, could never have been built were it not for Bonnie's mother. Later, her continuing contributions had kept the church in business. In the past few years, however, the congregation was comprised mainly of the town's small but growing Mexican population. This had done little to improve Mildred Gortner's sense of humor.

But her disposition, never droll to begin with, had now totally soured. After learning that Bonnie was pregnant, Mildred promptly fell prey to what she called an "attack of the vapors" and immediately took to her bed.

Bonnie was not impressed. She knew how obsessed her mother was with the elegant language and aristocratic customs of the Old South. As a young woman, Mildred had read and re-read "Gone With The Wind" until its exhausted pages were falling out of the book.

Yet whenever she and Bonnie had serious arguments, Mildred always dug up the bitter bones of her own not-so-genteel past. She had been raised in a trailer park that was little more than a shantytown, and as a child had heard the epithet "poor white trash" so often, she later became consumed with changing her station in life. When Mildred met Hubert Gortner, the path out of poverty finally became clear.

Just a few months before they met, Hubert had inherited ten thousand dollars from an uncle who speculated in oil and gas leases up around Odessa. He had gone broke more times than he could count; but luckily, for Hubert at least, the old man's fortunes were on the upswing at the time of his death.

Soon afterwards, Hubert and Mildred were married. Hubert's family earlier had lost its small ranch to both a drought and the Depression, and he was anxious to buy the place back from the bank. Mildred had other plans. She deposited the money into the same bank that had repossessed the ranch, and there the money stayed till Hubert returned from Fort Riley, Kansas, where he had been stationed for the duration of the Second World War.

When he came home from his noncombatant duty in the army, Mildred had their future mapped out, right down to the marble tombstones that would someday grace their graves. They promptly bought the local John Deere tractor franchise, and then spent most of their time making money and reinventing their poverty-stricken past. Gaining a Mexican son-in-law, especially a poor one, was not Mildred's idea of progress.

When she learned that Bonnie was pregnant, and that Val was not anxious to marry her, Mildred suggested an abortion. She knew a doctor in Dallas who might be willing to break the law, if the price was right. Hearing this, Bonnie bolted from her mother's bedroom, vowing never to speak to her again.

Mildred then decided on a two-pronged attack. The ideal solution was, of course, an abortion; failing that, she would demand that the "Mexican half-wit" do the honorable thing and marry Bonnie, then go to work at the Gortner tractor franchise.

Now, she and Bonnie were sitting together in icy silence in the front pew of Saint Jude's Church. The entire wedding party sat looking as if they were waiting for its cracked plaster ceiling to fall down on them.

Val had been baptized and received his First Communion in this same small, shabby church. But aside from those two non-voluntary appearances, he had rarely drifted back, though he liked the parish priest. Father Donovan seemed a real straight shooter. He looked tall and rugged, as if he should be punching cattle rather than preaching sermons.

Years before, Val's mother had made the priest a standing offer of free pie and coffee at the cafe; but she had done so, Val thought, to atone for hardly ever attending Sunday mass. Yet the pastor had taken her up on the offer often enough for Val to realize the tight straits he was in. It saddened Val to hear how the priest carried on, year after year, defiantly extolling the promises of his faith in a church usually filled with Mexicans too poor to leave much money in the collection plate.

Now, on the evening of the third day after Val had come into his inheritance, he was in that same church, on his knees in a dark box not much bigger than a phone booth. But this box had no phone. Not that there was anyone he could call for help. Maybe God, but Val doubted He would accept a call from a sinner who so rarely bothered to stay in touch.

Val was in the confessional of the only Catholic church in the one town in the world he despised. He had been born there; now, barring an act of divine intervention, Val thought he was probably doomed to die there. Maybe this very night, in the church itself. Already he could envision the local newspaper headline: Strange Mexican kid meets even weirder fate in rarely frequented setting.

Indeed, the somber voice coming from the other side of the gauzed partition sounded, Val mused, most appropriate for the Sacrament of Extreme Unction, the last rites of his erstwhile faith.

When Val had first entered the church, he had coiled up in the front pew, his mother on one side of him, Floyd on the other. His only avenue of escape seemed over the communion railing and across the altar itself; an option that struck even Val as slightly sacrilegious.

Just across the aisle, Bonnie sat boxed in between her own custodians. Her mother, stationed next to the passageway, was dressed in a frosted hairdo and a fancy coat that sported a glassy-eyed squirrel perched on one shoulder.

Father Donovan was addressing the little group, though Val couldn't hear much of what he said, mainly because of the groaning noise coming from the pipe organ.

Miss Violet, Noah Carson's secretary, had been recruited to play at the wedding service the following morning. She had unexpectedly arrived that evening to get in a little practice. Val thought she needed more than practice. Her rendition of "The Wedding March" sounded more like a funeral dirge.

But Val was not really listening to Father Donovan, anyway. Instead, he snuck glances at Bonnie's mother. She seemed the unhappiest person in the entire wedding party.

It would be funny, Val thought, if his only ally that night proved to be the person who most disliked him. Of course, he could pray to Saint Jude, the patron saint of lost causes. Saint Jude and Mildred Gortner would make for a strange alliance.

Val's only other potential ally was encamped by the side door of the church. Val had not planned to invite Clarence to the ceremony. But when he told him of his impending marriage, his friend had said he was the logical choice to be best man, since he was the best man Val knew; an opinion Val did not necessarily share, but at the time was too weak to contest.

Clarence sat wedged between Bonnie's prospective bridesmaids. Val didn't especially like either of them, though they didn't bother him near as much as Clarence bothered Bonnie. She thought him a hopeless case, and his brilliant grades and college scholarship only seemed to confirm her conviction. Bonnie's two bridesmaids felt the same way about Val.

Father Donovan was closing his battle-briefing. "So we're all set for tomorrow morning. Eleven sharp. Ceremony is gonna be hurried and sloppy, but best we can do on short notice."

Pausing, the priest announced what Val was dreading to hear. "Now I'll hear the confessions. You first, Bonnie. Give me a chance to hit my stride before I try tackling Val."

Bonnie rose, eased past her father, then quickly slipped down the side aisle into the confessional booth. A moment later, the priest joined her and closed the black door.

Then Miss Violet climbed down from the organ, and drifted toward the front door. As she passed Val's pew, she was, as usual, talking to herself. This time he couldn't blame her. Turning to watch her leave, his eye fell on his alleged best man.

Clarence stared at Val for a few moments, then slowly ran his finger across his throat. Val quickly looked away, afraid he'd either break out laughing or burst out crying.

Bonnie now came gliding out of the confessional, looking surprisingly cool and serene. She had been in the box for only a couple of minutes; Val saw this as an encouraging sign, since there was, of course, some duplication in their two sets of sins.

Val started for the booth just as Bonnie squeezed back in between her parents. Her mother peered up at her with a hard, inquisitive eye.

Now it was Val's turn. He stumbled toward the black box like a convict shuffling into the gas chamber.

"Forgive me, Father, for I have sinned," Val murmured, barely able to remember the proper words for confession. Then he began to itemize his most serious sins, along with their mischievous accessories. Not having been to confession in more than twelve years, Val had stocked up quite an inventory.

The black box grew hotter; a prelude, Val figured, to his inevitable journey down to that storage area famous for its lack of air conditioning. The walls of the confessional seemed to squeeze tighter.

Val intended to touch only on his major mistakes, then throw himself at the mercy of the priest. Yet once he started to speak, his feelings spilled over like water bursting past a dam.

"Geez, Val's been in there forever," one of the bridesmaids finally observed.

Clarence snickered. "Yeah, and he's always complaining about how dull this town is."

Father Donovan began to conclude the ceremony. Val peeked out past the gauzed window of the confessional. An old man was lighting some candles on the altar. Val glanced over at Bonnie's father, who was sitting closest to the black box. Hubert frowned as he glared at his wristwatch. He looked, Val thought, like an undertaker running late for his next appointment. But the others sat frozen-faced, as if expecting an earthquake at any moment.

Finally Val heard the priest whisper, "Okay, Val, I'll handle this," as he got up and moved out of the confessional. Then came a long silence. But what Val heard next almost brought tears of relief to his eyes.

"Forget it, folks," Father Donovan said in a soft voice. "The wedding is postponed, if not entirely cancelled."

Outside the confessional, it went quiet as a tomb. Most everyone was sporting a stunned look. Mildred Gortner, however, appeared strangely relieved.

"Well, I shall not pretend to be bitterly disappointed, though I do believe an explanation is in order," Bonnie's mother declared to the priest.

Father Donovan stepped back behind the communion railing, figuring, Val guessed, that he might need some form of protection in case of an all-out riot.

"The explanation is quite simple, Mildred," the priest said gently. What followed, however, seemed bound in barbed wire. "The boy is not ready to get married... and until he is, I'm not ready to perform the ceremony."

For a moment, it remained so still that Val thought Father Donovan had issued the final word of the evening. If Val had known otherwise, he might have stayed in the confessional.

But still savoring his freedom, he eased out of the booth and slipped into a pew near the rear of the church. Lupe turned to gaze at him with wounded eyes. Then she looked back at the priest.

"But Father, you no think my son have the duty to do the right thing?" Lupe asked in a crippled voice.

"We all have that obligation, Lupe," the priest answered with a bleak smile. "But I think your boy is wise to wait 'til he's sure. For most young folks today, marriage seems little more than a parlor game. Sometimes they get married just for the sheer novelty of it."

A mournful expression came over Father Donovan's harshly hammered features. It seemed the specter of hundreds of thousands of ill-matched young couples was marching before his eyes. The eerie silence was finally shattered by Mildred Gortner.

"Yes, both these children are too immature for marriage, and a damned sight too young for parenthood!" she abruptly declared. "But there is, of course, a medical way out of this situation."

Val wasn't quite sure what this solution entailed, but nodded in vague agreement. Bonnie's mother didn't seem so bad, after all. But nobody else appeared to share his opinion. Father Donovan suddenly turned on Mildred Gortner as if she had struck him with a cattle prod.

"The situation cannot be salvaged by simply murdering an unborn child," he quietly fumed.

The remark came with the swiftness of an uppercut. It seemed to stagger Mildred. "Oh, sweet Jesus and Mary, I hardly call the termination of a two-month old fetus an act of murder!"

The priest instantly retorted, and for several seconds their arguments bounced around like a tennis ball no one could squarely hit. Then, right in the middle of a volley, Bonnie leaped up.

"Stop it! Goddammit, stop it!" Bonnie yelled, glaring down at her mother. "You've been yakking about this since the moment I told you I was pregnant. But you've never believed in abortion any more than Father Donovan does—only in this case you're willing to make an exception. Because you simply can't stand the idea of me marrying a Mexican, especially a poor one whose mother runs a roadside diner!"

Mildred Gortner's mouth hung half open. "Now, Bonnie, I will not be spoken to in such cavalier fashion—and besides, there is a proper time and place to discuss such delicate matters!"

"Bullshit, Mother," Bonnie blared. "Right here, right now! And you'd probably let me go through half a dozen abortions, if you thought that'd keep me from marrying Val Cooper!"

Bonnie shot a withering glance in Val's direction. Her eyes filled with tears, but that didn't bank their fire. "But now I'm giving everyone here fair warning that even if I can't marry Val, nobody is going to take my baby away from me!"

Now that Val realized what Mildred Gortner had in mind, he couldn't blame Bonnie for being so furious. Putting the baby up for adoption still seemed the best idea. Yet it seemed the worst possible time to reintroduce the notion.

Mildred Gortner had started to stutter and stammer again. But before she could work the sounds into words, Father Donovan voiced what he hoped was a soothing sentiment.

"Now, Mildred, I'm sure we all, Val included, feel there is nothing sadder than an unwanted child who—"

"Oh, does he, now?" Mildred half-screamed, lurching to her feet. "Well then, if this can't be fixed in any other way, that good-for-nothing Mexican bastard is going to marry my daughter!"

Mildred turned to glare at Val. He knew Bonnie's mother had been humiliated, and wanted to get even with somebody. Val also knew that he posed the easiest target.

The priest interceded again. "Now, Mildred, I told you that until the boy is ready, I'm not going to—"

"Oh, he's not ready, is he?" Mildred exclaimed. "Well, he damned well better get ready— but then what could we expect, when his own father once did the same thing!"

Lupe quickly moved out into the aisle, as if preparing to get into Mildred Gortner's well-pampered face.

"Now *Señora* Gortner, please not get too personal about this if I was you," Lupe muttered with a steel-plated smile.

But Mildred Gortner, livid with fury, was speaking too fast to stop. "Hell, but like father, like son! The boy's own good-for-nothing father wasn't even responsible enough to hang around when—"

"*Señora*, better to shut up," Lupe fairly shouted. "Because if no, I slap your face right here in the church!"

Bonnie's mother now resembled a runaway truck. Her brakes had failed. To Val, looking on from near the rear of the church, there seemed a perverse fascination to the moment, like watching two vehicles racing at right angles toward the same intersection. Yet he sensed that in an ensuing collision, it would be him who would suffer the most damage.

"—And so what better place than a church for the truth to finally come out into the open?" Mildred was shrieking.

"Please, *Señora*! I give to you fair warning," Lupe barked.

Mildred turned toward Father Donovan. "And I'll tell you what's sadder than a child who's not wanted—a kid who's been lied to all his life. This boy's father isn't dead, never has been! He just ran away—"

Mildred Gortner didn't get to finish her speech before Lupe slapped her hard on the face. Yet Val felt as if he'd taken the blow himself. He suddenly became dizzy. Tears started to sting his eyes. For a long moment, everyone else became as inanimate as a photograph.

Finally, Mildred turned in a slow, jerky way back toward her husband, her eyes blinking an appeal for help. Hubert Gortner angrily came forward. But when he saw Floyd stride up beside Lupe, Hubert hit the brakes. Val couldn't blame him. The look in Floyd's eyes might have slowed down a freight train.

Bonnie's mother stood stewing for several seconds; then she marched toward the door. Bonnie and Hubert glumly followed after her. As they reached the rear of the church, Bonnie glanced back.

Val tried to smile. He had been touched by Bonnie's defiance. In that moment, Val had never been so impressed with Bonnie, nor had he ever come so close to thinking he truly was in love with her.

Clarence and Bonnie's bridesmaids had already slipped quietly out the side door, looking as solemn as if they'd just witnessed a near-fatal accident. Their mood seemed contagious.

The priest stared grimly down at the floor; then, with a sigh so heavy it sounded like a groan, he trudged behind the altar. Seconds later, Val heard a door quietly close.

Then Val saw Floyd put his arm around Lupe, something he'd never seen his stepfather do before. But then Val had never seen his mother look so defenseless. Suddenly he wanted to tell her that he forgave her for all the lies. What came out of his mouth next, however, didn't sound so merciful. "...Well, Mom, guess deep down I've sorta suspected this about my father for a long time. But did you have to let me find out like this?"

Lupe stood there looking like a badly beaten dog.

Managing to find the aisle, Val started for the door. As he walked out of the church, it suddenly hit him that this had been the most eventful night of his life. He had found a father, lost a wife, and gained a child.

Muffling a sob, Val pulled up the collar of his Levi jacket and stumbled off into the starless night.

Chapter 12

The Randolph Scott western had opened that night. Val bought a ticket and ambled into the musty old theatre. The place looked nearly deserted. Even Old Man Metcalfe was nowhere in sight. Val figured he was hiding off somewhere with his bottle of sour mash whiskey.

The movie that evening posed a different sort of challenge to Val's favorite film star. Its story seemed to stretch the actor in ways none of his other pictures had ever done, at least not in the ones that Val had seen. In the movie, the actor played an aging gunfighter who finally finds the respectable life he has always yearned for, only to realize it has come too late. He is a prisoner of his past.

The story reminded Val of a famous play he had been forced to read in his literature class at Big Bend High. He had thought the play crushingly dull; yet now, watching something similar unfold up on the screen, he thought the actor had beautifully brought it to life. But then Val knew he was hardly an expert on the art of acting. He was just another small-town movie junkie, mainlining celluloid every chance he got.

As he watched the movie, he also sensed that the actor had grown stronger for having taken such a risk. Not that he reasoned this out right away; rather he simply felt it in his heart. But even if he had fully understood it, it wasn't anything he planned to publicize. People would think it pretty silly that a movie actor, rather than a father, had helped him make one of the most important decisions of his life.

That night, as Val walked away from the theater after the last show, the lights on the marquee suddenly blinked off. His world of fantasy had finally come to a close; time to set aside those comforting illusions and run toward his rock-ribbed reality, even if the ensuing collision mangled him for life.

Val sensed that he could never have much of a future until he made peace with his past; nor could he ever become a good parent to his unborn child until he had confronted his own father. He would have to find Frank Cooper.

He also had to find a way to make things right with Bonnie, short of marrying her and forever miring himself in a town he despised. Something else troubled him. How had Bonnie's mother known about his father? Just one more thing Val had to discover. His list was growing longer.

>> <<

The farther out of town Val trudged, the lonelier he became. Hardly any traffic moved along the old highway at night. All he heard was the distant call of a coyote and the occasional chirp of a cricket lucky enough to have found a tree.

But as Val walked in off the road, and started past the diner and on up toward his cabin, he heard another sound: a Mexican love song was softly playing inside the diner. It was called *Solamente Una Vez*, his mother's favorite song.

The little ting-a-ling bell above the door sounded as he warily entered the cafe. Lupe was sitting at one end of the long wedding table, a half empty bottle of red wine parked in front of her. Apart from a solitary candle on the table, and the gauzed glow of the jukebox, the diner was dark.

Val thought it sad the way all the streamers made the room look now. The anticipated celebration had obviously turned into a one-woman wake.

"Well, I'm gonna go find my father," Val muttered, advancing toward his mother. "You can probably make it easier for me... but either way, I'm going. Before I do, though, I'd like to know how Bonnie's mother knew so much about him."

Lupe poured herself another glass of wine. "That is easy to answer. I tell her."

Val stopped dead in his tracks. "So you told that old witch something you shoulda told me a long time ago, huh?"

"So I make two mistakes," Lupe said, shrugging.

"Come on, Mom. I deserve a better answer than that."

Lupe sighed, and took a deep swallow of wine. "Okay, *hijo.* About six month ago, she come here one night. Look like it take her a half bottle of whiskey to get the courage. But there she is, standing outside my door. All smiling. She say she just learn Bonnie want to marry you, and only fair she say her family know more about you. Like who your father was. Maybe she think there was craziness in this family."

Val smiled to himself. The way he usually carried on, he couldn't blame the old lady for wondering. "So what'd you tell her?"

It took another long sip of wine for Lupe to answer. "The truth. But I also tell her not to say nothing to nobody else. Not even to Bonnie. Well, she swear never she tell nobody nothing— and like the fool, I believe her."

"Okay, so much for the past," Val said, slowly starting over to the window. "Now where can I find my father?"

Out along the highway, an eighteen-wheeler groaned past the diner. Its blapping sound had bled off into the distance before Lupe finally chose to evade the question.

"You not want to find your father, you know the real story."

"Try me, Mom. Please."

For a long moment, Lupe sat peering around the cafe, as if remembering what it had once looked like. "Well, the story start almost nineteen years ago. I still just the waitress here, but I got along nice with the old couple who owned it. This seem a good place to rest till I could get to the next one... and then I meet your father."

She paused, her eyes seeming to warm with the memory.

"Frank Cooper sometime come through here every few months, on his way from El Paso to Fort Worth to gamble. He speak Spanish better than I the English, so not take us long to become friends. Then one night, we get more friendly. So this is the story."

Staring off into the darkness, Val felt as if he were back in the confessional booth. "So then," he murmured, clearing his throat, "you two were never married?"

Lupe took another swallow of wine. She wasn't yet drunk, but well beyond being stone-cold sober. Ordinarily Val hated to be around her when she drank. Lupe had never been a happy drinker.

Val still remembered that when he was just a little kid, his mother sometimes started to drink just after she had closed up the diner for the night. Val would then see another part of her personality. The troubled and angry part.

She would sit quietly going over again and again all the slights she had suffered since coming to Texas. The cruel and cutting things Anglos had said and done to her. She seemed to have catalogued every one of them.

But later, after Floyd came into her life, the late-night sessions came to an end. Maybe Floyd had become her new audience. If so, Val now realized that he owed his stepfather a big favor. It had frightened Val to see his mother drink. She was his only protection, but when she drank she seemed just another scared and defenseless Mexican.

On this night, though, it would take dynamite to blast Val out of that diner.

"Married?" Lupe abruptly repeated, as if the subject were completely unknown to her. "No, Valentín, I think your father like me, but not so much to do nothing about it."

"Well, when I finally catch up with him," Val exclaimed, turning toward her, "I'm sure gonna do something about it!"

Shaking her head, Lupe smiled sadly. "Yes, and also you must thank him for giving to me the down payment on this cafe... and for the monies he left to you. *Y ya sabes que no tuvo que hacer nada de esas cosas para nosotros.*"

Val didn't know or even care what his father might have been legally required to do; the score he wanted to settle with Frank Cooper was not based on Texas law.

"So what happened after he came back to give you the money?"

Lupe's voice slowly began to break. "I never see him again. No phone calling, no letter. No postcard. Nothing."

Tears had welled up in her eyes. Despite the anger Val still felt, he walked over to put his hand on her shoulder. "Hey, that wasn't such a terrible story," he said. "You could have told me all this years ago."

"No, I wanted you to love him! If you think he die, instead of the other, it make it more easy for you to grow up feeling some fondness for him."

There seemed, Val thought, a tiny grain of logic in her argument. But that didn't make him feel any better. Drifting back to the window, he stood looking out toward the highway: the road he might soon be taking out of Big Bend.

"Did he walk out on us because we were Mexicans?"

The question seemed to sadden Lupe. "No, Val. Your father never think like that. Never. He was not a man to judge the people by the color of the skin. To him, was just two kinds of people. Those who win, those who lose."

Her answer made Val feel a little better. "So you still love him, Mom?"

Lupe seemed to be waiting for that question. Looking up from her wineglass, she stared wistfully at the front door. "I ask myself the same question, Valentín, for all the years of your life... What I know is still today each time the silly little bell rings, I look over, hoping to see him walk in the door. Yes, I miss him. Your father always made people feel life some game anybody could win... even a Mexican."

Lupe's voice suddenly choked with an emotion she couldn't control. It burned Val that this specter named Frank Cooper could still, even after eighteen years, so deeply affect her.

"Well, maybe you still love the bastard, but I sure don't," Val blurted out, in what he hoped sounded like a declaration of war. But Lupe wasted no time in trying to arrange an armistice.

"No, Valentín, you must to understand this: your father do for us all it was in him to do. He gave to us what he had in his heart, and much in his pocket. But I wanted the one thing he could not give me... and maybe this why I push you so hard to marry Bonnie. To be different from him, at least in this way."

It took Val a few seconds to work up the nerve to ask his next question. "Are we really alike, or was that just another lie you felt you had to tell me?"

Lupe sat studying the flickering candle in the middle of the table. Val held his breath. He could hear, off in the darkness, the forlorn call of a coyote.

"Little things, Valentín," Lupe said at last. "The way you always to see things so dramatic, like everything something from a picture show. Your father too. You have the imagination like him. I think he be proud of you, *hijo*."

Val turned away so she couldn't see what her words had done to his eyes. The coyote was still howling.

"So where do I find him?" he asked, peering at her image in the window.

Lupe's reflection slowly hardened. "No, forget your father. Leave the past in peace. You have enough trouble without going off to find more!"

"Listen, I know what Bonnie wants me to do," Val muttered, almost to himself. "Only right now it's the one thing I can't do. But maybe things will look different to me when I get back."

For a moment Lupe seemed to waver. Then her features froze. Val knew the discussion had ended. The court of last resort had rejected his petition.

"I say no for your good, Valentín. I help you to find your father, and you meet him, it only make you to feel more sad."

Val didn't see how he could feel much worse, but this seemed too flimsy a technicality to overturn her ruling. Walking to the door, he turned and noticed for the first time the hand-lettered sign hanging high over the counter. Bonnie and Valentín—Hoping they live happy forever.

The banner, Val thought, looked more like a funeral wreath.

Chapter 13

The following morning, after the breakfast trade had been pacified for another day, Val hiked down to a phone booth next to the highway. There was a phone inside the cafe, but for the call Val had to make that morning, he needed a little less noise and a lot more privacy.

Bonnie answered the phone herself. A stroke of good luck. If it had been either of her parents, he doubted they would have put Bonnie on the line. As he and Bonnie began to talk, cautiously retracing their steps through the events of the night before, Val felt as if he were walking through a minefield.

To his surprise, Bonnie didn't seem upset about the outcome of the previous evening; she probably thought, Val guessed, that he'd eventually regain what remained of his senses.

However, when he told her about his decision to go find his father, her feelings suddenly surfaced like a delayed depth charge. Bonnie thought Val's plan was about as smart as suicide.

"But, Bonnie, don't you get it?" Val said, straining to be heard over the rumble from the highway. "It's like last night, when you said having the baby was something you just had to do. Well, this is something I gotta do—because if I don't, for the rest of my life, I'll ask myself what might have happened if only I'd had the guts to face the bastard."

Striking out to find his father was a decision no longer open to general discussion; his attitude must have seeped through the line, because Bonnie now heaved a defeated sigh, and asked how long he planned to be gone.

"Oh, couple of weeks, anyway," Val replied, thinking it might be more like a couple of months. He had no idea of where to start his search. "I'll call you when I get back. Then we'll figure out what we're gonna do... And Bonnie, I was proud of you last night. Don't much agree with what you've decided to do, but I was still proud of you. And it'll be okay, you'll see... Yeah, I know. Bye, Bonnie."

Bonnie had ended the phone call by saying she loved him, and for a split second Val came close to saying he felt the same way about her. It wouldn't have taken much time or effort. But the night before, he had vowed to start facing facts, and his being in love with Bonnie wasn't one of them. But dammit, Val wondered, did honesty always mean having to hurt somebody?

Val was trudging back up toward his cabin when he saw Floyd wave at him. His stepfather was repairing the fencing on the far side of the cafe.

"Val!" Floyd yelled. "Mosey over for a minute, will ya?"

Figuring he was in for yet another general discussion, Val reluctantly changed course. Coming closer, he saw that Floyd had on a carpenter's apron. Suddenly, all the improvements his stepfather had made on the place over the past eight years rushed before Val's mind. Floyd had truly earned whatever life he had made for himself in Big Bend.

"Gonna try talking me out of going, might as well save your breath."

"Thanks for the warning," Floyd said, chuckling.

Standing on the far side of the fence, he was hammering in some new supports, employing no more than five strokes per nail. Val smiled. Floyd's carpentry, like his conversation, did not involve much wasted effort.

Val waited for the sermon to start. But Floyd didn't say anything until he had worked his way down to Val's end of the fence; then, as casually as if he were commenting about the weather, he said, "Think I know how you can find Frank Cooper."

It took Val a moment to recover. Floyd never volunteered much information.

"How do you know something like that?"

"Oh, your mother's talked about him enough," Floyd muttered, going back to his hammering.

"So how come you're willing to help me?" Val quietly asked. He felt like a moron looking a gift horse in the mouth.

Floyd frowned. There seemed a little more steam in the blows from his hammer. "Not just you I'm trying to help. Because if you do find him, and he still feels anything at all for your mother, I want you to bring him back here with you."

Floyd must be high on locoweed, Val thought, though he knew bonded bourbon was his stepfather's preferred vice. Then Val felt his face flush. His hands balled into fists.

"No sir," Val exclaimed. "I'll never bring that bastard back here!"

For a moment, Floyd said nothing. He laid up another crossbar. Val came forward to hold it for him. Only after Floyd had pounded the plank into place did he level his gaze on Val. Floyd's watery brown eyes, Val noticed, had never looked so kind.

"Oh, you feel that way about your father, Val, because you had him set up too high. But might find out he's an okay guy, if you ever give him a chance to—"

"Well, he sure never gave me much of a chance," Val whined. It felt good to wallow around for a moment in self-pity.

Floyd nodded solemnly, as if to say he understood how Val felt. Tucking aside his hammer, he reached into his shirt pocket for a cigarette. Val stared at him, wondering what sort of game he was playing. Knowing how much Floyd loved Lupe, Val could see little sense in what his stepfather had suggested.

"Anyway, you'd be taking the biggest chance of anybody if my father did come back."

"Yeah, suppose so," Floyd said, lighting up his cigarette. "But you see, Val, for a long time now I've also been living with the legend of Frank Cooper... Trying to compete with a person who seemed more myth than man. And after eight years of it, I'm a little tired of always coming in second. But maybe if he showed up back here, we could get this thing settled, once and for all."

It struck Val as strange that Floyd's reason for wanting to confront Frank Cooper was somewhat the same as his own.

"But what if you come in second again?"

Floyd's expression turned wistful. He peered down the highway. Eight years earlier, he had been mustered out of the army at Fort Bliss in El Paso, and for want of a better place to go, Floyd was on his way back home to Dallas when his bus had stopped off at the cafe for a lunch break.

So far, it had been a grim trip. Floyd dreaded returning to Dallas, as he had already been served with his wife's divorce papers. The last time he had spoken with her by phone, she had indicated that she and their daughter would soon be moving to Norman, Oklahoma. She didn't say why, but Floyd figured that was where her new boyfriend lived. So now, as if propelled by sheer instinct, he was going back to a home he knew no longer existed.

Sitting in a corner of the cafe that day, Floyd peered out the window and wondered in which direction his future truly lay. There was really nothing waiting for him in Dallas; or anywhere else, for that matter. He had been in the army for the past six years, and until he was seriously injured in the South Pacific, he had planned to make the service his career. In the army he had found the stability he so sorely lacked in civilian life.

He had come back from the war with a Silver Star medal, two fingers missing from his left hand, a six-inch scar across his stomach and five hundred dollars in mustering out pay. But other than that, Floyd had little else to show for his six years in the infantry.

Sitting alone in the cafe that morning, Floyd had been dwelling, however, more on his future than on his past when Lupe walked up with his order of ham and eggs. He'd grimaced when he saw the food. The ham was cooked to a crisp and the eggs were a watery mess.

"Lady, this place should get itself a real cook," he had said to Lupe. "Hell, we had better chefs in the infantry."

Looking up from his plate, Floyd had studied Lupe for a moment. The pretty Mexican waitress was obviously overworked, and it wasn't her fault the cook had so badly botched the breakfast. Floyd was sorry he had made the remark.

"You think you can do better?" Lupe asked, with a frazzled smile.

"Hell, anybody could, with a little practice," Floyd said, returning her smile. She was one good-looking woman, he thought.

"Well, the new cook we got been practicing for three weeks now," she muttered, glancing back toward the kitchen.

Floyd chuckled. "Just goes to prove that practice don't always make perfect, huh?"

Over the next half-hour, Floyd and Lupe had sandwiched in a bit more conversation between her trips to the kitchen. When the bus for Dallas finally rolled back onto the highway, Floyd had not been on it.

Now Floyd was staring down that same highway, remembering a morning that seemed a lifetime ago.

"Well, Val, I was headed east eight years ago, when I first came through here... and guess that's the direction I'd go in again. But least I'd leave knowing that your mother got whatever she'd been hoping for, and was finally happy."

It surprised Val that the prospect of Floyd leaving should sadden him; yet if his father did come home, Floyd would have to leave. He had tried so hard to please Lupe, but had never been able to become the person she really wanted.

Years before, Val had read somewhere, or more probably heard in a movie, that people are basically formed, or deformed, by both those who loved them, as well as by those whose love they wanted, but couldn't win. Floyd seemed living proof of that. He had been crippled, Val thought, by Lupe's coldness as surely as if he'd lost a leg in the war.

"Well, young fella, do we have a deal?" Floyd finally asked, extending his hand across the fence.

"Yeah, okay," Val muttered, shaking Floyd's hand. "So now where do I locate this so-called legend?"

Floyd tossed away his cigarette. "Well, best place to start, I think, is about two hundred miles west of here. El Paso... and a good friend of yours right here in Big Bend can probably tell you exactly where in El Paso."

"Geez, hope so. I hear El Paso's a mighty big place."

"Now your friend here in town might pretend he don't know nothing about your old man. But stay after him... because I sorta suspect your friend would also like to get this finally settled. One way or another."

Val had guessed who Floyd had in mind. What was harder to figure was why Noah Carson might have some personal stake in the matter.

Chapter 14

When Val told Noah Carson he knew about Frank Cooper and planned to hunt him down, the lawyer bolted for his bottle of brandy. Then he started to stalk around his cramped office like a caged tiger. Val could almost hear Carson growl every time he glanced in his direction.

"But Mr. Carson, if Floyd's willing to help me, don't see why you can't. Heck, he's got a lot more at stake than you do!"

"Oh, come on, Valentín, stop the goddamned baby talk," Carson snarled. "Doesn't matter to me what your stepfather decided. What counts is that you're running away from your responsibility to Bonnie and that unborn child!"

In any other town, how Noah Carson had found out about Val's impending parenthood might have posed a mystery. But not in Big Bend, where Val had often observed that bad news travelled faster than a flying saucer.

"But like some oversexed jackass," Carson continued, "thought you could have all the pleasure without any of the pain, huh?"

This was not entirely accurate, but Val knew better than to argue technicalities with a lawyer.

"And you have this notion," Carson went on, "that personal freedom doesn't have a price tag, that once you hit the open road, you're free and clear to—"

"No sir, I don't think—"

"But boy, let me give you a news flash: you're going to have one mean companion every step of the way!"

"Who's that, Mr. Carson?" Val timidly asked.

"Not who, what—your conscience!" Carson thundered. "And it's not going to give you a single mile's worth of peace, no matter how far nor how fast you run!"

Carson paused for a refill, which gave Val a chance to catch his breath. He felt as if he was bucking one hell of a head wind, yet sensed it would soon get stronger.

"But the trouble you're running toward, Val, will probably be far worse than what you're trying to leave behind," Carson snapped, taking another slug of brandy.

"Why's that, sir?" Val softly inquired. He didn't really want to know, but did want Carson to think he was paying close attention.

"Why—? Because I know your father! Frank Cooper was, and undoubtedly still is, a nickel-plated bastard! Totally incapable of loving anything other than a pat hand of poker! People, he treats like little more than wind-up toys which—"

Carson abruptly stopped. He seemed embarrassed that his feelings about Cooper obviously ran so deep. Sitting down, Carson stared past the statuette of Clarence Darrow at Val. A sheepish look snuck across the lawyer's imposing features.

"But aside from that, Val, I think your father is one of the most fascinating men I've ever met."

Val shrugged, hoping to imply that this characteristic ran in his family. "But Mr. Carson, I'm not asking you to like him. Just want you to help me find him, that's all."

Mumbling something in the direction of his drink, the lawyer said, "Well, I never had anything personal against him. Just that I didn't much like what he did to your mother."

"And I didn't much like what she did to me," Val heatedly replied, though he was careful to stay close to the door. "All those lies for all those years—and now she won't even help me find him, so I can get the truth for myself!"

The argument didn't seem to impress Carson. For a long and painful moment, he simply glared at Val; then he turned toward the scruffy mountains out past his window. Val figured it was time to leave. But as he was about to thank Carson very much for nothing, the lawyer started to speak again; and something in his voice told Val the battle was not yet lost.

"Can you really blame your mother for not wanting to help you? Think she's pleased at the prospect of having her heart broken all over again by the same man?" Carson asked quietly, still staring at the mountains.

Val couldn't see his face, but the tremor in his voice made him think Carson was now heading toward uncharted terrain.

Finally, the lawyer rose up to his full height and heaved a heavy sigh, as if reluctant to continue the trek, but aware he had gone too far to turn back.

The silence lasted for several seconds. Fearing he might be pushing Carson too hard, Val decided to ease off a little.

"You seem to know a lot about everybody in this town, Mr. Carson. But nobody knows nothing about you... Not even why you ever chose to settle here in Big Bend."

Noah Carson smiled to himself. He had been able to keep his history where it belonged. In the past. Carson had first come to Big Bend some eighteen years earlier. But on the day he arrived, he had not been smiling.

Though still in his early forties, his future had seemingly already been used up. Only the year before he arrived, Carson had lost his wife, his health, and his reputation. Carson's wife had died of cancer, and in despair he sought refuge in alcohol. His law practice in Fort Worth suffered severely, and within months he was close to being disbarred for neglecting his clients.

Then the crowning blow came when he contracted tuberculosis. If he hoped to live much beyond his next birthday, his doctor suggested he seek out a much drier climate.

Piling what remained of his belongings into his 1934 Dodge, Carson drove west, bound for Arizona. He had bought the car new the year before, but just outside Big Bend, it snapped an axle. Yet what seemed at the time a serious setback would later turn into a blessing of sorts. In the two weeks it took for another axle to arrive from El Paso, Carson had decided not to drive any farther west. The climate in Big Bend suited him, he liked the people he met, and of the town's population of some 25,000, there was only one lawyer.

One of Carson's first clients had been Val's mother. Lupe had recently come into enough money to make a down payment on the roadside cafe where she worked as a waitress. Carson had drawn up a contract that was fair to everyone except himself, joking to Lupe that he would take his legal fee out in free coffee. From that day on, he became the cafe's best customer, and would remain so until a summer morning in 1946, when Floyd Dalton went to work in the kitchen of the cafe.

In the nearly ten years that followed, Carson had rarely been back to the restaurant. Lupe had married Floyd; but Carson could not quite let go of Lupe, and by way of staying in her life as best he could, the lawyer became both friend and mentor to her only child.

Yet Lupe still stirred something deep inside him, and when Carson now turned to face Val, his eyes were wistful with the memory of what might have been.

"You know, son, back in those days, your mother was about the prettiest, most gallant little lady I had ever met. A man could have gone a long way with a woman like Lupita by his side. But your father had on king-sized blinders. Was a classic case of casting pearls in front of pigs... What the hell Cooper was looking for, I'll never know."

Val tried to keep from smiling. It seemed that Noah Carson, for some mysterious reason of his own, had obviously changed his mind about helping Val find his father. But not wanting to push him too far too fast, Val simply said, "Well, guess whatever he was looking for is what I need to find out for myself."

The room grew very quiet. Then Carson took a file from out of his desk drawer. He was muttering to himself as if he'd been taking lessons from his secretary, Miss Violet. Pulling a scrap of paper from the file, Carson sat down, drew his phone closer and dialed the long-distance operator.

"Good morning, Hazel. This is Noah Carson speaking... Fine, thanks. Listen, like for you to connect me to a number in El Paso. It's Logan 5-7541. Thank you kindly, dear..."

For the next several seconds, time seemed to stand still. Val started to inch toward the desk. But his legs seemed to go out from under him, and he felt as if he was sliding forward on his stomach.

"Hello, I'm calling for Frank Cooper," Carson murmured into the phone. "I see... Well, how soon you expect him back in El Paso? All right, when he gets in, or calls, please ask him to telephone me. Noah Carson in Big Bend. He has my number and will know what it's all about... Thank you, sir."

Slowly setting the receiver down, Carson swiveled his chair around, and once again faced the window. Several seconds crawled by before he finally spoke. "I've always been able to reach your father through the Cattlemen's Hotel in El Paso. They say he's due in there tomorrow morning, but not expected to stay for more than a day or two. So now it's your call, boy..."

"Listen, sir, even if I don't get to spend more than fifteen minutes with him, I'm going... And thank you!" Val hoped he sounded a lot more positive than he really felt. Carson turned to study him for a moment. Then he smiled grimly. "Better wait till you get back before thanking me, son—and that's assuming you live through the experience."

Val shrugged his shoulders. Carson continued to peer at him in a curious way, as if trying to determine whether Val was a lot tougher than he thought, or simply much dumber than he had ever dreamed.

≫ ≪

Two hours later, Val was wondering the same thing himself. In his tenuous state of mind, he had been waiting for the first little thing to go wrong, anything that might give him an excuse to cancel his plans. Earlier he had withdrawn fifteen hundred dollars from his brand-new bank account, more than half what his father left him. Val wasn't sure why he wanted to take so much money with him, but simply sensed he might need it.

Clarence had gotten permission to go with him, though he'd lied to his parents about the destination and exact purpose of the trip. Clarence had said that he and Val wanted to drive up to Midland to see a major-league baseball exhibition game.

His parents, surprised by his sudden interest in baseball, and not realizing that the major league regular season had already begun, still thought he had earned a vacation for working so hard to win his scholarship, and reluctantly granted him permission to make the trip.

Val and Clarence were to rendezvous back at the diner at twelve noon.

Returning to the restaurant, Val announced his intentions to his mother. He told her how much money he was taking, and how long he planned to be gone. Val had expected to encounter some flak, but neither Lupe nor Floyd uttered a word of protest. It wouldn't have mattered anyway. Val wasn't about to take his money back to the bank; certainly not after he'd bragged to all the tellers about his travel plans.

He had told Clarence they'd be shoving off at high noon, and right on the dot, the little pickup skidded to a stop in front of the diner. Val had hoped to make an inconspicuous departure, with as few people in the bon voyage party as possible. But his pal's noisy arrival blew away his plans.

Grabbing the secondhand cardboard suitcase he had bought that morning, Val hurried toward the truck just as Clarence came bounding out of it.

"Saddle up, pilgrim," he bellowed, loud enough, Val thought, for even John Wayne, wherever he was, to hear. "Let's take 'em to Missouri!"

"Geez, thought I'd seen too many movies," Val said, tossing his suitcase into the back of the truck. "Come on, let's ditch this dump before we draw a crowd."

But just then Clarence whipped off his cowboy hat, and waved it in the direction of the diner. Lupe and Floyd were standing just past the screen of the front door. Val warily angled toward them. Clarence, sensing his mood, instantly folded up his wild-west act, and meekly got back into the truck.

Val stopped well short of the diner door. He and his mother stood staring at each other through the screen. Val had already said his piece, and figured she felt the same way. But no such luck; and to make it worse, when Lupe started to speak, her voice sounded to Val as mournful as a graveside eulogy.

"Este es el segundo mas triste día de mi vida."

Lupe had called this the second saddest day of her life. Val wondered what the most sorrowful day might have been. He figured it was either when her father had left her in south Texas, or the day Frank Cooper had bolted out of Big Bend.

"No puedo recordar ningun tiempo cuando has hecho una cosa tan contra de lo que quiero," she said, after a long pause.

"Well, guess there's never been another time when I had to go against you, Mom."

Lupe seemed uncertain of what to do or say next. She turned back to Floyd, who smiled reassuringly and handed her a paper sack. Then she came out the screen door, walked a few feet past Val, and stopped. Without looking back, she thrust the sack in his direction.

"Roast beef sandwiches Floyd make for you boys... from the wedding dinner last night."

Taking the sack, Val nodded his thanks to Floyd, then turned to Lupe and dropped his voice to a whisper.

"If I find him, Mom, anything you want me to tell him?"

Lupe turned to gaze off toward the old road to El Paso. "Yes, Valentín... tell to him the business here come out good and always I be grateful to him for helping me to buy the cafe."

When she finally turned to face Val, she had tears in her eyes. "And remember this... No man ever living up to what I put all these years into your head. So do not go expecting too much, and maybe you come home with less disappointment, eh?"

Giving Val a hurried hug, Lupe strode back into the cafe. Watching her go, Val now realized that despite all her tough talk, she must have always felt, deep down, like just another frightened Mexican trying to keep body and soul together in what she perceived as the hostile territory of West Texas.

With not much more to do or say, Val waved goodbye to his secret benefactor. "So long, Floyd. Thanks... and take good care of that jukebox, will you?"

Floyd flushed up a troubled-looking smile, and waved. It seemed they both shared a dislike for long goodbyes. But for a fleeting moment, Val wondered why he should feel this way. Other than the night many years before when he and Clarence had hitched a freight train down to the next town, this was the first time he had ever gone anywhere.

With a final wave, Val climbed into the truck. Clarence sounded the cavalry charge as they went fishtailing across the gravel toward the highway. Glancing back, Val saw Floyd put his arm around Lupe. That image of her and Floyd huddled together at the door would linger in his mind for the next several miles.

Clarence had cracked open a six-pack of beer, and was trying to keep Val interested in the only game Val could beat him at; Val figured it must have looked like he needed cheering up.

"Okay, next question: For a hundred bucks, name one of the few movies John Wayne ever died in?"

Prying open a beer, Val took a swallow before answering. But it wasn't the size of the bet that made him pause; from their previous movie guessing games, Clarence already owed him more than ten thousand dollars. Val's problem went lower. They had travelled no more than ten miles, but already his feet had grown very cold.

Clarence's smile grew bigger with each passing second. Then Val finally answered. "The Sands of Iwo Jima."

Arching his back as if Val had stuck a knife in his spine, Clarence said, "Oh, balls, that's a hundred bucks I already owe you!" he groaned. "But now it's get even time, folks. Name the last Marlon Brando movie where he got to keep the girl."

Val clammed up again, though this time for a different reason. He couldn't remember the name of the goddamned movie.

"For a thousand bucks!" Clarence chortled, kicking the bet as Val hesitated. Then Clarence sensed the real reason behind Val's silence. "Well, pilgrim, you're some world traveler—barely ten miles out of Big Bend, and you're already homesick!"

"No, not really," Val lied. "Just thinking what I'm gonna say to my father, when I finally meet up with him."

Clarence must have considered this a tough question, Val thought, because for several seconds his friend actually stopped moving his mouth.

"The problem is: do I hug my father before I hit him, or afterwards?" Val asked.

The query seemed to unsettle Clarence. Only now did it dawn on Val that his friend had said very little about Frank Cooper's miraculous resurrection; maybe deep down, Clarence resented it. He had probably grown pretty used to having a fatherless friend, and was not too keen about making an abrupt adjustment.

Already Clarence had slid into a sullen silence. Then he spotted a mileage marker up ahead. "Elll Paassoo!" he announced in his best railroad conductor voice. "One hundred and eighty-five miles. Next stop: wine, women, and song!"

Then Clarence started to sing the Marty Robbins song "El Paso." Only at breakneck speed. He sounded like someone trying to sing as he nervously bailed water out of a sinking canoe. He must have figured the only reason Val had asked him to come along was just to keep their spirits afloat.

Val started to sing along with him. He had always liked the song. Now Val wondered if he would also like the city; and the more he thought about it, the louder he sang.

⇒ PART THREE ⇐

Chapter 15

Gamblers don't believe in good luck. Rather illogically, however, they say there are some people who simply never have it. Now Frank Cooper, sure he wasn't among those luckless souls, was driving hundreds of miles to a poker game he figured he'd already won. Even so, uncertain of exactly how much he might win, he had brought along Blue Morgan as his insurance policy.

They had been cruising south from Reno since early morning, but were still more than seven hundred miles from El Paso when Cooper leaned back to announce: "Hey, think I better call on ahead, just to make sure the game's all set for tomorrow night. Say, you still alive back there?"

Creeping into view from the back seat, Blue carefully held her head as if it were a pane of glass. She had thrown a going-away party the night before. The celebration proved so rowdy, however, that by morning she hadn't wanted to go anywhere but back to bed. Now, besides having a blinding hangover, her ulcer had turned carnivorous again.

Squinting out at the parched countryside, Blue uttered her first words of the day. "Damn, don't this desert ever get tired of being a desert? Hell, even Kansas looked better than this!"

"Say, you're cranky as a six-year-old brat without breakfast," Cooper said, chuckling. "I better buy you a hamburger right quick."

Rolling her eyes, Blue sank from sight. "Whatever you say, big spender. Just make sure it comes with a gallon of milk," she groused, and said no more until she got the hamburger, which was still fifty miles away.

➤➤ ◄◄

At about sunset of that same day, Val and Clarence finally arrived in El Paso. In the spectacular hues of late afternoon, the border town was a colorful sight. Lights were twinkling like fireflies almost as far as the eye could see. To the south, the waters of the Rio Grande shimmered in the dying glow. Beyond the river, Mexico lay beckoning like an exotic and mysterious woman.

From a road that ran around the rim of the large mountain which overlooked the city, they stood sizing up the territory. Val had heard that the population of both El Paso and Juarez, its sister city across the river, numbered some half-million people. But peering down at the huge expanse, he had just one person in mind.

"Big, huh?" Clarence remarked. The sheer size of the two towns staggered him. Like Val, Clarence had never ventured more than twenty miles out of Big Bend.

"Yeah, big, all right," Val echoed. "But hell, next to our hometown, almost anything would be." Then, lowering his gaze to the downtown area of El Paso, Val's mood seemed to drop. "Okay, let's go check, see if he's gotten into town. Then we'll get a motel, maybe go see a movie, huh?"

Clarence looked as if he'd just gotten dirt in his mouth. "Damn, Val, if seeing movies is all we're gonna do, coulda done that back in Big Bend!"

Val grinned warily. It didn't take a genius to guess the alternative program Clarence had in mind.

"No, Clarence, I'm a little nervous. Besides, from what I hear, all the girls in the whorehouses over in Juarez look a bit like baby elephants." Val had never heard any such thing.

"Yeah, but after we down a couple of drinks, we're probably gonna think we're elephants ourselves—and with enough booze in us, just about anything is gonna look beautiful!"

Clarence's attempt to sound experienced made Val laugh; at eighteen, his friend was still a virgin, though Clarence blamed this entirely on the frigidity of Big Bend's female population.

Val decided to call Clarence's bluff; a man could only take so much, even from his best pal. "Hey, I'll bet twenty dollars you're too chicken to score even in a whorehouse—and if you lose the bet, don't even have to pay me."

A gleam came into Clarence's eyes. Thrusting out his jaw, he declared: "Val, you just lost twenty bucks—because after I toss down a couple of tequilas, those Mexican *señoritas* gonna think they've tangled with a sailor who ain't had shore leave in a very long time."

Suddenly Val didn't think his bet looked so good. Strange things had happened recently—and if his father could manage the miracle of returning from the dead, it seemed vaguely possible that even Clarence could get laid.

❧ ❧

The Cattlemen's Hotel sat right in the heart of downtown El Paso. The ten-story building had been built back in the booming twenties, and no cost had been spared to make it an oasis in the desert for those wealthy enough to handle the cover charge. The lobby, all gleaming brass and mahogany wood, looked, Val thought, only slightly smaller than his high school auditorium.

The pinched-faced clerk behind the registration desk gave Val and Clarence a withering look before he finally spoke. "Yes, how may I help you?"

Val cleared his throat. "Yessir, we're, uh, looking for somebody..."

"Anyone I might know?" the clerk muttered, turning to sort through some mail.

"Yessir... Frank Cooper."

The desk clerk abruptly wheeled around, something vaguely resembling a smile settling over his features. "Is Mr. Cooper a friend of yours?"

That was a hard question to answer. "No, not really," Val quietly said. "Just like to know if he's got here yet."

For a moment, the clerk seemed rather stumped himself. Val could almost hear what the man was thinking. He obviously had little regard for the two young hicks standing before him; but on the other hand, Frank Cooper was one of the hotel's most valued patrons. It might not be wise to insult anyone even remotely connected with him.

"Mr. Cooper is due in tomorrow morning. Would you care to leave a message for him?"

Val backed away from the desk. "No, thanks. I'll deliver it in person."

Then, getting instructions from the hotel's doorman, Val and Clarence started toward the bridge that led over the Rio Grande River. Val sat gawking at the sights. Tall buildings, wide boulevards and huge movie theaters—and all playing pictures that would probably take another five years before they limped into Big Bend.

Val grew quiet as he and Clarence reached the river, and crossed the wide span of steel and concrete into Mexico. He had never before set foot in his mother's country, and knew that her birthplace of Chihuahua City was only two hundred miles south of the border.

He wondered what the place looked like, and whether she had any relatives still living there; somebody who was part of her past, as well as his. He also wondered why his mother had so rarely spoken about the city where she had been born.

But Juarez didn't seem the best place to begin his exploration of Mexico. The town looked like the setting of a carnival movie with Spanish subtitles. Val was disappointed.

He had expected to see *sarape*-clad women beating on stones and horsemen with bandoliers across their chests, like characters out of "Viva Zapata."

Clarence, however, looked delirious. He felt sure they had hit the mother lode of adult entertainment. Over the next few hours, they sideswiped several bars and strip joints. The main drag in Juarez was an endless stream of blazing neon, where it appeared the tourists celebrated New Year's Eve every night. Yet no one made more noise than Clarence; and with each tequila he drank, the louder he became.

Then, around midnight, his noise box suddenly went so quiet, it seemed its cord had been jerked out from a wall socket. He and Val were recuperating in a drowsy cantina about half a block from the main boardwalk, when Val reminded him of their bet.

He figured Clarence had gassed up enough to make a run at it; what Val didn't know was that it was now all Clarence could do to simply walk.

Clarence didn't realize it, either. Swiveling around on his barstool, he happily announced to the general crowd that he was off to the first whorehouse he could find. But when he slid off the chair, he couldn't even find the floor until he hit it with his head.

Glaring down at Clarence for a moment, Val peeled him off the concrete floor, then draped him around his shoulders and weaved toward the door. Val felt pretty drunk himself, but he was still sober enough to itch with mortification.

Yet as he struggled down the full length of the bar with his friend strapped across his back, not a single Mexican paid them the slightest attention. Maybe they were accustomed, Val thought, to the sight of Americans falling off barstools.

≫ ≪

By nine o'clock the following morning, Val and Clarence were stationed in the lobby of the Cattlemen's Hotel, awaiting the arrival of Frank Cooper. The huge room was filled with stuffed animals. Mounted heads of wild boar, buffalo and mountain lions hung on every wall. Val thought they all appeared to be glaring at him.

He and Clarence were perched on a cowhide sofa that sat about a hundred feet from the main entrance. From there they could see everyone who came in through the front door.

But Clarence was not much help. With his hangover, he seemed unable to focus on the potted palm sitting right next to him. For the better part of the next hour, they sat there glassy-eyed and frozen faced; looking, Val supposed, like a couple of mounted heads themselves. By now some of the hotel's personnel were shooting semi-hostile stares in their direction. The desk clerk Val had spoken with the previous afternoon was nowhere in sight.

As for the others, Val figured their unfriendly interest had something to do with the shade of his skin. The night before, over in Juarez, he had hardly seen anybody with a different color than his own; now, just a few miles north of the Rio Grande, they seemed as rare a breed as the buffalo hanging over his head.

Feeling a sudden urge to hide behind something, Val picked up a travel folder someone had left on the sofa, and held it up close to his face. But though the folder was about California, all Val could think about was the dusky color of his skin.

His dark complexion had embarrassed him for most of his life. In grade school, many of his classmates had regarded him as some sort of freak. But by the time he reached high school and became a good football player, most of them no longer seemed so seriously troubled by his mixed breeding. Football in West Texas was nearly a religion; winning was its central creed. If a mixed breed could help them avoid a losing season, then it was an easily forgivable sin.

More trouble had come at Val from an unexpected source. The pure-blooded Mexicans in Val's high school were few in number, but all meaner than cornered coyotes. They resented what they perceived as his attempt to pass as a deeply sun-tanned Anglo. Many a hellish afternoon had been spent giving Val what they called an "adjustment of attitude."

So if anybody had ever asked Val how he'd liked growing up a half-breed in Big Bend, he might have responded with the old line that "excepting for the honor, he would just as soon not have."

Val was remembering all this when someone walked through the front door of the hotel who looked very much like the faded image he had of Frank Cooper. Yet never having seen him in person, Val couldn't tell for sure. But if ever anyone matched the myth he'd been nurtured on, it was this tall, ruggedly handsome man now striding across the lobby of the Cattlemen's Hotel as if he owned it.

Watching Cooper, Val could feel his stomach turn over. For a moment, he thought he might be sick right there on the gleaming hardwood floor of the lobby. Then the sensation passed, but was followed by another almost as unsettling. Val's hands began to tremble as both fear and anticipation swept over him. Cooper seemed a ghost who had returned from the grave to assume the form of the man standing at the registration desk.

Right behind him had hobbled an elderly valet carrying two large pieces of luggage. One of the bags was pink. Val figured it belonged to the blonde walking a few steps behind Cooper.

She was the most gorgeous woman Val had ever seen, either in or out of a movie house, with a figure that more than matched her face. Val nudged Clarence, nodding toward the front desk, where Cooper was being greeted by several of the hotel's employees.

"Think that's him?" Clarence asked, trying to focus his bloodshot eyes.

"Hey, you've seen his picture a hundred times," Val said.

Clarence squinted harder. "Yeah, but that picture's almost as old as you are. Well, only one way to find out."

Groping around for his legs, Clarence looked as if he planned to walk over and ask to see Cooper's driver's license. Val grabbed his arm, and hissed, "Hey, sit down! Damn, those tequilas musta permanently bashed your brain."

Clarence's expression turned queasy. He slowly sank back down, his face pale as the white part of the cowhide sofa. "Val, if you value our friendship, please refrain from mentioning even the name of that particular beverage."

Val turned away. In the distance, Cooper was shaking hands with a dapperly-dressed man who had just come out of his office.

"Welcome back to El Paso, Mr. Cooper," the manager said.

"Good to be back, Herb," Cooper said, signing the register. "Everything all set for tonight?"

"Just like always, same suite, same supplies, and same stock of our best drinking material."

Cooper smiled. "Well, now let's hope I have the same luck."

The manager chuckled knowingly; then, sorting through a small stack of notes, he handed Cooper a piece of paper. "And you have a telephone message here. Came in yesterday morning from Big Bend."

Glancing at the note, Cooper's expression went sour. Looking up, he saw that Blue seemed worried about this sudden change.

"Herb, could I make this call from your office? You can just bill my room for the charge, can't you?"

"Of course, sir," the manager replied. Cooper started around the desk. "And you take all the time you need, hear?" the manager said, softly closing the door behind Cooper. Blue stood with a perplexed frown. It seemed obvious Cooper didn't want her to overhear the conversation.

Some hundred feet away, Val scrunched further back on the sofa. He tried to keep from staring at Blue, but it was no use. It troubled him that Cooper was travelling in the company of such a beautiful woman. She had made for another wild card in a deck that already seemed loaded.

"I don't think that's him," Val lied.

"Just don't like seeing him bound up with all that blonde stuff," Clarence muttered. "Gonna make it tougher to take him home with you, right?" Clarence wasn't wrong, which made his remark all the more annoying. Val raised his hand as if to smack him. But Clarence quickly closed his eyes and emitted a snoring noise.

Then Val saw Cooper come out of the office. Glumly nodding his thanks to the manager, he started across the lobby toward the elevators. Blue and the elderly valet hurried after him.

"Honey, have you just seen a ghost?" Blue asked, struggling to catch up with Cooper.

Cooper strode toward the elevators, his head held rigid. But out of the corner of his eye, he was scanning the lobby.

"Was that the ghost you called on the phone?" Blue quietly asked.

"The ghost's lawyer," Cooper muttered. "Tells me his client has come to El Paso looking for me."

They arrived at the elevators. The valet hit the button. Cooper stood staring at the closed doors. Blue, sensing something was seriously wrong, inched closer to Cooper.

"Who's this lawyer's client?"

"Some kid, I guess. Maybe his mother, too."

"What does this kid want from you?" Blue softly inquired.

"Money, probably... Maybe even worse, he wants me," Cooper murmured, glancing sideways to make sure the valet was out of earshot. "Little bastard is laboring under the impression that I'm his long-lost father."

If Cooper expected an incredulous laugh, he didn't get it. Blue had heard enough gamblers' double-talk over the past twenty years to have developed an almost infallible bullshit detector.

"Well, maybe the kid won't show up," Blue said.

One of the elevators had opened. As they all moved into it, Cooper said, "He already has. I think that's him sitting on the other side of the lobby." Startled, Blue turned and caught a glimpse of the two young men seated across the way just before the elevator door closed.

Watching from the distance, Val and Clarence sat sporting entirely different expressions. Then Clarence let loose a low whistle. "Man, that blonde's some kind of sexy stuff, huh?"

Suddenly Val regretted having asked his friend to come along with him to El Paso. But he was far more angry with himself. Why hadn't he just walked up to Cooper and introduced himself, then let the chips fall where they might? A humiliating thought struck Val like a blow to his already troubled stomach. He had come two hundred miles only to prove himself a coward.

Chapter 16

When the elevator opened, Cooper charged out like it was on fire. Blue, hoping to lift his spirits, hurried after him. "Hey, that dark-skinned kid sort of favors you. Nice-looking boy!"

Striding down the hallway, Cooper shot Blue an over-the-shoulder snarl. "And you think he's gotta be ugly and pearly white to make trouble for me, huh?"

"Okay, scratch that last observation," Blue muttered. "But listen, if his presence pesters you so bad, why not go back down to the lobby, tell him to get the hell lost?"

Cooper growled an obscenity. "Miss Morgan, I'd like to find a more subtle way of avoiding him."

Blue looked dubious. "Yeah, well, suppose you could sneak in and out of the hotel by the fire escape."

The elderly valet lugging their bags also looked skeptical. Arriving at their suite, he unlocked the door and started inside with the luggage. Blue was about to follow after the old man when Cooper stopped her short.

"Listen, honey, do me a favor?" he murmured, glancing back toward the elevator as if he expected to see Val dash out of it at any moment. "Go ask that damned kid downstairs what the hell he's doing here, and exactly what the hell he wants from—"

"Oh, and just how do I approach a total stranger with all these personal questions?"

"Oh, now come off your high horse, Miss Morgan. I gotta tell you how to approach strangers?"

The corrosive smile stung Blue worse than the words. For a moment, she fought back the urge to scream; then she stormed into the suite, slamming the door behind her. Cooper knew he had made a tactical mistake, and gave Blue a couple of moments to calm down before starting after her.

But the door had locked from the inside. Cooper had to knock on the door of his own suite, which did nothing to sweeten his spirits. As the valet came scurrying out, Cooper clapped on a smile, and dug into his pocket for some money.

"How about it, Harry?" he drawled. "Double or nothing?"

The old man cheerfully shook his bald head. "No, Mister Cooper, I don't do much gambling no more. Me and good luck parted company years ago. Now I just take whatever's coming to me, and grateful to get it."

"Harry, that's good advice," Cooper said, chuckling as he handed him a ten-dollar bill. "But don't sound like much fun."

Flashing a hit-or-miss smile, the old valet ambled away. Cooper advanced cautiously into the suite. He always took that same suite, number 507, because he was rather superstitious. Five and seven were his favorite numbers.

But he also liked the way the suite was decorated in a mode that could best be termed Western Outrageous. Its walls were hung with stuffed animals' heads and large Remington prints; the two bedrooms sported swinging saloon-style doors, and the long wet bar came complete with a foot railing, brass spittoons, and little stools outfitted with saddle seats.

Blue sat perched on one of the saddles, mixing herself a drink from the hotel's complimentary stock of liquor. Glancing back, she saw Cooper enter the suite. He looked unsure of what to say or do next.

"Blue, I am truly sorry," he finally grumbled, grinding down hard on each word. "Didn't mean to insult you. Sometimes I say things I don't exactly mean—"

"Oh, I thought the fabulous Frank Cooper never says nothing he don't mean?" Blue barked, pouring a splash of bourbon into her tumbler of branch water. To hell with her ulcer.

"And hey, cowboy, I didn't come all the way down to El Paso just to get my past pushed in my face—though I realize that is exactly what is now happening to you."

Cooper frowned. Taking off his Stetson, he sent it sailing toward a large cowhide sofa. "Well, I ain't gonna enter a formal plea just yet to any past misdemeanors. But plead guilty to the charge of accidental insult. Yet I hope my steady attendance at Sunday School might convince the court to go easy on me."

His mock-penitent mood vaguely amused Blue. "Okay, Frank. Gonna let you off on probation this time."

"Can I choose my probation officer, ma'am?"

Blue chuckled. Setting aside her drink, which already was aggravating her stomach, she slowly walked over to the window. "Guess I'm just a little sensitive about my own past. Think I need to shine back up the one talent the Good Lord gave me, so maybe someday... I'll be able to say: Hey, folks, I'm a saloon singer. Nothing more, but nothing less, neither. Damn good at it, and damned proud of it, too."

Gazing down at the hundreds of people on the street below, Blue wondered how many of them could make such a boast about their own lives; not many, she mused. She remembered the old line her mother sometimes quoted from the Bible: "Many are called, but few are chosen."

Cooper lowered himself into a chair, and now sat gazing down at his feet. "Well, Blue, I'm pretty fair at what I do, but ain't never felt especially proud of it," he murmured, checking out the wear on the heels of his boots. "But maybe if I hit big with that poker game back up in Reno, be worth a try to get into something a bit more respectable, for a change."

"What's your idea of something more respectable?" Blue asked quietly. "Cattle rustling?"

"Oh, can't say for sure," Cooper said. "But that nightclub notion of yours didn't sound so bad."

Turning away from the window, Blue studied Cooper. When she finally spoke, her voice was no louder than a whisper. "Now you wouldn't try to hustle a hustler?"

"Hey, honey, I've pissed money into a lot worse places than a little nightspot," Cooper groused, still peering down at the three-hundred dollar snakeskin boots he'd been forced to hock on more than one occasion.

Blue smiled. She was too old to believe everything a man like Cooper might tell her, yet still young enough to want to.

Picking up Cooper's Stetson off the sofa, she started toward him. "Well, Frank, here's my business forecast: with your brains and your looks, we might make one hell of a combination."

Cooper grinned, though the joke didn't appear to lift his spirits by more than an inch or two. "I sure need something brand-new in my life, tell you that. Or maybe I'm just starting to feel my age... But the nasty notion of wasting the rest of my days struggling to fill inside straights sometimes gets me a bit spooked."

Cooper's confession touched Blue. In the three days and nights they had been together, this seemed the only time he had let her see behind his freewheeling façade. Taking his head in her hands, she cradled it against her chest.

For the first time since they had met, Blue thought they might have a future together.

Then Cooper broke loose from her grasp. "But meanwhile, there's chores to be done," he said, handing Blue a hundred-dollar bill. "So you mosey on down to the beauty parlor. Get all gussied up. Then buy yourself a gallon of sexy perfume. I'm counting on you to distract the hell outta them other poker players tonight. Hear?"

Blue sparked right up. For a long period in her life she'd been absolutely sure of her sex appeal. But those comforting days were now history. Twenty years in a soul-sapping business had beaten her down to the nub. Blue no longer took anything for granted anymore.

Cooper knew this. Spotting other people's weaknesses was part of what made him a successful gambler. Now, playing off her insecurities, he had managed to keep his insurance policy paid up in full.

Buried in bliss once more, Blue gave him a grateful kiss, propped his hat back on his head, and started into one of the bedrooms to change her clothes.

≫ ≪

To better shield themselves from the hard stares still coming at them from the main desk, Val and Clarence had moved to a table closer to the hotel's novelty shop. Just before making this strategic move, Val had drifted into the shop.

In his muddled state of mind, he bought the first thing that caught his eye, a pegboard puzzle that later seemed designed to make him feel stupid.

After giving it his best shot, Val passed it on to Clarence, and was delighted that his friend couldn't figure it out, either. But, failure usually made Clarence even feistier.

"So Val, if you're too chicken-livered to actually face your father, why not just call him on the phone?"

Val responded with what he thought was heroic temperance. "And exactly what do I say when I've got him on the line?"

"Keep it simple," Clarence replied. "Ask him what he wants for Father's Day."

The idea of strangling Clarence had just popped into Val's mind when he saw Blue Morgan step out of the elevator. Blue was now wearing form-fitting Levis and an even tighter-tugging red gingham cowboy shirt. Val watched her sashay over to the novelty shop, where she began to browse through a rack of post-cards.

As yet Val had no notion that she and Cooper knew who he was; but Val did know that unless he quickly mustered up a lit-tle courage, he would soon be making a long and humiliating retreat back to Big Bend.

Blue was starting toward the beauty shop across the lobby when Val made his move. "Say ma'am," he called out, hoisting a limp smile. "Listen, could you explain to us how this little game is played?" Val pointed down to the pegboard. The ploy seemed as weak as his grin, but Blue didn't appear to mind.

She smiled and started toward him. Val noticed the closer she got, the prettier she became. He also noticed that Clarence was now making strange little sibilant sounds.

"Dammit, stop vibrating," Val whispered to Clarence, as Blue came up to their table.

"Oh, hell, has that little chicken-squat game got you boys buffaloed?" Blue asked.

Clarence started to stammer. "Well, not really, really, but sort of... manner of speaking, of course. You like to play this game, ma'am?"

Blue snorted. "Tell you what I'd really like—and that's to strangle the sadistic son-of-a-bitch who designed it."

With a nervous laugh, Val stood up and offered his chair to Blue, hoping she wasn't already bored by the conversation.

"Well, okay," Blue moaned, easing into the chair. "I'll give this game one more chance, just to be sociable."

No sooner did Blue get the weight off her feet when Clarence passed her the pegboard. "Thank you, sir," Blue murmured in a husky voice that Val thought went perfect with the rest of her equipment.

"Now... with whom do I have the pleasure of breaking my brain?"

Like a shot, Clarence's hand sailed across the table. "Hi, my name's Clarence Kendall, and this here is—"

"Roger Worthington," Val interjected, then felt himself blush with embarrassment. Why the hell had he chosen such an unlikely name? With his dark skin, pitch-black hair and mixed-up manner, he could more plausibly have passed himself off as an Indian called Water on the Brain.

Blue pumped Clarence's hand, then did the same with Val. "My name's Blue Morgan. Delighted to meet both you boys," she said, smiling. "But I do wish it was under less taxing circumstances."

With the formalities out of the way, Blue pretended to concentrate on the game. Val started to slowly walk around the table, figuring a moving target might be harder to hit.

Then Clarence, staring at Blue so intently Val thought his horned-rimmed glasses might fog up, asked, "That your real name, ma'am, 'Blue Morgan'?"

Blue laughed. Her teeth, Val noticed, looked absolutely perfect. Damn, he thought, don't this lady friend of Cooper's have at least one flaw?

"Honey," Blue replied to Clarence, "most folks can't even pronounce my real name. So I just never bother with it." Then, glancing over her shoulder in Val's direction, Blue said, "And what about you... Roger?"

"What about me, ma'am?" Val warily asked.

"You any good at this here game?" she politely inquired.

Breathing a little easier, Val nodded nonchalantly. "No, ma'am, it's not exactly my kind of game."

"What is your kind of game, Roger?" Blue casually asked, still pretending to be engrossed in the pegboard game. When Val didn't answer, she raised her green eyes and fixed him with a strange stare. Blue suddenly seemed rather sad.

Then, looking as if she'd made up her mind about something, she smiled. "Roger, you must be a poker player, way you hold your cards so close to the vest... and now there just happens to be a little game tonight that—"

"Oh, no, Miss Morgan," Clarence interjected. "We'd be way out of our league, just a couple of boys from Big Bend—"

"I'd like to play. Thank you, ma'am," Val quietly declared.

Blue nodded thoughtfully. Val had the eerie feeling she was trying to do him a favor, though he couldn't figure out why. Then Blue pushed the pegboard game away, and rose from her chair.

"Yeah, Roger, sorta had you figured for a player. Well, I gotta go get my hair overhauled. But hope to see you boys this evening. Suite 507. Just get off the elevator and head for the noise."

With a cheery wave, Blue started across the lobby. Val and Clarence sat watching her walk toward the beauty parlor, each of them nursing a different notion.

"God Almighty," Clarence uttered with awe. "Seems like every part of her moves at the same time, don't it?"

He wasn't wrong, but this seemed to Val hardly the ideal moment for a discussion on the mysteries of the female body.

"Hey, come on, Clarence," he grumbled. "We got more serious stuff to think about than—"

"Oh, maybe you do," Clarence chortled, as Blue disappeared into the beauty shop. "But I ain't the geek going up against any professional gamblers tonight, am I?"

"Hey, wise-ass, you forget I've played a lot of poker in—"

"Yeah, but most of the time with a bunch of bimbos, using bottle caps for chips," Clarence hissed.

Val could offer no rebuttal. Still, he had learned the game from no less an expert than Noah Carson; but as Clarence had reminded him, never in a game where anything but bottle caps had been used for chips.

There was, however, another consideration, though Val knew his friend would think it totally irrational.

"Listen, Clarence, I gotta get close to Cooper in some way, even if it costs every dime he left me to do it," Val said, slowing getting to his feet.

The reaction was about what Val expected. Clarence's eyes grew grave with mock concern. Putting the palm of one hand over Val's forehead, as if to ascertain just how high his fever had climbed, Clarence guided him back into a chair, all the while murmuring what someone might say to a retarded child.

Clarence's diagnosis, Val suddenly realized, might not be that far wrong.

Chapter 17

When Blue got back up to Cooper's suite, he was sprawled out on the bed, Stetson nesting on his face. She figured he'd earned a rest, having done all of the driving from Reno. Blue sat down and started to pry off her boots as quietly as possible; a task ordinarily accompanied by much groaning and cursing.

"That boy still lurking around down there?" Cooper finally muttered from under his hat.

His voice startled Blue. "Geez, why didn't you tell me you was awake? It's tough to take my boots off without cussing!"

"Is that kid still downstairs?"

"Yeah, I talked to him," Blue said, struggling with her last boot. "Nice guy. Says he likes to play poker. I told him we was having a game tonight and gave him an invite."

Cooper slowly hoisted his hat and squinted sideways at Blue. "We musta miscommunicated. I wanted you to obtain information, not disclose it!"

"Oh, come on, Frank," Blue murmured. "What's it gonna cost you just to get acquainted with—"

"Madam, that is exactly what I'm worried about," Cooper grumbled, dropping the Stetson back over his face.

Blue suddenly realized there might be worms in the can she had so blithely opened down in the lobby. Hoping to cap shut the can, she nestled next to Cooper and started to stroke his bare chest. This was the first time she had initiated anything of a sexual nature with him. She was not quite sure what was stirring inside her; certainly she was immensely attracted to him, yet there seemed something more. Maybe his predicament with the kid downstairs had something to do with it.

"Just all heart, ain't you, cowboy?" she murmured, her husky voice coming over him like a caress. Cooper slowly lifted up his hat again to more carefully assess the situation.

"Yeah, and right now, that's all I am. Just heart, nothing else. Hey, I'm bushed. So good night," he grumbled, dropping the lid back over his face.

Blue was not so easily discouraged. Getting up, she moved to the foot of the bed, where she took hold of Cooper's boots and started to tug them off. "Come on, cowboy," Blue said, shearing him loose from his snakeskins. "About time we got somewhat better acquainted. Besides, a little loving shouldn't take that long."

The next question came from beneath Cooper's hat.

"Yeah, but what about the recuperation time?"

Blue paused to ponder the situation, then tried another tack. "Might at least take your mind off your miseries."

No response from beneath the hat. Cooper seemed to have no interest in Blue's notion of mental therapy, which of course did little to improve her own frame of mind. Finally, getting his boots off, she hoisted them high, then dropped them. They sounded like heavy rocks hitting the floor.

Still no reaction. Blue was quietly stung by Cooper's lack of enthusiasm; on those rare occasions when she had been either very attracted to a man, or couldn't safely talk her way out of a dangerous situation, she had gotten top dollar for her sexual favors. Now she couldn't seem to give them away. So, hoping to get a rise out of Cooper, one way or another, she fired off a loaded question.

"Is that kid downstairs your son? Dammit, yes or no!"

A short spell of silence ensued.

"... Yeah, guess the odds are in favor of that," Cooper wearily mumbled from beneath his hat. "But that don't make me like it. Him, neither, for that matter. Now come on, Blue, let me get a little shut-eye, will ya?"

Blue instantly felt rather tired herself. Laying back down, she burrowed in next to Cooper. But she didn't say anything more for such a long time, he must have thought sure she had fallen asleep.

"Ever in love with the kid's mother?" she finally asked.

A groan crawled from underneath the Stetson.

"Well, yes or no?" Blue persisted.

"... Yeah. For about three hours, as I recall."

"So what happened?" Blue asked, persisting some more.

"Nothing happened... Just back in those days, I figured if I ever stayed in one place for more'n a few days, somebody would start pouring concrete over my feet."

"Oh, come on, Frank, what really happened? I mean, the lady is the mother of your child, you musta felt something for—"

"Say, why all the sudden concern over this brat?" he asked, still speaking through his hat. "Thought you was my probation officer, not some goddamned social worker."

A sorrowful look swept across Blue's eyes. She remembered a morning some thirty-five years before, when her father had left to find work in another town, and then the day her mother finally told her he was never coming home.

"I know what it feels like not to be wanted, that's all."

Blue felt an impulse to tell Cooper more about her own painful past, but quickly changed her mind. She had, however, already told him more than she thought.

Cooper could read a person's voice almost as accurately as a lie detector machine; and he might have been touched by what he'd just heard, for his own voice now went softer.

"Okay, honey... Gonna tell you the truth, exactly how it was. You see, something happened between me and the kid's mother... that was so tough to take, I finally had to get the hell out of there."

"Yeah... like what?" Blue asked, abruptly sitting up.

Cooper slowly lifted his hat to look Blue in the eye. "It was this way: like you, the kid's mother also wouldn't let me get no goddamned sleep!"

With that, Cooper dropped the hat back over his face. But it didn't stay there long. Blue quickly lifted up the Stetson, and gave him a chaste kiss. Then she gently replaced the cover over his face and laid back across the bed.

Finally she smiled and said to herself, Prudence Patricia Nikolsolski, you are happier now than you have been in a very long time.

Chapter 18

Soon after their conversation with Blue Morgan, Val and Clarence left the lobby of the Cattlemen's Hotel; much to the relief, Val suspected, of its entire management staff. Returning to their own three-dollar a night motel, Clarence collapsed and slept through the afternoon.

This suited Val fine, though his friend made almost as much noise asleep as he did when awake. Val was too nervous to sleep, anyway, and spent the rest of the day watching soap operas on television. Ordinarily he hated such shows. Yet they now served a therapeutic purpose; all the emotional mayhem on the TV screen made his own troubles seem trivial by comparison.

Still, by the time he and Clarence left to head back to Cooper's hotel for the poker game, Val felt like an unranked fighter about to go up against a world champion. The butterflies in his stomach felt strong enough to lift him off the ground.

Arriving at the hotel, they were entering the elevator when the elderly valet they had seen that morning crowded in with a cartful of beer and whiskey. The sight caused Clarence to turn green at the gills again.

Coming up to the fifth floor, the old-timer took the cart rattling down the hallway. Val and Clarence tagged along behind him, searching for the suite number Blue had mentioned. She had told them to head toward the noise, but all Val could hear was the clanking of bottles and the flapping inside his stomach.

"Hey, check it out," he whispered to Clarence, as the valet stopped right outside room 507. "Look where he's taking all that booze."

"Good," Clarence muttered. "You're gonna need it."

It seemed, however, they had come to the wrong room; for a long moment no one answered the valet's knock. But when the door finally opened, Val knew they had found the right place. Raucous laughter was erupting from inside the suite; and not the kind, Val thought, that one might hear at a PTA meeting.

Blue Morgan had opened the door, and when she saw Val and Clarence, she clamped hold of their arms as if making a citizen's arrest. The valet braced his spindly shoulders, and pushed the cart into the room.

"Well, about time, dammit," Blue said to Val and Clarence. "Thought sure you boys musta overdosed on that pegboard game!"

Blue was wearing a low-cut, formfitting red dress, which for the moment caused Clarence to forget his hangover. But Val was more interested to see that the old valet had come wheeling out with another cart loaded with at least twenty empty beer bottles.

Then the sound of a voice Val had often fantasized about caused the butterflies in his stomach to grow as large as eagles. He knew the voice belonged to his father.

For a fleeting moment, Val considered following the valet out the door; but the old gentleman quickly closed it. Val paused to allow the lump in his throat to pass, then slowly crabbed into the room.

The suite, which seemed only a slightly smaller version of the lobby, was filled with oversized personalities to match. Most of them were gathered around a large circular table that sat in the middle of the main room. Over by the bar, two young, good-looking women sat perched on the saddle-style stools.

Six players sat surrounding the table. Two of them looked as if they might be wealthy oil men; but another couple of middle-aged men seemed to be at the wrong game, maybe even in the wrong part of the United States: button-down types, Val thought, who in the movies were always taking commuter trains into New York City.

The only woman at the gaming table, a sharp-eyed old lady, wore a Boston Red Sox baseball cap, and was puffing a cigarette through a long plastic holder.

But the obvious star of this sextette was Frank Cooper.

Back in Big Bend, Val's mother had warned him that no man would be able to live up to the image she had created of his father. But up close, Cooper looked like no one Val had ever seen before; outside of a movie house, anyway. Val thought that with his dark tan, blue eyes, and perfectly chiseled features, Cooper could have been a film star himself, had his destiny taken him in that direction; and yes, he did look a bit like Randolph Scott.

Then Val looked for some semblance of himself in Cooper's face. But there was none. There was, however, a charm about his looks that caused Val's anger to suddenly deflate. Cooper seemed the type of man who might be impossible to dislike, even while one loathed everything he did or said. Feeling his rage seeping away, Val hated himself for surrendering so easily.

Cooper was telling a story as Val and Clarence walked into the suite. "—So then this night-court judge demands to know how we're all gonna plead to the charge of gambling. Well, everybody starts in fumbling and mumbling, and finally they end up pleading guilty..."

Pausing, Cooper glanced at Val. Something sullen swept past his eyes, but it vanished in a second. With the other players hanging onto his words as if they were game-winning hands, Cooper went on with his story. Yet Val's presence seemed to throw him offstride, and the vibrancy in his voice dropped perceptively.

"But when it comes my turn," Cooper continued, "I plead not guilty. So the judge leans over the bench and asks me how come, seeing as the cops caught us all red-handed. 'Well, Your Honor,' I says, 'correct me if I'm wrong, but for anything to be legally considered gambling, gotta be an element of uncertainty to it—and since I ain't ever once lost to this group of mental midgets who now stand before you, how can I possibly plead guilty to a charge of gambling?'"

One of the oil men, the shaggier, more serious-sided of the two, fixed his hound-dog eyes on Cooper. "Now you ain't telling us that there judge fell for such a load of fertilizer!"

"Hell, no," Cooper said quietly. He seemed to have lost interest in his own story. "The old bastard fined me double for contempt of court—but setting him straight sure made me feel better."

As the laughter died down, Val felt Blue take him by the arm again. He and Clarence were then led right up to the table; not exactly the furtive entrance Val had hoped to make.

"Hey, everybody, got us a couple more suckers here," Blue announced, as if introducing the contestants in a pig calling contest. "Smart-looking boy is named Clarence, and this dark, good-looking kid calls himself Roger. Let's give 'em a big hand, folks."

"But this here, honey, is a closed game," the old lady said to Blue. "By invitation only." The old woman was the official hostess, though the game was being held in Cooper's suite.

"I invited these two boys to the game," Blue muttered, with a touch of menace in her voice. The craggy-faced old woman leaned back in her chair and let loose a cloud of cigarette smoke. "Old friends of yours?"

"For a couple of hours, anyway," Blue said. "And how many friends you got with such long-standing status?"

"Well, may I ask just what their qualifications might be?" The old woman apparently took her role as referee seriously.

Blue snickered. "What, you wanna examine their family tree? They're qualified, Miss Irene, because I say they're qualified!"

"But how do we know they ain't holdup artists, just posing as young punks?" the leaner of the two button-down types asked.

"Hell, they're probably thinking the same about us—and they'd be right!" Blue exclaimed. "Besides, I already seen the color of their money—and they got plenty to lose," Blue lied.

Listening to this brief debate, Val hoped the protesters might prevail. He needed an excuse to make a hasty retreat back down to the lobby. But the climate suddenly improved. Smiling, the old lady backed off. "Just making sure that you're sure, dear. Don't want anybody here accusing me of dereliction of duty." With that, a few of the players reluctantly extended their hands to Val and Clarence.

Then Cooper finally recognized their presence. "What, you boys just killing time 'til the movie house opens up?"

Cooper had addressed both of them, but was staring up at Clarence, who wasted no time in surrendering. "Oh, no sir," he stammered. "I'm just riding shotgun on this trip. It's my friend here who's crazy enough to think he knows where he's going—"

"Then sit down, young fella," the hatchet-faced old lady with the baseball cap barked, grabbing Val by the arm. "Start bringing me some luck!"

Val could barely see the old lady through the smoke coming from her cigarette. But her talon on his forearm didn't leave him much time to dawdle. Then somebody wedged another chair up to the table, and just that quick Val was in the game.

Cooper began to shuffle the cards faster than Val had ever seen them handled before. They were just a blur before his eyes. Then his father began to deal the cards out across the table. Sitting opposite him, Val stared down at his hands self-consciously. Why the hell hadn't he remembered to clean his fingernails?

"You like seven card stud, kid?" Cooper casually asked.

"Fine," Val muttered, deciding on a strategy that called for as little conversation as possible.

"Then maybe you wouldn't mind putting up your ante. This ain't no charity function we're running here," Cooper grumbled.

Val cursed himself. Damn, not even at the table for more than a minute, and already he looked like exactly what he was: a small-town hick trying to step up in class.

He tried to smile. "Sorry. What's the ante?"

The old woman flashed what seemed to be a set of second-hand teeth, yet as yellow as any bunch of bananas Val had ever seen. "Five dollars, honey."

"Okay," Val murmured, after letting another lump pass down his throat. In the last game he had played back in Big Bend, the ante had been a bottle cap.

The old woman made a chuckling noise that sounded sinister. "But why doncha start with just three hundred dollars worth of chips. Sorta sneak your way in, huh?"

Fishing into his Levis, Val extracted a wad of money, and holding it just below the table, he counted out the three hundred and handed it to her. Miss Irene flashed the ocher-colored smile again and passed Val a pile of chips. Then she stuffed his money into a large jar sitting on top of the table. The jar was half-filled with hundred dollar bills. Val thought his own ten-dollar bills made for a pretty crappy comparison.

Clarence had meanwhile walked toward the bar; drawn in that direction, Val hoped, by the two ladies and not the liquor. The present company might not prove as tolerant of his drunken dives as the Mexicans had been over in Juarez the night before.

The heavy-set oil man brought Val's attention back to the game. "Well, what about it, Miss Irene?" he asked, all sly smiles after the first few cards were dealt out. "Has this young Mexican buck brought you any luck?"

The old woman frowned and jerked her cap down tighter. "Gonna cost you to find out, squirt," she grumbled, letting loose another screen of cigarette smoke. Catching the brunt of the barrage, Val started to cough. Aside from his other problems, it was now becoming difficult to even breathe.

The leaner of the two oilmen made the first bet. Encamped behind some chips he had placed in a semicircle—as if sentries guarding his position—he drawled: "I open with the maximum bet. Thirty-five dollars, U.S. money. Ain't as good as Confederate, but all I could raise on short notice." As he spoke, he glared at Val, as if trying to scare him out of the game.

One of the commuter-train types quickly tossed in his hand as if it were a hot potato. The others called him Harold J. This seemed the right name, Val thought, for a chubby little guy with a nonexistent chin, nasal voice, and bold black eyes that bounced around a lot behind his horned-rim glasses.

"Oh, thirty-five dollar opening bet way too fast for my track," Harold J. groaned.

Val emitted a small sigh of relief. He wasn't the only low roller at the table. But the old woman didn't seem amused by the man's penny-pinching attitude. Blowing through her cigarette holder as if to clean it, she snorted: "Harold J., you remind me of a quarter horse trying to run with the thoroughbreds. Next time, get yourself a game over at the Salvation Army."

Then Miss Irene matched the bet. As she was scolding Harold J., Cooper studied his own hand. Now, laying it aside, he dealt out another set of cards, then turned to Val for the first time. Val felt a trickle of sweat start down the side of his body.

"What about you... Roger?" Cooper asked, studying Val with some interest. It seemed that he too was looking for a resemblance between them.

Val had a pair of fours and might have drawn another one, but the prospect didn't seem worth anywhere near thirty-five dollars. "Think I'll wait for a little more help," Val muttered, tossing in his hand.

Cooper grinned, then said to nobody in particular: "Yeah, ain't wise to get in any deeper than the length of your rope."

As the game continued, Val stewed over Cooper's rope remark. With the five dollars that had just dropped down the drain, and the money he'd already spent on the trip, as well as the fifty dollars needed for his retreat back to Big Bend, Val had about thirteen hundred dollars worth of rope left.

⫸ ⫷

Over the next few hours, Val lost more than seven hundred dollars. But what galled him worse was his putrid performance. Early on, he had realized his skills were no match for those of the other players. His only hope was to get good cards, and then push his luck to its full length. Yet, though he'd gotten several decent hands, he had worked them in such sorry fashion that even when he won, the pots were hardly worth counting.

Val imagined that Cooper and the other players were secretly laughing at him. Cooper seemed to be weighing Val's every move, and whenever he made a dumb decision, Val could feel his skin crawl with embarrassment.

Except for Blue, everyone else around the table seemed to have branded him a bum. But every now and then Val would catch Blue staring at him, and her smile told him she was still in his corner.

On the last hand almost everyone had folded early. That left just Val and Harold J. Val figured that even if the fat little man was holding three of a kind, they probably wouldn't be better than his own trio of kings.

"Well, Roger," Harold J. murmured, twisting his thick neck around as if he had a crick in it. "I'll have to raise another three hundred dollars." He slowly parceled out six fifty-dollar chips and tossed them into the pot.

Val felt stone-stupid for not calling on the previous raise. Harold had boxed him in. He was fast running out of money. Yet staring down at his three lonely-looking kings, Val remembered Noah Carson once saying that even more important than winning was losing like a man. Another player might take your money, but he couldn't swipe your self-respect; that you had to give away yourself.

Recalling Carson's words, Val slapped a smile on his face and threw in his cards. Harold J. seemed startled. Then he reached out his pudgy hands and pulled in the prize.

"Roger, you are a wise young man," Harold J. proclaimed. "Discretion is always the better part of valor."

"Valor, hell," Cooper abruptly exclaimed. "Stupidity be more like it. Kid shoulda seen that raise and called. I'll wager all the money in that Mason jar he has the better hand."

Looking disgusted, Cooper rose from the table and ambled over to the bar. Watching him depart, Val angrily dug back into his Levis. Setting aside the fifty dollars he'd need to get home, he handed the rest of his money to Miss Irene. She counted it, stuffed it into the jar, then doled out what seemed to Val the final installment of his future.

Handing him the chips, Miss Irene released another mustard-tinted smile. She had won more than two thousand dollars, yet this was her first grin in what now seemed to Val like several weeks.

Clarence had been following the game, and what he saw was almost enough to sober him up. "Wow, another beating like that one, and we're gonna have to hitchhike home," he said in a voice loud enough for everyone to hear.

"Yeah, downright tragic watching a rich kid lose his weekly allowance," one of the young women observed.

"No, that's his inheritance he's playing with," Clarence mumbled. "And it took him eighteen years to get it."

Val felt his stomach turn over again. Clarence had become a double-barreled disaster. When not falling off barstools in front of Mexicans, he was divulging private information to strangers. Especially to Cooper.

≫ ≪

It was the biggest pot of the evening. Cooper, along with Harold J. and Val, were the only players left in the game. The others had slowly dropped out, reluctantly leaving behind a pot worth more than nine hundred dollars.

The other players watched with fallen faces, looking as if they hoped nobody would win. Clarence and the two young ladies had gravitated closer to the table, sensing, Val supposed, that the final disaster of the night was about to descend on his head.

Val had matched one raise after another, marching forward like a dispirited soldier heading for the frontlines; yet this battle he would not be bluffed out of winning. His cards were good enough to stick with right down to his last chip, which was now only a few more away.

"I'll see your raise, Frank," Harold J. groaned, carefully laying a fifty-dollar chip over the pot as if placing a cherry on top of an ice-cream sundae. Then he turned to Val. "I trust you are still with us, Roger?"

Val tossed out all but his last fifty-dollar chip. He was in for the full ride, even if he had to walk home.

"I'll see that raise and call," Val quietly said. Then he noticed Cooper staring at him; there seemed something akin to compassion in his father's eyes.

"You heard the boy, Harold J.," Cooper drawled. "He's calling your bluffing ass."

The suspense seemed to suffocate Harold J. Taking a moment to control himself, he then carefully laid out his cards faceup on the table. "Bleeping bluff, my ass," Harold J. sputtered. "Hell of a way to talk about my pretty little pair of pairs."

Two pairs, tens and aces. Loveliest sight Val had ever seen. His relief, however, was short-lived.

"So how about it, kid?" Cooper asked. "Can you whip that pair-salad, or am I gonna have to?"

Trapping his breath, Val slowly turned up his hole cards, one after another. Noting the final result, Cooper laughed, then said in what sounded to Val like a proud voice, "Triple queens! Hey, Harold, this young fella just whipped your pair-salad into mashed potatoes!"

Harold's face folded to about half its normal size. "And you got triple aces, I suppose?" he fairly shrieked at Cooper.

Cooper made no immediate response. Instead, he turned away from the table and flashed his hole cards in Blue's direction. She leaned over, as if to make sure she'd seen what she thought she had, then mustered up a thin smile.

Her reaction, however, didn't compare with the one she had when Cooper abruptly rose from the table. "Harold, if I could beat this boy, I wouldn't be folding over. Your pot, kid."

Blue hurried around the table to give Val a big hug. A few of the other players gave him a reluctant handshake. Yet in the midst of this tepid celebration, Val remained cemented to the same spot. Clarence quickly began to stack Val's chips.

Cooper, leaving his cards facedown on the table, ambled over to the bar, where he poured himself a tall glass of orange juice. "Well, Miss Irene, you're the one who actually did me in," he carped from behind the bar. "I don't know exactly how much I won this evening, but would bet it'd be a lot more if it hadn't been for you."

"And hadn't been for you, handsome," Miss Irene croaked, "I'd be a lot richer myself. But ain't no use hanging around any longer. Players who still got money, I can't beat—and them I can whip are now broke."

Cooper chuckled. "Yeah, guess we gotta go find us a fatter flock of pigeons, huh?"

Blue joined Cooper over at the bar, where most of the other players had straggled, looking like sun-struck prospectors whose water had run out.

"So where you gonna find these pigeons?" Blue nervously asked. "Up on the roof?"

"Oh, there's usually a good crap game somewhere over in Juarez," Cooper drawled. "But I'll be back by sunrise, honey, broke, bent, or otherwise—"

"Hey, cowboy," Blue heatedly interjected. "I ain't about to be left in charge of this here funeral service—besides, least you can do for this used flock of pigeons is take them across the river and treat 'em to a little bird-seed."

"But first comes payday, honey," Miss Irene called over, opening up the jar now crammed with thousands of dollars.

"Payday, hell," Harold J. snorted. "For yours truly, gonna be more like Judgement Day."

"Well, me, I'm gonna take a shower and like ole Pancho Pilate, wash my hands of this entire mess," Cooper said, heading for the bedroom. "Miss Irene, you cash me out, will ya? I've never been stupid enough to return to the scene of the crime."

Blue followed Cooper into the bedroom, still protesting his travel plans. Miss Irene, flashing another flaxen smile, started to convert the chips into greenbacks. Clarence had stacked Val's chips into neat little piles, and slid them over to the old lady.

Val's mind, meanwhile, returned just enough for him to handle some simple arithmetic. Even with his previous losses, he had managed to hit the finish line just a hundred dollars shy of breaking even. Damn well worth the money, he thought. Five hours of instruction by a world champion had cost him less than twenty dollars an hour.

Then came what seemed a bigger bargain.

As Val watched Miss Irene convert his chips into folding money, he noticed Clarence slyly turn up the hand that Cooper had earlier discarded. Val studied the cards for a long moment, then looked at Clarence. His dumbfounded expression confirmed what Val thought he'd seen. Suddenly, and for the first time, Val realized the main reason he had gone searching for his father.

He had hoped that when they finally met, Cooper would become his friend. More than anything else, Val wanted the man he had loved all his life to at least like him.

Now, staring down at Cooper's winning full house hand that he had folded over in deference to the three queens, Val saw the proof of his father's affection. Then his vision began to blur as his eyes slowly filled with tears.

Chapter 19

"Man, I've died and gone to Heaven," Clarence cried, as the heavy roll of drums rumbled across the crowded cabaret. An arm sporting a long white satin glove had peeked out from behind a curtain; attached to it was the sexiest-looking young woman Val had ever seen. Then, as if carried forth on a cloud, she slowly swept onto the stage.

The stripper was wearing a graduate's cap and gown, and aptly enough the band shifted into "Pomp and Circumstance"—only with a mambo beat a lot meaner than the version Val had heard at his own graduation from Big Bend High.

He and Clarence were sitting below the stage, barricaded along with Blue, Miss Irene, and Harold J., behind a tableful of beer bottles in a Mexican strip joint over in Juarez; waiting for Cooper to return from his crap game.

The stripper had peeled down to her G-string and fluffy bra when Val noticed Cooper coming across the smoke-filled, neon-streaked room. He looked strangely subdued.

But what fascinated Val far more was what the stripper wore attached to her crotch: a little beribboned diploma which now seemed up for grabs, as if she were offering it to anyone who felt entitled to such a degree. Clarence shot up his hand, as if asking to be included in this category.

"So how'd the crap game go, Frank?" Blue asked, as Cooper sank into the chair next to her. He peered up at the stripper, swaying toward their table.

"Hell, just lucky to get out of there with my clothes on," Cooper quietly groused.

Blue gently patted his hand. "Well, don't pout, precious. Mama's gonna buy you a pony for your birthday."

If Blue had made a joke, Cooper didn't seem to get it. He sat there, staring at his hands. Val was staring at something else. The stripper had advanced to the edge of the stage, where she stood leaning over toward the table. She hung there like an exotic bird of prey, her beautiful, bronzed body slowly swinging in time to the sensuous music.

Her gyrating pelvis almost hypnotized Val. He felt stupid sitting there gawking in the general direction of her G-string; so, pretending as if he caught this type of act every night of the week, he casually turned away.

The cabaret, Val noticed, was packed with people. Colored lights bounced around the room, making it hard to see anyone's face clearly; just as well, Val thought. Most of the middle-aged Anglos in the crowd looked as if they'd rather not be recognized.

Val felt someone poke him in the ribs. "Hey, Val, she's looking right at you, man," Clarence sputtered.

Glancing up just long enough to confirm this, Val snarled in Clarence's face. "What, you cross-eyed, on top of being blind?"

"You the one who's cross-eyed, Roger," Miss Irene chortled, appearing a bit confused that Clarence had called Val by another name.

Then the stripper, lowering herself down on her haunches, said something to Val in Spanish. Clarence started to rake his rib cage again. "Hey, dammit, this ain't fair! What the hell's she saying?"

"Wants to know if we're enjoying ourselves," Val explained. Hitting his smile button again, Val rattled off some stuff to the stripper he hoped sounded like Spanish.

"Hey, Val," Clarence bellowed. "In English, dammit!"

"Told her you couldn't enjoy yourself much more, without having to do it in private," Val lied.

Clarence went red in the face. But Cooper was smiling. Yet his grin bothered Val. His father seemed to know something about the situation that he didn't.

The stripper again aimed her voice in Val's direction.

"Oh, my God, now what?" Clarence shrieked, bobbing around as if all his wheels were about to drop off.

Val suddenly felt a little off-keel himself. "She, uh... wants one of us to dance with her."

Clarence nearly fell out of his chair, something Val had been expecting for the past few hours. "Oh, hell no, physical impossibility," Clarence stammered. "But hey, tell her I don't dance to slow music, okay? Don't want to hurt her feelings!"

Val suddenly felt a fat hand on his arm. Harold J. was half-hauling him out of his chair. "Well, Roger," Harold giggled, "get up there, show your friend how it's done!"

Val was about to jerk his arm away when he noticed Cooper staring at him. There seemed a subtle challenge in his eyes.

"Okay, you asked for it," Val murmured, starting toward the stage.

"Attaboy, Roger," Blue called out, hurriedly fishing a little flashbulb camera from her purse.

As Val climbed onstage, the stripper quickly took him in her arms, and away they waltzed. The band shifted into a sensuous tune as they slid around the floor in slow motion.

Val had done his share of close dancing before, but never like this. The stripper stuck to him like a Siamese twin, her crotch nailed to his, her hands fiercely clamped to his rear end. It seemed she expected a hurricane to hit at any moment, though her thickly-lashed brown eyes were blinking brazen signals even a blind man could read.

Then Val heard tiny titters of laughter. The customers, he thought, were enjoying the show. But as the music swelled up to a booming finale, the stripper dropped her death grip on his rear end. Her hands then started to jerk and yank in every direction. Val was aghast. It seemed she was having a fit of some sort.

But it was the crowd that had the fit, as she yanked off her wig, bra, and G-string. Then the male stripper scurried across the stage to disappear behind a curtain. Val was left to face the audience, which now resembled a mob of howling hyenas.

There were only two avenues of escape: backstage, or off-stage. Val began to wade through the crowd. By now most of the people had calmed down a bit. But one guy was still yelping: a big-bellied biker, with a long, black beard that hung halfway down his bloated gut.

Across his T-shirt was stenciled I HATE MOST EVERY-BODY. That apparently included Val, for as he eased past his table, the big man grabbed his wrist. Val winced with pain. The man had the grip of a pipe wrench.

"Hey, you little faggot," the big guy boomed. His breath smelled like a brewery. "What wouldya done if that'd been a real woman?"

The three other men at the table, all pot-bellied clones of the guy, broke into hysterics. The remark didn't seem that funny to Val, but he grinned anyway, and tried to continue on. But he had moved no farther than the length of his arm when the black-bearded man snapped him back like a rubber band. Then he laid what felt like meat hooks on Val's shoulders, and launched him toward another table.

There were several small-sized Mexican men at the table, who got very wet when their pitchers of beer went tumbling over on them. But the Mexicans realized that Val had been propelled into their party through no power of his own.

In only the time it took Val to scramble back to his feet, the Mexicans charged into the big-bellied bikers. Val thought they looked like Chihuahua dogs attacking a herd of elephants.

War was immediately declared between the Mexicans and the gringos. Recruits from both camps rushed forward from every corner of the cabaret. The musicians, staying safely off to one side, began to play bullfight music.

Val was pondering how best to demonstrate his neutrality when he saw Cooper charge into the fray. Harold J. waddled along behind him, Clarence and Blue half-heartedly bringing up the rear. Cooper immediately stunned the bearded man with a jarring blow to the jaw.

This sight so delighted the locals, they broke out in a cheer. Then the battle began to resemble a replay of the Mexican-American War, with Cooper and Val standing on the southern side.

But the southern brigade was getting badly blistered. Both Val and Cooper hit the floor more than once. Val had just gone down for the third time when he noticed a lifeless-looking body under a nearby table. It was Harold J. The skin around his beady eyes was badly scruffed up.

Val thought about Clarence. The brawl seemed no bargain for a little guy with glasses and wired-together teeth. Focusing his eyes, Val looked around for his friend.

But the first thing he spotted made him so mad, his vision steamed up again. The stripper, wearing only jockey shorts and high heels, was hopping around the stage, screaming in a freaky voice that sounded neither male nor female.

Then Val saw that the big biker who had started the war was now pounding a little Mexican into pulp, holding him upright with one hand, beating him senseless with the other.

Blue stood nearby, taking one picture after another. But the sight of the little Mexican getting ground into mush stopped her in her tracks. Setting aside her camera, she grabbed an empty beer pitcher.

Taking it through a long swing, she brought it crashing up against the big guy's shoulders. Val thought sure Blue had killed him. But his back must have been made of something stronger than heavy glass; instead of falling, he teetered back and forth for a few seconds, finally careening off at an angle, slicing through the mob like an ice-breaking boat. Then Val noticed Clarence.

Carefully sauntering through the battle zone, Clarence seemed to be looking for a fight with anyone smaller than himself. Val doubted that Clarence had thrown a single punch. He knew his little friend hadn't taken one, as one was usually his limit.

Then the big guy with the beard, now appearing as if he had no more than a few seconds of flying time left, bumped into the back of Clarence. Startled, Val's friend wheeled around and flung forth his fist. But when Clarence saw where it was headed, he tried to cancel the attack. Too late. What remained of his punch landed flush on the big man's jaw.

It didn't look as if the blow could have stung much worse than a mosquito bite. But apparently Clarence's anemic effort was enough to take the behemoth beyond the point of no return. He slowly fell to the floor like a ship sinking into the sea.

Clarence watched, mesmerized, as the man's belly sank lower and lower, till at last it flattened out on the sawdust floor. Having no idea of the man's previous encounter with the beer pitcher, Clarence stared admiringly at his right hand, marveling at the power he never knew it possessed.

Then he unleashed his presumed power once again: a soft shot to the cheek of a tall American, who till now had steered clear of the general mayhem. The tall man casually shook off the blow, then stared incredulously down at Clarence.

Blinking nervously, Clarence waited for the man to topple over. Only the man didn't topple; instead he simply smiled—and an instant later, he took Clarence by the seat of his pants, lifted him up onto the bar, and then hustled him through half a hundred beer bottles. Clarence's head finally met the register at the far end of the bar.

❧ ❦

When the police arrived, it didn't take them long to restore order; Val was amazed how fast their clubs convinced the crowd to calm down. What took time was for the cabaret owner to calculate the damages.

Every man was charged an equal share. But feeling partially responsible for inciting the riot, Val offered to pay for his entire table. Cooper happily rejected the offer.

"Oh, no, I'm picking up the tab for our table," he snorted. "Hell, ain't had this good a time since I attended the funeral of my worst enemy."

By the time Cooper and the big biker with the long beard ambled over to cover their share of the damages, the cabaret had almost emptied. Two Mexican cops had stationed themselves on either side of the owner, watching the financial transaction with what seemed more than idle interest.

"—Anyway, what the fuck was us Americans fighting each other for?" the big-bellied biker affably asked Cooper. "Shit, was them lousy little spics we shoulda been smashing, right?"

The bruiser glanced derisively in Val's direction, then extended his hand to Cooper. "So no hard fucking feelings, huh?"

Cooper chuckled and took hold of the man's hand. But instead of shaking it, he pulled it—jerking the biker forward and smack into a crushing left jab.

The big man went down like a shot, and as he fell he hit his head hard on a foot railing. The big guy heaved a groan, then lay very still. With his ample white belly pushing past his I HATE MOST EVERYBODY T-shirt, Val thought he looked like a beached albino whale.

This unexpected finale brought the two cops out from behind the bar; but Cooper, peeling off a few more twenty-dollar bills, managed to slow their advance.

"Oh, but here, this should cover that last bit of damage. Okay, amigos?" Cooper casually drawled.

The two cops mulled this over for a moment. Then each man pocketed one of the twenties. The older policeman tried to maintain a somber expression. The younger cop smiled.

"Correct, *Señor*," he exclaimed to Cooper. "And for no more charge, we keep here your sleeping friend a little while. For his own protection, of course." Cooper chuckled and glanced down at the big man still snoozing in the sawdust.

At that moment, Val felt very proud to be Cooper's son; proud enough to now make an impulsive decision. Leaving the hotel earlier that night, Val figured he would soon be saying goodbye to Cooper, and if he was lucky he might get a chance to speak privately with him before they parted company.

Either way, Val knew he already had come out a winner. He would not be returning to Big Bend broke; better yet, his father, in allowing him to win the final pot of the evening, had proven his friendship, though he probably still had no idea of Val's true identity. To expect much more, Val thought, might push his luck well past its limit.

Val knew now, however, that if given the chance, he would stay with Cooper for as long as he could, no matter where the path might lead. The problem was Clarence. Val already knew that Cooper's life-style allowed for little excess baggage.

As Cooper started for the door, Val and Clarence followed along behind him. Clarence still seemed dazed by his encounter with the cash register. The large lump on his forehead, incurred in falling off the barstool the night before, had been joined by another big bump on the top of his head. Val felt a twinge of guilt for getting his friend into the brawl.

But nearing the exit, Val spotted something which lifted his spirits. The male stripper, slumped over a table, sat chugging down a glass of bicarbonate of soda. The evening's violent finale had obviously given him a bad case of indigestion.

※ ※

A half-block away, some Mexican kids were giving Cooper's convertible a spit shine. Blue was sitting inside the car as Cooper came walking up. He had covered the half-block from the cabaret as if he expected the big biker and his clones to catch up with him at any second. Hurrying along behind Cooper, Val was worried himself, though not for the same reason.

By now, he half-suspected that Cooper had finally guessed his real identity, and wanted to get out of town before Val could open up any ancient wounds.

Arriving at the car, Val knew he was fast running out of time. His long-awaited chance to cement some connection with Cooper seemed to be slipping from his hands like quicksilver.

"Well, Miss Morgan," Cooper snorted. "One expensive idea you had about bringing everybody over here to Juarez!"

"Yeah, I know, cowboy," Blue murmured. "I can get real dumb when I've been drinking... So what's next on the program?"

Cooper went for some pocket change, which he passed around to the kids. "We gotta head north. Hell, ain't nothing more'n dry sand around here now."

As Cooper settled into the car, Val shot Clarence a nervous look. The fresh air had revived him somewhat, and getting the message, Clarence ambled off toward his truck. Val glanced back at Cooper. An unwelcome thought bolted through Val's mind. He felt like a TV game show contestant, with no more than thirty seconds to come up with the correct response.

Muttering a fast prayer, Val crouched down next to Blue's window. "Can I talk to you, Mister Cooper?" he asked.

"Make it quick, boy," Cooper said. Val could almost hear a clock ticking off his precious thirty seconds.

"I'd like to pay back the money you let me win."

Cooper turned to Val with a chuckle that seemed half-loaded with contempt. "What money, young fella?" he quietly inquired. "Talk American, kid, so's I can understand you."

"I'm talking about that full house you folded over, when all I had was three queens."

Val's remark surprised Cooper. "Hey, hot shot," he drawled, "didn't whoever taught you to play poker so good tell you it's bad form to turn over a discarded hand?"

Val glanced over his shoulder to make sure Clarence was safely away. "I didn't do it, my friend did. But it was me you helped, and I'd like to make it up to you."

For what seemed to Val a full minute, Cooper said nothing. Val wouldn't have survived this long lull without fainting if it hadn't been for Blue. She was smiling at him in an encouraging way. Val figured she still wanted to help him.

When Cooper finally broke the silence, his manner seemed as deliberate as if he were carefully stepping across a stream, one stone at a time. "Kid, why don't you stop looking a gift-horse in the mouth, and head for home, huh?"

"Just dumb, I guess," Val replied. Val held his breath, waiting for his father's next move.

"... You play blackjack as well as you do poker?"

Val flashed a wide grin. "Mister Cooper, I play blackjack better'n I do poker."

For a few seconds, Cooper studied Val as if he were a hand of poker. Then he smiled. So did Val. Cooper had finally crossed that pepple-strewn stream.

"Go get your bag, Roger," Cooper said softly. "You just made the traveling squad."

It took Val about five seconds to travel over to Clarence's truck. Then he glanced back to make sure Cooper was waiting for him. In the distance, Cooper and Blue sat watching Val with two entirely different expressions.

"Ain't this gonna be a little dangerous?" Blue asked.

"Yeah, the kid could be setting me up for a fall."

"And you gotta bring him along, just to see how he does it, huh?" Blue observed, still rather startled by this sudden change in the program. "Besides, I'm mean dangerous for the kid, not you. Hell, you could survive inside a sackful of scorpions!"

Back up at the truck, Val had explained the situation to Clarence. "But hey, come with us, no big deal," Val exclaimed, fearing that Clarence might accept the offer. Val knew that his reservation on his father's Express was only for one.

"No thanks," Clarence mumbled, gingerly touching the knot on the top of his head. "I've had me enough big-city excitement for a while."

Val heaved a sigh of relief. But his friend's crumpled look worried him. "Hey, you gonna be okay?" he asked. Clarence looked as if his head was still ringing. "Wanna go find a doctor?"

"Naw, just wanna find the road back to Big Bend..."

"Well, you gotta take this same street back to the bridge," Val said hurriedly. His father looked as if he might be leaving at any moment. "Then once you cross over, head straight on till you get to Highway 80. Cut right and put her on automatic pilot. Okay?"

Clarence seemed less than sold on the idea. "But you ough-ta come on home with me, Val. Now, while you're still ahead. Know what I mean?"

Val knew exactly what he meant. It suddenly dawned on him what a great friend Clarence had always been. Then Val remembered something else.

"Oh, you're gonna need money to get home," he said, fishing into his Levis. Counting out five ten-dollar bills, he handed them to Clarence. "This should get you back to Big Bend in one piece—that is, if you can keep from whacking anyone else who weighs three times more'n you do."

Clarence counted the money, then managed a forlorn smile. "Yeah, thanks, Val. Be more'n enough... But it's you I'm worried about."

Taking a deep breath, Val reached into the cab of the truck for his cardboard suitcase. "Clarence, I don't go with him now, I'll spend the rest of my life wondering what might have happened... But thanks, partner. Thanks for getting me this far. And do me a favor, will you? Call my mom when you get back."

Clarence frowned. "She's gonna yell at me for letting you be so dumb."

"Yeah, I know," Val muttered, extending his hand. "Tell her I hit my head on something."

"She already knows that," Clarence said, as they shook hands. Val waited for his pal's parting shot, almost always an exit line filched from some movie; but that night, the line never came. Val laughed, however, just as if it had, then started back toward Cooper's convertible.

Tossing his suitcase into the back seat of the car, he climbed in after it. The car moved off toward a galaxy of neon lights. As it passed Clarence's truck, Val turned to wave.

A wave of sadness swept over him. One large part of his life seemed to be ending. He had made it safely past a fair stretch of years; and many people, Val now realized, had helped him along the way.

Sure, maybe his mother, Floyd, Bonnie, even Noah Carson, hadn't been all he wanted them to be; yet each, in their own way, had helped to point out the sharp curves and deep chuckholes that had lain in his path. Suddenly it didn't seem his first eighteen years had been near as bad as he had always believed.

⇒ PART FOUR ⇐

Chapter 20

For the first hours out of El Paso, Blue kept jumping from one safe subject to another, trying, Val thought, to ease them all into a less edgy frame of mind. Her favorite topic was the history of gambling up around Reno, her stomping grounds for the past twenty years.

The gambling started with the Paiute Indians, who used to wager by rolling gopher bones in the sand, covering their bets by putting up their horses and women; which was why, Blue chuckled, back in the old days you'd see so many Paiutes walking down the road all by themselves.

Val was curious why gamblers often ruined everything else in their lives just to keep wagering. Blue's answer surprised him. Betting, she said, was considered a religion. When a gambler won, he took it as a sign that God favored him.

Blue also believed that gambling appealed to the spoiled child in every adult. At a certain age, many children expect the best of everything, and are absolutely astonished when they don't get it. Gamblers, she mused, were little more than pampered kids who never grew up.

How much of this Cooper was buying, Val could not say for sure; about the only sound his father made was a sporadic grunt. Val wondered whether that was a yea or nay.

But when Blue had the floor, she didn't like to share the space with anyone. She was the best talker Val had ever met. What he didn't know was that she had become a good conversationalist in self-defense.

Basically shy, Blue had developed an outgoing personality for two reasons: first, to bring in business, then to avoid the sticky situations this business often created. She had discovered that many of her clients often settled for a subtle compliment in lieu of sex. But she prided herself on honest service, and never promised more than she delivered.

Val was fascinated by her sparkling personality. But when they reached Lordsburg, New Mexico, a couple of hours out of El Paso, Blue suddenly stopped in mid-sentence.

Leaving the border town, Blue had changed places with Val, so she could stretch out in the back seat. Now, within seconds of her last truncated thought, she fell fast asleep. The life of the party had gone home, leaving Val and Cooper stranded out in the middle of a conversational wilderness.

Val tried to go on talking, but every subject seemed a one-way street. He sat racking his brain, trying to think of a topic that might hold Cooper's attention; he even considered telling Cooper the truth about who he was, and what he wanted from him, though Val hadn't yet decided on this last part.

Springing his surprise so early might be dangerous, but Val figured the worst Cooper could do was slow down to sixty and shove him out of the car. Still, it was a beautiful night for walking: full moon and a desert sky studded with bright stars. Of course, he might be hauled in by the highway patrol, but maybe they'd think he was simply another Paiute Indian trudging home from a dice game.

Val had just worked up the courage to make his confession when Cooper abruptly broke the silence. "Okay, I got good news and bad news. You awake, Miss Morgan?"

Dead silence; then a murmur from the back seat: "Depends on how bad the bad news is."

Blue's hands clamped onto the top of the front seat. Val glanced back. She appeared to be girding herself for the worst.

"Well, Blue, it's like this: we managed to escape from El Paso in fairly good shape, though woulda done best to steer clear of Juarez," Cooper conceded. A sigh slipped through his teeth. It sounded, Val thought, like a warning whistle. "So we're still about fifteen thousand bucks shy of the twenty-five I need to get into that game back up in Reno."

What game back up in Reno? Val wondered.

"How about it, Blue?" Cooper drawled with a casual smile.

Blue cleared her throat, something she always did when about to disappoint somebody. "Yeah, cowboy, I have some money saved up," Blue muttered, slowly drawing herself forward. "But could be all that's gonna save me from having to sell apples in my old age."

Cooper's expression went slack. For a moment, the car seemed as quiet as a crypt.

"But hey," Val piped in. "What sort of a game takes twenty-five thousand dollars just to get into it?"

A hard glint came into Cooper's blue eyes. "It's a high stakes poker game, boy," he grunted. "And nobody, including me, wants to allow some rummy to take a shot at the big money with nothing more than piss in his pocket. Hell, be like giving him the chance to beat us with our own goddamn money!"

Cooper didn't sound happy. Val doubted his father ever did much explaining about anything to anybody. He looked as if he'd rather chew on cut glass.

"Listen, Blue, I been waiting months for this game. I know just about every player who'll be there. Their style of play and how their so-called brains work," Cooper said. "Your money'll be almost as safe as sitting in some bank—and it could make you a hellava lot more interest. But deals like this don't grow on cherry trees."

Blue sat very still for several seconds. Then she loudly cleared her throat again. "Yeah, I know you win a lot more'n you lose, cowboy. But with my luck, this lifelong trend of yours will probably reverse itself just for this one game. No, that little piano bar I told you about still seems the safer bet."

Val wasn't aware of this other 'bet' but he sensed that turning Cooper down might eventually prove detrimental to Blue's future with him. She had sensed the same thing, and quickly slid into the shadows of the back seat.

Val sat holding his breath. Then, out of the corner of his eye, he saw Cooper's rigid expression soften somewhat.

"Well, okay. No big deal. Ole Doc Cooper's just gotta find hisself another solution to the situation. So now don't you go 'blue' on me, Miss Morgan."

Val let out a sigh of relief. His father had seemed to take Blue's refusal like a real gentleman.

"Hey, can always get into another game," Val said, hoping to tint the scene a rosier color.

"Well, kid, ain't gonna stay underwater while I'm waiting," Cooper declared. "You see, I don't get invited to many parties. Winners get reputations, just like losers do. 'Cept losers—rich losers, anyway—are a lot more popular. I wouldn't have gotten the invite to this party up in Reno, but the guy sponsoring the shindig owed me a couple of favors."

Val wondered what those favors might have been, and how recently they'd been rendered. "So what now, Mister Cooper?"

"Oh, ain't a question of what, Roger, but where. We'll try Lake Tahoe first. Then after that, play it by ear. If we still got our ears, that is."

Val frowned. He had no idea where Lake Tahoe was; but not anxious to showcase his ignorance, he tried to skirt the issue. "Lake Tahoe, huh?" he lamely observed. "But that's a bit out of the way to Reno, isn't it?"

Cooper ground out a grim smile. "Yeah, couple of hundred miles off our line of march. But the casino folks up that way don't know me so well. Besides, boy, just how far you willing to go to pay me back?"

Val wondered the same thing himself.

Chapter 21

Cooper covered ground in fits and spurts, driving at ninety miles an hour for long stretches, then abruptly pulling over to sleep for a spell, or settle inside a roadside diner, lingering over a cup of coffee as if he had all the time in the world. Val was strangely gratified that his father seemed to actually enjoy sitting inside a roadside restaurant.

Val and Blue had slept a bit the night before, so whenever Cooper pulled off the road, they'd usually take a little hike. The countryside, though still desert, was a great improvement over the pile of rocks back around Big Bend. Val thought Southern New Mexico possessed some style; yucca trees twenty feet tall, wild bushes blooming with most every color, the air pure and clear, the sky a cobalt blue.

It seemed to Val his father had the perfect life. He went wherever he wished with whomever he wanted, and did pretty much what he craved when he got there. Val couldn't resist comparing this life to his own. Cooper's life won, hands down. It sure beat sweating over dirty dishes, cleaning toilets and selling soda pop in freezing weather.

Blue didn't do so bad herself. She had a knack for finding pleasure in the simplest things and least promising places, and often, during these roadside hikes, she would collect rocks. By the time they pulled into Santa Fe late that afternoon, she was packing about five pounds of ore in her purse.

Val was personally not that crazy about rocks. He had seen enough of them in Big Bend to last him a lifetime. Yet whenever Blue went looking for specimens, usually while Cooper slept, Val had tagged along behind her. He enjoyed her company, and also liked to watch the fluid flow of her hips when she walked.

It struck Val as strange that he and Blue had become friends so fast. She must have known, as he did, that in a way they both were competing for the heart of the same man. This should have made them natural enemies, but Blue was the type, Val figured, who rooted for all the underdogs of the world—even when there was a good chance any one of them might bite her.

Cooper did not seem similarly inclined, though by this time, conversing with him had become less of a chore for Val; but about all Cooper talked about was the manner in which he planned to fleece the casinos in Lake Tahoe, so he could buy his way into the big game back up in Reno. That's where Val came in.

He soon learned that Cooper was what the casinos called a counter: a person who can add up the cards so fast in a game of blackjack, the odds almost always tilt in his direction. Driving toward Santa Fe, Cooper occasionally demonstrated just how quick he was. Passing a mileage sign, he'd take the numbers on it—as if they were the first cards dealt out to a couple of players—then add another set of numbers like they were the second cards laid out. After that, he'd determine which hands should take another card, stand pat or double down—and all this in less than ten seconds.

Hearing this, Val smiled, remembering how hard it'd been for him to correctly add up the customer's checks back at the diner. Lupe often told him that he had inherited many of his father's characteristics, but Val figured the mathematical gene had been out to lunch when the transfer was made.

"Anyway, while this 'counting' is technically legal," his father explained, "the casinos naturally take a dim view of any system that cuts into their ill-earned profits. Hell, I been barred from playing blackjack in every damn casino in the entire state of Nevada. Quite an honor, when you think about it—and that, Roger, is where you enter the scenario."

Val tried to maintain his smile. Luckily, there were many miles to go before they reached Lake Tahoe. Val hoped that when they got there, he might still have a little courage left. Damn, why the hell had he told Cooper he wanted to come along to pay him back for letting him win that last hand of poker? Couldn't he have used another excuse?

Cooper had finally tired of driving, and when they arrived in Santa Fe that night, he checked them into a fancy hotel right on the main square. After eating a steak dinner, the best Val had ever tasted, they walked through the town for a while.

Santa Fe had been built around a plaza that could have been, Val thought, a movie set for a western. Better yet, several of the townsfolk sported the same skin color as his own. Val no longer felt like a chunk of chocolate in a sea of vanilla.

Cooper believed there were only two ways to travel: first class and no class, so he booked them into the hotel's swankiest suite. Val just wanted a bed that didn't collapse in the middle. But no sooner was he trudging off toward his bedroom when Cooper called him back into the living room.

He wanted to go over the battle plan again. Managing to keep from groaning out loud, Val sank down on the sofa, and cursed himself once more for having offered to pay Cooper back the money he'd let him win down in El Paso.

Blue strolled over to the refrigerator to get a glass of milk, then went to watch some TV in the bedroom she was sharing with Cooper. Val wasn't very keen on the housing arrangement. He would have preferred his father sleep on the sofa. But now there were other slightly more important things to think about. Blue was just walking back into the living room when Val voiced his first reservation about Cooper's plan.

"But what happens if the casino people get wise to us?"

Cooper looked as if he intended to gloss over this detail. But seeing Blue enter the room, his eyes went grim and his voice fell to a hoarse whisper.

"Oh, they'll just bash our brains in," he grumbled. "Then after that, they'll really get mad. But by then, we won't be feeling much pain, anyway."

Val had suspected as much; hearing it so starkly confirmed, however, suddenly turned his steak dinner upside down. But

Blue's presence had affected his own behavior, as well. He didn't want her to think him a wimp.

"Well, I'm no stranger to danger," Val muttered, employing a line from a western he had seen back in Big Bend.

Blue looked unimpressed. Val figured she had seen the same silly movie. She turned to glare at Cooper. "Frank, you're laying an impossible load on this young kid's shoulders—and it's gonna end up breaking your own goddamned back!"

Cooper sighed heavily, took another swallow of bourbon and quietly declared to his glass: "Well, Old Dame Fortune sometimes can force a fool in the damnedest direction."

"Oh, that's bullshit," Blue snorted. "You expect this boy to learn in two days what it took you twenty years to—"

"I am simply priming this lad to play one small part in this here desert drama, that's all," Cooper drawled.

Cooper turned to Val with a smirk. "And with me handling the tutoring chores, them casino clowns gonna think ole Roger here is smarter than a tree full of owls."

Blue muttered something and stalked back into the bedroom. Watching her go, Cooper found a sly smile, as if something good was about to come his way. But what that might be, Val was now too tired to figure out. Hauling himself up from the sofa, he headed for what had been his original destination.

"Good night, Mister Cooper."

"...You're a smart kid, Roger," Cooper said softly as Val walked past him. "We're gonna do just fine together, son."

The comment hit Val like a shot of adrenaline. This was the first time his father had complimented him. Yet for the moment, all Val did was give his all-purpose smile and walk on into the bedroom.

But after closing the door, he raised his arms in triumph. Damn, he thought, I am finally getting through to the bastard!

Chapter 22

The trouble started at Lake Tahoe; yet never would Val have guessed from looking at it. He had never seen a more peaceful-looking place on earth. Towering spires of pine cradled the lake's blue-green water, the forest to the north sweeping off into a humbling infinity.

Luckily the scenery they'd crossed through had been building up to this finale; if he'd gone directly from Big Bend to Lake Tahoe, Val mused that he might have been stricken with a severe case of the bends. Gasping as he caught first sight of the lake, Val figured he must look to Cooper and Blue like the gawky-eyed, small-town Mexican rube that he was.

Cooper had the Cadillac's top down so they could better enjoy the scenery. But Blue didn't seem impressed. She sat mute as a department store dummy in the back seat, hiding behind a big pair of sunglasses. She owned what seemed more than a dozen pair, and wore them in both bright weather and bad, indoors and out. She did take them off at night, but always rather reluctantly. If Val hadn't known better, he would have sworn Blue was on the FBI's Ten-Most-Wanted List.

A couple of miles farther on, almost everybody looked like they could be on that same list. Cooper had pulled into the tiny town of State Line, passing out of California and into the state of Nevada. The town was populated by the strangest-looking people Val had ever seen. They reminded him of the desperate, haunted-eyed prospectors he'd seen in old photographs of the Klondike gold strike in Alaska. The characters clamoring around State Line seemed cut from the same bolt of badly frayed cloth.

Cooper noted Val's interest. "Well, Roger, for a fella who's never been out of Big Bend, this must be about the most colorful collection of crazies you've ever seen."

Cooper's question blind-sided Val. His father hadn't said anything in quite a while, but he'd been watching Val, snorting now and then when he'd catch him gawking at the passing parade. Val had not mentioned Big Bend before. Had Cooper made the connection? he wondered.

Then something up ahead caught Val's eye. Two of the fattest women this side of a carnival sideshow stood alongside the road, holding a cardboard sign. WILL DO ANYTHING FOR THE GAS MONEY TO GET HOME! Cooper laughed and honked his horn. Val gave them a cheery wave. He hoped the two large ladies had brought along plenty of warm clothing. It could well be winter before anybody took them up on their offer.

"Carload of characters, huh, kid?" Cooper said, smiling.

"Yeah," Val admitted. "Biggest bunch I've ever seen. Outside a movie house, anyway."

Cooper seemed to want to say something important, but what he mentioned next didn't give Val much of a clue. Cooper sometimes spoke as carefully as if he were studying a hand of poker.

"You see a lot of movies, kid?"

Val shrugged his shoulders. "Why not? Cheap way to travel. What's wrong with that?"

"Nothing," Cooper muttered. "Just thinking how much alike we are, that's all."

"Yeah, how's that?" Val nervously asked.

"Well, you watch movies, I gamble. Both of us trying in our own way, I guess, to avoid all the Big Bends of this old world."

Val suddenly felt like a fish watching somebody cast a line in its direction. How and when had Cooper found out about Big Bend? He must know, Val thought. But he'd be damned if the mere mention of it would make him take the hook.

"Really?" Val replied, coolly slithering on downstream. "You don't gamble just for the money?"

"The money's just a way of keeping score," Cooper said, bringing the convertible to an abrupt stop. Then he nodded

toward a blockhouse building fifty yards farther down the road.
"And that's whose money we're gonna heist tonight."

The casino looked as impregnable as a frontier fortress. Val
wondered from what angle Cooper planned to attack it. Then his
father leaned over to take from the glove compartment a large
wad of bills. Counting off ten one-hundred dollar bills, he handed them to Val.

"Okay, boy, here's a thousand to get you started," Cooper
said, as casually as if he were ordering a hamburger and french
fries. He turned toward the back seat. "Wake up, Miss Morgan.
It's showtime."

"I am awake," Blue grumbled, slowly leaning forward with all
the enthusiasm of a robbery suspect stepping into the lights of a
police line-up. "But I still think this is one show that ain't gonna
make it past the first act."

Blue's attitude was contagious. Val swallowed what felt like a
large marble. He stared at the ten hundred dollar bills, still stuck
to his hands like flypaper.

"...But I thought we were gonna rest up, maybe go see a
movie tonight, then start all this tomorrow, when—" Val lamely
protested.

"Got no time to see a movie, kid," Cooper exclaimed. "We
gotta produce one of our own—and we have only another few
days to make it."

"But I'm not really ready for this! What happens if I lose all
this money?" Val said, as the marble settled on his stomach like
a five-pound rock.

Cooper gently patted Val on the shoulder. "Don't worry
about the money. You just remember our signals."

Gulping down another lump, Val climbed out of the car. Blue
followed Val out. For a painful moment, they simply stood there;
probably looking, Val thought, like a couple of unwanted kids
who had just been dropped off at an orphanage.

Blue slammed the car door shut. Cooper winced. He babied
his convertible as if it were his best friend, often referring to it as
'George.' On the long trip north to Lake Tahoe, he had often
mentioned that 'George' was thirsty or hungry whenever the car
needed water or gasoline.

"Well, Frank, you ain't asked for my advice, but you're gonna get it, anyway," Blue quietly declared. "For openers, I think this shitty scheme is way too heavy for your son here to handle, and besides that..."

Blue's voice trailed off. She had finally turned up Cooper's hole card; yet for several strained seconds, the three of them simply stared off into space. Then Cooper smiled and extended his hand in Val's direction.

"Hell, about time we was properly introduced. They call you Val, right?"

"...How long you known about me?" Val asked, taking Cooper's hand as if it might be holding an electric shocker.

"Oh, just after I got to the hotel in El Paso, I had me a brief but most informative conversation with that lawyer friend of yours, Noah Carson," Cooper drawled. He looked rather pleased that everyone's cards were finally faceup on the table.

"...Did you see me sitting in the lobby?" Val asked, blushing with embarrassment. He was reliving that morning all over again.

Cooper chuckled. "Yeah, I spotted you right off, boy."

"I didn't think you'd seen me."

"Well, that's what makes me a pretty good card player," Cooper said. "Anyway, I'm real happy I don't have to call you Roger no more. That handle didn't quite fit you."

Val felt more relieved than pleased. Years earlier, he had toyed with the notion of someday becoming an actor. But now he realized what tiresome work it was, pretending to be somebody else. Val decided that 'Roger' was the last character he would ever play.

"How come you didn't say nothing when we first met?" Val exclaimed. Now he worried that Cooper might decide, just moments after they had been properly introduced, to say goodbye and leave him stranded hundreds of miles from home.

"How come I didn't say anything? Well, I could ask you the same question," Cooper slyly answered. He seemed to cast his fishing line out again.

"Guess I was afraid you'd decide to disappear before—"

Blue interjected with a loud snort. "Yeah, I'll bet that when he gets the itch, old Cooper's as expert at disappearing as Lamont Cranston himself."

"Who's Lamont Cranston?" Val asked.

"He's the 'Shadow,' dumbo," Blue said, smiling. "Doncha ever listen to the radio?"

Nodding as if he had just remembered, Val turned to Cooper. It was his turn to go fishing. Tossing out a line, he asked, "So what do we call each other now?"

Cooper knew what Val hoped to hear, but he was a little too nimble to take the bait. "Well, kid, for now let's settle on partner, huh?"

Val chewed on this for a moment. But before he could decide whether he liked the taste, Cooper started up the convertible. "Okay, guys, I'll go get us booked into the Last Chance Motel, then change into my work clothes. See you all inside the casino in about thirty minutes."

¡Dios mio! Val thought. Thirty minutes till game time, and he still didn't know all the plays. There were a hundred questions yet to be asked, but before Val could get his mouth to work in tandem with his brain, Cooper pulled a U-turn and rolled away in the opposite direction from the casino.

Watching the convertible disappear, Val tucked the thousand dollars into his Levis, and said a silent prayer that he would not let his father down. Cooper had entrusted him with a huge amount of money, and if he lost it, Val feared that his brand-new relationship with his father would probably go with it.

Then he turned, half-expecting to find that Blue had also disappeared. Yet though she hated what they were about to try, now that they were committed to the plan, Blue seemed determined to give it her best.

Flushing up a flimsy smile, she hooked her arm in Val's and they trudged off toward the casino. It was just getting dark, and a galaxy of glittering lights suddenly snapped on. Despite the dancing neon, the casino still looked like a fortress.

As they cautiously approached it, Blue began to softly sing. The song was not quite appropriate to the situation; but even in Val's shaky state of mind, Blue's version of the famous lyrics made him laugh out loud.

"We're off to see the Lizard, the wonderful Lizard of Oz."

Chapter 23

After booking two rooms at the Last Chance Motel, Cooper took a leisurely shower, then grabbed a short nap. He had told Val and Blue he'd see them within thirty minutes; but it didn't really matter if he showed up at all. His casino scheme was no more than a sham.

Leaving El Paso, Cooper realized that in the short time he had to make the fifteen thousand dollars he still needed to get into the game back in Reno, his best bet was Blue's bankbook.

But so far she had failed to take the bait. Cooper needed to cast out another line, one that might touch Blue's heart instead.

Val would be the bait. Regardless of whether they won or lost that night, Cooper decided that in the morning, he would tell Val he had realized that the shell game with the casino was simply too dangerous. Posturing as a concerned parent, he would proclaim that he did not want his son involved in such shenanigans. Then he would give Val a thousand dollars, bid him a sad farewell, and send him back to Big Bend.

Of course, the scene would be played in front of Blue, preferably in a forlorn little bus station; and if his seemingly heroic sacrifice did not finally get him next to Blue's money, chances were that nothing would.

Mulling over his plan of attack, Cooper felt a slight twinge of regret. He had, despite his protective instincts, grown rather fond of Val. The kid had plenty of moxie, and under less pressing circumstances Cooper would have liked to get to know him better. But the race between friendship with Val and Blue's bankbook was no contest. The kid ran a poor second.

≫ ≪

An hour later, Cooper still hadn't shown up. But the time had slid by so slyly, Val could see how it was possible to lose track of it altogether inside the big casino; it was difficult to even tell if it was day or night, an illusion fostered by the heavy drapes over all the windows, the large dividers in front of the doors and the absence of any clocks.

The atmosphere inside the casino reminded Val of the movie house back in Big Bend. Secretive, mysterious, and fraught with impending drama; a place where dreams could come to life. Val loved it.

He and Blue were playing the nickel slot machines. Val was up by more than thirty dollars. But it had been an uphill battle until he chanced upon a little reverse psychology. The idea came from a toothless old woman playing the slot machine right next to him. The old lady, dressed in carpenter's overalls, would drop in a nickel, then turn away and start to sing. Always the same song, same verse. "California, here I come, right back where I started from, where bowers and flowers bloom in the spring." The woman wouldn't look back at the machine 'til it had completely stopped spinning.

At first Val thought this sort of silly. But it certainly seemed to work. The machine, perhaps intimidated, he thought, by her show of indifference, kept belching out one small pile of nickels after another.

Val decided to borrow a bit of her act, though he did drop the sound-track. Besides, he wasn't from California, though he certainly planned to go there someday. So after cranking his own machine, Val peered around as if he couldn't be bothered with the outcome.

Blue employed her own system. She'd crank one machine, then start a few more before the tumblers stopped on the first one; at one point, three machines were whirling at the same time, yet her mind seemed somewhere else. She cranked the handles as if she were flushing a toilet.

Val was pretending to ignore his machine again, when he noticed a tall man coming down the main aisle. The man wore a baggy windbreaker, a crumpled baseball cap, and reflector-style sunglasses. He was also wearing a scruffy pair of tennis shoes.

But it was his limp that caught Val's eye. The man carried his gimpy leg with a certain pride, as if it might have come from an old war wound. Val should have recognized him right away, but not until the man nodded in his direction did he realize that Frank Cooper finally was reporting for action.

Blue also noticed his arrival. Watching him walk toward the blackjack tables at the far end of the spacious room, a wistful look wandered into her eyes. Val had seen that same expression in Bonnie's eyes, and knew what it meant.

"In love with him, aren't you, ma'am?"

The question surprised Blue. Then she smiled, which only made her look more melancholy. "Yeah, now that you mention it, afraid so," Blue uttered. "Which makes for a sorta silly situation between you and me, huh?"

Val nodded, though he wasn't sure of exactly what situation Blue had in mind.

"Yeah, some sad sort of fix," Blue said, still smiling. "You probably came to take Cooper home to your mother—and me, I'd like to take him back to Kansas to meet mine."

Blue wasn't wrong, but before Val could muster a reply, his slot machine started to clang, belching forth a pile of nickels. Dropping to his knees to gather up the coins, Val had a fleeting thought: this gambling gig was one highflying occupation. Hell, no wonder Cooper liked it so much!

Blue quickly let the air out of Val's balloon. "Beginner's luck, Val," she said, with a smile which looked like a warning. "But grab it up good. Might be all any of us gonna win tonight."

⇒ ⇐

Besides Val and Cooper, there were three other players at the table. Cooper sat to Val's right. To Cooper's right was a stolid stump of a man who looked like one of those Paiute Indians Blue had mentioned. He was wearing a solemn expression, as well as about a half pound of turquoise around his thick neck.

In the two hours he'd been at the table, the Indian hadn't said a word. Even when he busted out, about all he did was belch. But he hadn't busted out very often. If his luck held, he would certainly not be one of those Indians walking home broke that night.

To Val's left around the curved table sat a pert little blonde who reminded him of another blonde, though the girl looked a couple of years older than Bonnie. Val's mind drifted for a moment. What was Bonnie doing that night? he wondered. She probably had locked herself in her bedroom, so she wouldn't have to listen to her mother going on and on about what a no-good she was. Val felt a sudden stab of guilt. He had left her all alone to face the music, which no doubt by now had come to resemble a funeral dirge.

Val turned back to the blonde sitting next to him. She and her husband, parked on the other side of her, were on their honeymoon. But from the look of their luck, they would be the ones walking home broke that night if they didn't get a divorce first. They had been squabbling for the past hour about the way the other one was playing.

Blue was standing behind Val, cheering him on; and for those first few hours there was plenty to cheer about. Val was up by almost two thousand dollars. Cooper was even better at counting cards than Val thought; his signals, however, had become tougher to read. But Val figured this was good; if they had been that easy to spot, he and Cooper wouldn't have been able to fool the dealer for very long.

The tension was burning a hole in Val's stomach, though not only because he was fearful of getting caught. What Val dreaded most was disappointing his father.

Cooper had been drinking throughout the game, and was now acting rather rowdy. Had Val not been so nervous, he might have enjoyed watching the act.

The toughest problem was to catch Cooper's signals without having to glance toward him. That's where Blue came in; standing to Val's left, she could peer past him without drawing too much attention. When she saw a signal, she'd relay it to Val by using just the slightest amount of pressure on his shoulder.

The other obstacle was the dealer: a nasty-looking slug with a face that seemed blasted out of pure granite. What bothered Val most was the Coke-bottle glasses the dealer wore. When the light hit them just right, his eyes grew as small as a snake's.

The dealer had just dealt out the second card, faceup, of a new hand when Cooper anxiously muttered: "Hit me, pal—but not hard enough to break anything."

The man pulled a seven from his card shoe. Cooper groaned as if he'd just been served with a summons to appear in court. As he threw in his hand, the dealer turned to Val—and in that split second, Val got the signal.

The dealer raised his head slightly, like a hunting dog that's caught the scent. The move made Val more jittery.

"Go ahead and make your move, Pancho," the dealer hissed past the sizable gap between his two front teeth. How sweet it'd be, Val mused, to widen that gap with a screwdriver. Then he felt Blue's fingers tighten on his shoulder. She was relaying a signal from Cooper to double up on his bet. Val did so.

The dealer's cratered face backed off a bit. Then he dealt out another two cards to the newlyweds, after which he laid out one more card for himself. Turning up his hand, he said, "Dealer pays on twenty."

Both Cooper and the Indian had already busted out. The bride and groom now followed them, having taken as usual one card too many. That left just Val and the dealer. Val almost felt afraid to show his hand. Blue leaned past him to turn up his hole card.

"Hey, honey, you're hotter than hell tonight," Blue said. "Twenty is exactly what you got!"

The dealer's expression soured. Pushing a pile of chips in Val's direction, the dealer took off his Coke bottles and stood slowly wiping them with an embroidered hankerchief. His eyes never seemed to blink.

Val felt the sweat beginning to stream down under his arms. Blue had finally grown a bit overwrought herself, and now leaned over to give Val a hurried peck on his cheek.

"Great, cowboy," Blue gushed, dumping her words directly into his left ear. "Somebody is smiling sugar on you tonight. That's the fifth hand in a row you've won."

One hand too many for the big Indian, who let loose his loudest belch of the night. Cooper turned toward him, as if the sound had been his cue to speak. "Yeah, that's the word for it. This young squirt's luck has given me a stomachache, too. Come on, Chief, I'll race you back to the reservation."

Abruptly swinging off his stool, Cooper started away into the crowd. A smart tactical retreat, Val supposed, though it left him and Blue in the middle of an immediate mess. He could quit playing, or go on for a while, though in far less expert fashion. Val flipped an imaginary coin in the air, and remained at the table.

Stripped of Cooper's play-calling signals, however, he was no match for the slit-eyed dealer. The marked difference seemed to set off one more alarm bell in the man's brain.

Val quickly lost more than three hundred dollars. Yet he couldn't seem to muster the will to simply get up and walk away, dreading something far worse than merely losing money. He could almost feel the hand of the casino's boss about to grab him by the throat.

Blue had read the situation, and now made known her desire for a steak dinner. But when Val hesitated, Blue announced that if he wouldn't spring for the steak, she would find somebody who would.

Gathering up his chips, Val slid away from his chair. Arm in arm, he and Blue started across the floor, heading nowhere in particular, looking, Val figured, like two orphans out in search of a family.

By this time, both he and Blue felt as if they'd worked a full shift in a coal mine. After Val cashed in his chips, they wandered around for fifteen minutes looking for Cooper.

"Let's go back to the motel," Blue finally muttered.

"Remember the name of the place?" Val asked.

Blue let loose a quiet curse.

So there they stood, with all that money, but without the slightest idea of where to take it.

"Well, nothing to do but walk around in circles till either Cooper or the buzzards find us, huh?" Val muttered. He felt so tired, there didn't seem much difference between the two parties.

Chapter 24

Half an hour later, Val spotted a familiar-looking pair of tattered tennis shoes on the next aisle over from where he stood. But the shoes were no longer connected to the rest of Cooper's costume. The battered windbreaker, crumpled baseball cap and reflector sunglasses had been ditched.

Cooper himself, however, appeared to be all in one piece. Intently cranking away at a slot machine directly across from Val and Blue, he acted as if nothing less than the rest of his life depended on the outcome.

Val nudged Blue, who was leaning over her own machine as if she wished it were a bed. Seeing Cooper, she quietly cursed him for having left them stranded. Cooper pretended not to notice them, and went on negotiating with his slot machine. Taking their cue, Val and Blue re-cranked their own one-armed bandits.

"But why did you cut out?" Val finally asked, posing the question directly to his machine. "We was still going good—"

"Naw, that dealer finally woke up," Cooper muttered.

"Just as we were falling asleep," Blue sighed. "Anyway, we still cleared more than fifteen hundred bucks. So why not call it a night?" Her question was aimed at Cooper's tennis shoes.

Val nodded to second the motion. But the expression in Cooper's eyes stopped him cold. His father was glaring at Blue with what seemed profound contempt. When she looked up, however, his features quickly shifted.

He looked to be waiting for Blue to suggest an alternative program; when she remained silent, Cooper shrugged. "Well, Blue, I know it's been one hell of a long night," he conceded, cranking his machine one more time. "But I got me less than four days to round up more'n thirteen thousand bucks."

Blue started to protest, then simply plopped her head down on Val's shoulder. She was dead on her feet. Val felt the same way. Cooper stared at them as if they were the two most pampered brats on the block. Then he smiled.

"Well, shoulda known better'n try to get any serious work outta you two Girl Scouts," he drawled. "Okay, see you squirts back at the motel."

"Hey, where is that motel?" Val thought to ask.

"Back down the road a few blocks. The Last Chance Motel. Can't miss it."

"You're not coming with us?" Blue asked in a stunted voice.

"Naw, night's still young. I'll try another casino. Maybe find me a couple of drunks to roll on the way over... But you did good, guys."

Damned right they did, Val thought, waiting for Cooper to further praise their merits; those few words, however, were apparently all his father could muster.

Watching Cooper stride toward the door, Val and Blue started to jerk away at their slot machines again; they probably looked, Val thought, like poor neglected mutts who even asleep could not stop scratching their fleas.

Finally, gathering what remained of their strength, Val and Blue made for the far end of the casino. They had sidestepped most of the crowd, and were no more than fifty feet from the main door when two men intercepted them.

"Congratulations, young fella," a tall, slick-looking man in a shark-skin suit said, reaching for Val's hand. "You just won our first door prize of the night."

If Val had been less tired, he might have shown a little more enthusiasm. But it was all he could do just to hang onto the man's hand. Then the second man, a butterball type sporting a necktie about half as wide as his face, tried to clear up the confusion.

"Oh, don't think you've done anything so special, young man," the chunky man exclaimed, laughing as he handed Val what looked like a raffle stub. "Just every now and then, we select one of our patrons at random for a door prize."

"So what's the prize?" Blue asked, warily climbing into the conversation.

"Dinner for the lucky winner and his guest," the sharkskin replied. "We take the young man's picture for our publicity department, then treat him and his guest to the best prime rib dinner in the entire state of Nevada."

"Prime rib, huh?" Blue murmured lazily, stopping just short of licking her lips. She and Val hadn't eaten a thing since breakfast.

The tall man seemed to read their stomachs. "In case you're wondering, our main restaurant is still open—and this little picture-taking session shouldn't last more'n a few minutes."

Blue still seemed skeptical.

"Come on, Blue, let's go for it," Val said. "What do we have to lose, except our hunger pangs?"

Blue finally nodded, and they all started toward a set of double doors about a hundred feet away.

As they arrived at the door, however, Val glanced away to spot something that almost instantly raised the hair off the back of his head: a small, yet blinding light coming from one of the blackjack tables. Then something shifted, and Val saw what was behind the light. The Coke-bottle glasses. The blackjack dealer was staring at Val, eyes swimming with satisfaction.

A split second later, Val felt himself being pushed through the door. The man in the sharkskin suit then started to hustle him down a long, dimly lighted hallway. Val could hear Blue walking behind him. From the shuffling sound of her boots it seemed she too was being pushed from behind.

Then Val heard the quick clickety-clack of her heels on the concrete floor. But the sound didn't last long. No sooner had Blue made a move back toward the double doors when a huge man came charging into view. He had been watching them through a little window in one of the doors. When he saw Blue racing toward him, he had hurried into the hallway. Blue meekly rejoined Val.

Now they were surrounded, as well as outnumbered.

The procession stopped just outside the door of a restroom. The tall man in the suit disappeared inside. A moment later, he came back out, wearing a strange smile.

Val blinked with disbelief. Maybe it was the dim lighting, but the man's face seemed to change right in front of his eyes. Out on the main floor, the dapperly-dressed man had looked like just another of those slick, shiny types meandering around the casino like oversized cockroaches.

But in the semidarkness of the hallway, Val thought the man looked far more dangerous than a cockroach. His patent leather hair, angular features, and lifeless eyes could have gotten him cast in a movie as a hired killer, a killer in that line of work for more than just the money.

"I'll handle it from here," he purred to the fat man. "But you make sure me and my Mexican girlfriend are not disturbed."

The guy with the wide tie grinned, and loosened his grip on Val's left arm. The scary-looking man clamped hold of his other arm. Val winced. The man had the grip of a Doberman pinscher.

"Well, sweetheart," he muttered with an eerie smile, "let's go get your door prize."

Val felt his legs go limp. Then he seemed to shrink several sizes right on the spot. The sharkskin now looked a full foot taller.

Blue cranked up a brittle smile. "Now, come on, fellas, it can't be casino policy to rough up anybody who's managed to win a little money..."

The slick-looking man holding Val with the mad-dog grip flashed another smile. "No, lady, we're just freelance hustlers, same as you and your two partners. Little smarter, that's all."

Then, having finished the introductions, he guided Val into the restroom as gently as a church usher leading someone to an empty pew.

The restroom was long, narrow, and windowless, with some ten stalls. Across from them were the urinals and washbasins.

The room, lit by strips of blue-colored neon along the top of all four walls, seemed as quiet as a mortuary.

The sharkskin hustled Val over to the mirror above the washbasins. When he started to speak again, he looked only at their reflection in the mirror.

"I lied to you, greaser," the man murmured to Val's image. "You see, it's really me who's gonna collect the prize... And I ain't had a kid as sweet-assed as you in quite a while."

A kidney punch ripped into Val's side like a rocket. As he keeled over the washbasin, the man hit him again in the same spot. The sharkskin had found his most vulnerable spot. Val had injured his right kidney playing football. Gasping with pain, Val saw himself slide below the mirror.

Gulping, he felt the man take him by his hair and yank him back up toward the mirror. For a moment, Val didn't recognize himself. He was white as chalk, with his features twisted around as if he'd suffered a stroke. But what shook Val worse was the look on the other guy's face.

In the weird bluish light, his dead-looking eyes seemed to finally come alive. "Now listen up, greaser: You can make this easier for both of us," he muttered, gazing admiringly at his own image in the mirror. "Or be a tight-ass about it. Which I'd enjoy even better. Now where do we find the tall cowboy you was working with?"

"Go to hell," Val sputtered. He had just gotten his breath back when the big man took it out of him again. The shot to his stomach seemed to climb all the way to his chest. Val keeled forward once more.

As he stood there on wobbly legs, the man started to rifle through his pockets. Earlier, the man had divined which part of Val's body could take the least punishment; now he went directly to the left breast pocket of Val's coat, where he was carrying all of the casino's money, as well as the thousand dollars Cooper had given him to start the play. Val had his own money hidden in his boot.

But what the man in the sharkskin suit found still came to more than twenty-seven hundred dollars; Val prayed it would be enough to calm him down. Making a fast count, he stuffed the money into his pocket, then turned to stare at Val's reflection in the mirror. Again the same sick smile.

Val knew the dismantling job was about to continue. Then he was momentarily saved by the sound of a flushing toilet. The man spun around, startled that they'd had company all this time.

A small stump of a man stumbled out from one of the toilet stalls. He had a tuft of gray hair that rose straight back from his forehead, and cheeks so ballooned he might have had a case of the mumps. Val thought he looked like a chipmunk. A very drunk chipmunk.

The bruiser smiled at the little man, as if to assure him that everything was under control. Then he began to carefully wash his hands. Val could see in the mirror that the little man was standing about ten feet behind him, his features scrunched tight with scorn.

"Fuckin' Mexicans," the chipmunk said to the shark. "Can't hold their firewater any better'n them pukey Paiute Indians!"

The chipmunk veered drunkenly toward the door. For a fleeting moment Val thought about pleading with him to run for help, yet Val knew the message would never get through. The two men out in the hallway would whap the little man the moment he walked out the restroom door.

"... Now, kid, I'm gonna ask you again: where do I find the tall cowboy you was working with?" the sharkskin man said. He was no longer addressing Val's reflection in the mirror. "You see, kid, I figure your partner is packing a bigger roll himself. So after I pass him the collection plate, we'll be through for the night. What do you say, sweet-ass?"

Val cursed his luck. The man had asked him to do the one thing in the entire world he couldn't do. If he betrayed Cooper, their relationship would never get the chance to grow into love. No choice now but to try and fight his way out of that restroom. He would worry about what awaited him in the hallway when he got there.

Rearing back, Val unleashed a right cross, catching the man on the side of his jaw. But the blow carried more surprise than sting. The man simply shook his head and smiled. Then he fired off a shot of his own, again aimed at Val's right kidney. Val flinched just enough to make it miss. By now his kidney was throbbing so badly, if the bruiser had asked him, Val would have gladly exposed his other one, to more democratically divide up the pain.

The man had missed his main target, but still rammed Val's rib cage with a blow that dropped him to the floor. With his face flush on the tile, Val saw the guy with the wide tie watching from the doorway. He seemed to be enjoying himself. Then his expression suddenly soured.

"Sorry, gentlemen," the fat man said, hoisting a tentative smile. "This here restroom's outta order."

"Yeah, who the hell ordered that order?" came a booming voice from somewhere down the hallway. "What kinda crummy joint you running here?" Judging from the fat man's nervous twitch, the owner of the voice was large enough to pose a sizable threat.

But to Blue, warily appraising this sudden twist, the threat seemed more like an opportunity. From where Val lay, he couldn't see Blue as she bolted for the double doors. But it sounded as if she wasn't going to slow down till she hit the outskirts of her hometown of Hutchinson, Kansas.

Meanwhile, the man with the cement-mixer voice was joined by a friend who sounded every bit as big. The fat man began bouncing from one foot to another.

"Yeah, fat boy, all the money these clip joints rake in," the second voice exclaimed, "and can't even keep their fucking water pipes in working order!"

Then the cement-mixer voice growled, "And if I don't get into a restroom pretty damned quick, I'm gonna spring a leak in my own water pipe!"

A hand the size of a Virginia ham grabbed the fat guy by his necktie, and yanked him away from the doorway. A scuffle instantly ensued; from the sound of the brawl, Val's benefactors were greater in number than he had first thought.

Now or never, Val decided. Scooping up what remained of his strength, he cocked his leg and sent it hurtling upward. The heel of his boot caught the sharkskin square in the crotch.

Letting out a screeching howl, he went careening past the washbasins, then tailspinned into an open toilet stall and tumbled to the tile floor. By the time he collapsed, Val had already reached the hallway.

The cement-mixer was still unloading on the fat man as Val hobbled out from the restroom. Seeing Val, he tightened the necktie around the fat man's throat.

"Hey, thought you said this restroom was outta order!"

The fat man couldn't do much more than gurgle, though this did little to crimp the interrogation. "Yeah, why the hell do the American people hafta be continuously lied to?" a barrel-chested man demanded to know.

The barrel-chested guy, dressed in a Hawaiian shirt, was with a group of men sporting the same type of shirts. They all looked as if their hobby might be busting boulders with their bare hands.

Then Val saw Blue charging down the hallway with a couple of angry-looking security cops in tow.

"Hey, what the hell's going on?" one cop yelled, drawing forth his pistol.

The guys in the gaudy shirts quickly started to hike in the opposite direction. The fat man loosened his tie so he could breathe again, then went hurrying in the same direction as the Hawaiian shirts.

Taking up the chase, one security cop went racing past Val; but the second guard came to a stop. Drawing his pistol from its holster, he cautiously entered the restroom.

As the cop disappeared from view, Blue put her arm around Val, and gently herded him back toward the double doors. With the adrenaline slowly seeping from his system, the pain now hit him with its full force.

Yet as they hobbled away, Val heard something that almost made him smile: the voice of the guard, inside the restroom.

"Hey, come on now, mister," the voice growled. "You wanna lay down somewhere, go get yourself a hotel room!"

Then came a weak, high-pitched whine. Val had apparently kicked the sharkskin-suited man in the crotch hard enough to temporarily turn him into a soprano.

Chapter 25

An hour later, lying flat on his back in a cabin at the Last Chance Motel, Val thought the place rather aptly named. Earlier, Blue had taken him to an emergency clinic, but about all he could remember was the slot machine in the waiting room. After that, everything had gone white for a while.

Back at the motel, Blue told Cooper what had happened at the casino. Val was too weak to say much himself. Besides, there was no way he could top Blue's dramatic rendition of what had proved the evening's main event. She even dimmed all the lights, either out of fear, or to heighten the theatrical effect.

Listening to the story, Cooper looked as whipped as if he'd taken the beating himself. He was sitting on the bed, while Blue stood guard back near the door, as if expecting the shark squad to bust in at any moment.

Dreading the same thing, Cooper got up to go peek past the drapes. When it seemed everything was all right, Val closed his eyes. This had been the longest day of his life.

Turning away from the window, Cooper said, "Val, did them scumbags get your own money?"

"Had it in my boot," Val murmured, trying to smile but making a mess of it.

Cooper sat down again. Leaning across the bed he patted Val on the shoulder. Val flinched. Every inch of his skin felt as though he had the shingles. Noting his reaction, Cooper winced a bit himself.

"In your boot, huh? Smart... Well, better get some sleep now. We'll talk in the morning. Okay, partner?"

Val faked another smile. Cooper clicked off the lamp next to the bed, and walked over to the door. He and Blue stood quietly talking for a moment. Val could barely keep his eyes open, but he could see that Blue still seemed terribly upset.

"The doctor at the clinic thought Val had been run over by a half-ton truck," Blue muttered, a subtle sting in her voice. "But your boy wouldn't tell those slime balls at the casino who you were, or where you were. Probably coulda saved himself most of them bruises if he'd told them what they wanted to know."

Cooper turned toward Val. "Yeah, he sure took his licking like a man."

Blue softly shot back, "Especially considering it shoulda been your licking."

Nodding solemnly, Cooper hung his head. Val doubted that they realized he could hear them. But it wouldn't have mattered much to Blue. Cooper didn't appear crazy, however, about continuing the conversation. He reached over to unfasten the chain lock on the door.

"Big mistake I made was not making sure you all was safely out of the casino before I left," Cooper whispered, peering outside the door.

"Tell me something I don't know," Blue quietly growled. She wasn't interested in hearing Cooper's confession; she had one of her own to make, and though she kept her voice low, Val could tell she was fast losing control of her emotions.

"I'm grabbing a bus back to Reno tomorrow morning," Blue declared to no one in particular. "Oh, not that I've got much of a life up there, but I've sorta made my peace with it by now. It don't tear up my insides anymore. Not like they're torn up now, anyway..."

Cooper turned back in Val's direction. Speaking very softly, he said, "Well, guess that just leaves me and the boy."

Then, gazing off into the darkness again, he ushered Blue outside. He shut the door and double checked that it was locked. Then Cooper followed after Blue down the vine-covered walkway that ran alongside the cabin. They hadn't gone more than ten feet when Cooper stopped to pick up the conversation. It was a warm night and past the drapes, all the windows were open. Val heard every word that came next.

"Well, Blue, just want you to know one thing," Cooper said. His voice sounded as forlorn as the lonely call of a lost ship. "I ain't got much of a life back up in Reno myself... anywhere else, for that matter... And I don't rightly think the kid has much of a life back in West Texas. So what we got here is three people still searching for something they ain't yet found. Only maybe they have, but don't know it..."

Cooper paused, as if struggling to find the exact words he wanted. Blue finally broke the silence.

"Listen, I'm gonna tell you the same thing you told Val down in Juarez: speak American, so's I can understand you."

"Well, guess what I'm laboring to explain is that this big poker game up in Reno is important, not just for me, but for you and Val, too. If I win, it could be the start of a brand-new life for all three of us..."

Inside the cabin, Val waited for Blue's reply. But the quiet lasted so long, he thought Blue had walked away, leaving Cooper to talk alone with the softly rustling wind. When Val finally heard her voice again, he could tell she wanted to believe what Cooper had just told her.

"Not still trying to hustle a hustler, are you, cowboy?"

"Hey, lady, best back off now," Cooper drawled, a hint of humor in his voice. "Like I told you before, Frank Cooper don't say nothing he don't mean."

That was the last thing Val heard. Blue and Cooper had walked away. But what Val overheard gave him plenty to think about; especially what Cooper had said about how the game up in Reno could change all three of their lives.

His last thought that night, however, was not about the future, but rather the recent past, Val was thinking about that prime rib dinner he had never gotten to eat.

≫ ≪

That next morning, Cooper bought them all sirloin steak, eggs, and hotcakes; the best breakfast Val had ever eaten, though he missed the *chile casera* he'd grown up putting on or in almost everything but his coffee.

After they finished their meal, Blue was still suffering from battle fatigue and retreated to her room. Val felt even worse, though he no longer thought he might not live long enough to see his nineteenth birthday.

With Blue safely tucked away, Cooper led Val down toward the edge of the lake for a little talk; yet for a long while, neither of them said a word. Strange, Val thought, how some places could discourage idle conversation. There, under an azure, cloudless sky, next to glistening blue-green water and trees as tall as cathedral spires, Val felt as if he were walking through a gigantic church.

Cooper was also unusually quiet. Val's courage the night before touched him in a spot he thought had long been sealed over. It had been many years since anyone had cared enough for him to offer the painful sacrifice Val had made on his behalf.

Earlier that previous evening, Cooper had planned to make a production number out of sending Val home, but now he knew that regardless of what Blue might eventually do, he wanted to keep his son by his side. Very little in life impressed Cooper like a raw display of courage. His son had shown a valor that Cooper thought had gone out of style.

But there was still that fifteen thousand dollars he needed to get into the game up in Reno.

Val had also made a decision, but thought it wise to let Cooper make the opening move. Blue's remark the night before about catching a bus home had made Val think about doing the same thing. It seemed Cooper had read his mind.

"Well, Val, even if you're sorry you came looking for me, can't really take off now, can you?"

"Not sure yet. About coming or going," Val said. But he was glad he had come; he simply wondered whether he should now leave. Cooper studied him for a moment, as if trying to discern which way Val was leaning.

"But you take off now, Val, be like walking out on a play right in the middle of the second act. Hell, ain't you sorta curious how this little drama's gonna come out?"

"You still think this plan of yours will work?" Val asked, avoiding Cooper's question.

"Yeah, up the road a piece, it might," Cooper drawled. "Hell, we almost pulled it off last night, and we ain't even practiced that much."

"But what if those guys are still around?" Val shuddered at the mere thought of a rematch.

"Naw, them type twirps usually scatter after they've made a score," Cooper retorted with a dismissive wave of his arm.

Val wasn't so sure. "Yeah, but I bet every casino in Nevada got their own guys who—"

"Val, that muscle last night weren't working for the casino. Just in cahoots with that one blackjack dealer," Cooper replied. "If they'd been clowns from the casino, they woulda just taken the money, figuring that alone would discourage you from coming back... Assault and battery is considered a serious felony, even here in Nevada."

Val didn't know enough about Nevada law to argue the point; he did know that the discussion was bringing him no closer to the decision he would soon have to make. It was time to turn up his hole card.

"Listen, I haven't mentioned this before, but... I left a girl pregnant back in Big Bend," Val muttered. "I'm not crazy about getting tied down, but it isn't something I can exactly ignore. Or is it, Cooper?"

Cooper reared back like a fish that had caught a hook in its mouth. Then he started down to the edge of the water. Val thought he might be thinking of making a swim for the far side of the lake. However, when Cooper turned around, he seemed almost amused by the situation.

"Hell, boy, you asking my advice on something like that?"

Nodding, Val waited for his answer; then, realizing that the lake would probably go dry before he got a reply, he fired off another question.

"Maybe you can answer this one: didn't care enough for my mother and me to wanna hang around?"

The first question had startled Cooper; the second seemed to stump him. Looking back toward the lake, he started to skim some pebbles out across the water.

Val figured he'd struck out again, and was thinking up an easier question when Cooper finally answered the last one.

"Yeah, Val, maybe that's what it came down to. I was fond of your mother, but back in them days I needed to be free to ride the open road. Afraid everything else came in second."

"Would it made any difference if my mother hadn't been a Mexican?"

The question rankled Cooper. "Now why the hell ask me a fool thing like that?"

"I don't know," Val lied, shrugging his shoulders.

"Well, think I know, even if you don't," Cooper quietly said. "Her being Mexican was neither here nor there to me—but it makes a great deal of difference to you."

Val started to file a mild protest, but Cooper raised his hand to stop him short. "No, now hear me out, boy—because I've suspected something about you from the moment we first met back in El Paso. Saw it in your eyes. Heard it in your voice. Truth is, your skin color and your mother's race are something you're ashamed of... But if you knew anything about anything, you'd realize you been lucky. Your mother gave you a heritage born of some of the greatest bloodlines ever known to man. Don't believe me, try reading a goddamned history book. Hell, I'm full-blooded Irish and I'd swap pedigrees with you any day!"

Cooper paused to light a cigarette. Val wasn't sure how to respond to what he'd just heard, though a little appreciation seemed right.

"Well, thanks for the history lesson," he said, meaning it.

Smiling wryly, Cooper said, "Hell, I just hate to see you hung up for all the wrong reasons. Life usually provides us with enough real cause to get discouraged, without us having to cook up any phony problems. Know what I'm saying?"

"Yeah. For a change, I do," Val said, grinning.

"Now, about your mother. Can't say I'm especially proud of that little episode. I did try to help her with some money, but couldn't quite throw in my freedom, as part of the deal. Anyway, maybe you can understand better'n most the fix I was in, huh?"

Cooper wasn't wrong, though Val didn't think that was cause enough to let him off the hook. Val still carried a deep wound and it hurt far worse than his bruised kidney.

Yet some instinct told him to tread carefully. Cooper seemed as skittish as a wild horse. He would have to proceed with great caution if he hoped to tame him.

"Well, what went on between you and my mother was a long time ago. What happens now?" Val hoped Cooper would catch his meaning without having to spell it out in flashing lights.

Turning back toward the lake, Cooper started to skim pebbles across the shimmering water again. Val inched up beside him.

"Val, gonna tell you the same thing I told Blue a few days ago," Cooper finally said. "I've gotten pretty damn sick of the idea of trying to fill inside straights for the rest of my life. Like to finally settle down in one place, if I just had me the money. That's the God's truth, if I'm still any judge of it."

Cooper's smile seemed rueful. But Val couldn't quite figure out what he'd just said. Then Cooper grunted something and began to walk away.

It burned Val, the way his father had of letting him get close for a second, then say or do something that killed off the moment. The time had come to force the issue.

"What I'm asking, Cooper, is if you think we could go on together?" Val said, trailing after him. "I hope you'd at least level with me. I'd do the same for you."

There, he'd said it. He had let Cooper know how important he was to him; and if it didn't work out between them, it wouldn't be for lack of trying on his part.

Cooper stopped. But when Val caught up with him, he started to walk again. When he finally spoke, Cooper weighed his words so carefully, he might have been measuring some precious substance.

"For years now, Val, I've sorta suspected that we'd run into each other some day. What I didn't expect—the Joker in the deck, so to speak—was that I'd come to care for you as much as I have. I was damned proud of the way you held your water last night. So here's the deal, son: you stick with the program for just a few more days. Help me talk old Blue into staying on the team. She likes and trusts you, will listen to what you say. Then, if I do win big back up in Reno, you and me will go partners on a little ranch somewhere. How's that sound...?"

Val frowned. When Cooper pressed on, there seemed a quiet urgency in his voice. He was looking at Val, but seemed to be addressing some situation much further back in time. The faraway look in his eyes reminded Val of his mother's expression the morning he'd asked her if she had any special message to give his father.

"Now I might not always be around, Val, but the place will be there for you, whenever you want it. That ranch could be the first permanent address I've had in a long time. Yet somehow that don't spook me near so bad as it used to... So how does that sound to you, son?"

It sounded to Val like the best deal he could make, though earlier he had dared to dream that maybe he could bring Cooper home with him. But by now, he'd realized that Cooper just wasn't cut out to be somebody's husband. Not his mother's, anyway. He would never be able to supply her with the love and devotion that Floyd had given her; yet his mother was still in love with a myth, and had no idea what a good man she'd found in her short-order cook.

Beyond all that was Val's dream of someday trying to break into the movie business. Cooper had said he might not be staying around that ranch. Yet Val might never be there. He'd seen enough barren spaces and parched cactus to last him a lifetime.

"Oh, one more thing, Val," Cooper said, stopping to stare him straight in the eye. "When this little adventure is over, use that money I left you to get a decent education. Don't want to see you end up riding a road to nowhere, like some folks I could mention."

"Then when would we see each other?" Val asked, annoyed. This thing about him going to college was starting to look like a nationwide conspiracy. As usual, Cooper read his thoughts as if they were printed up on a billboard.

"I'm not the first person who's given you that advice, huh?" he said, chuckling. "Anyway, that's what them school vacations are for, ain't it?"

"Yeah, that's right," Val muttered, trying to screw up his courage. "But I'm thinking about going out to California."

"What's in California?"

"The movie business. I want to get into it, even if it's nothing more than the guy who carries around the coffee."

Something akin to compassion came into Cooper's eyes.

"Yeah, I know what it means to have a dream. Or used to, anyway. But from what I hear, that film business is about the toughest racket in the world... And if you get an education, then while you're waiting for that big break, you'll be able to fall back on something a bit more dignified than panhandling."

Val stood weighing his options. Then Cooper, expert gambler that he was, lightened the bet.

"Hell, boy, at least promise me you'll sign up for some night school courses, will ya?"

"Okay," Val finally muttered. Cooper drove a hard bargain. Yet Val knew he had gotten the better end of the deal. Extending his hand to Cooper, he tried to bridle back his emotions. "It's a deal," Val mumbled, past the lump in his throat.

Chapter 26

Val would later learn that gamblers have much in common with actors. Both sometimes exist in a personal vacuum, and often alter parts of their personality to reinvent themselves.

Frank Cooper was no exception. After his discussion with Val down by the lake, he suddenly became somebody else. To Val's amazement, Cooper was now as warm-hearted and outgoing as any man Val had ever met. It was as if he had grown tired of playing his last role, and was now affecting a near perfect imitation of Noah Carson.

That afternoon Cooper took Val shopping for some clothes. He wanted his "junior partner" to be the best dressed member of the brand-new firm of Cooper & Son. But Val had worn Levis and T-shirts all his life, and lacked appreciation for the finer points of sartorial splendor. Noting this, Cooper took charge of the expedition.

He selected five pairs of expensive serge and flannel pants, a beautiful western-style corduroy coat, and a half dozen of the store's finest cowboy shirts. When Val gasped at the expense, his father gave him a bit of advice.

"Always reach for the best, Val. Better to own one really fine thing than ten that don't make the grade... And besides, ever get down so far you gotta hock your clothes, the good stuff will still have some resale value, the bad stuff only fit for ripping into cleaning rags."

This advice appeared to apply to more than just clothing.

Late that afternoon, while Blue grabbed another nap, Cooper and Val drove around the lake. Cooper was curious about Val's life back in Big Bend. He was not, however, much interested in hearing about Bonnie, or even Lupe. He seemed to have a blind spot, Val noticed, when it came to women.

But Val was far more interested in getting answers than in fielding questions. He feared he might never again have such a great chance to discover more about himself by finding out more about his father. But Cooper seemed reluctant to talk about his personal life.

His three favorite subjects were gambling, history, and travel. He had read boxes of history books, mainly about Ireland and Mexico. Cooper had also studied the Bible, claiming there'd been a time when he could carry on a conversation by repeating nothing more than quotes from the Good Book. Politics and sports bored him, though he did seem proud that Val had been good at football.

After a few hours, Val felt comfortable enough to ask a question that Cooper had earlier avoided.

"So what do you think I ought to do about my girlfriend?" he finally asked. Cooper was silent for a long while.

"Well, son, there's a fine line between the freedom you owe to yourself, and whatever you owe everybody else... Just try to handle it a bit better'n I did. Because no matter how fast you run, your conscience will always be a little swifter."

➤➤ ➤➤

That night, they had driven north of State Line to a small casino a few miles off the main highway. There Cooper & Son would go back into business. The plan was basically the same as the night before. Val and Blue would enter the casino first, then rendezvous with Cooper at the blackjack tables. The only refinement on the previous program was that this time they'd leave the casino together, or not at all.

Of course, Val didn't know that the plan was another sham production, designed only to hold Blue in place until she finally opened up her bankbook.

He and Blue were feeding nickels into a pair of one-armed bandits, as they waited for the star of the show to make his appearance. Blue had agreed to bump back her trip home by a few more days, though it had taken some fancy talk by both Val and Cooper to convince her to stay over. Blue had realized, however, that win, lose, or draw, she'd soon have a free ride home.

The situation seemed simple to Val: if they didn't score big that night, Cooper's hope of buying into the poker game up in Reno would sink like a torpedoed ship, taking all hands and assorted dreams down with it.

Half an hour after Val and Blue walked into the casino, they received the first surprise of the evening. Val had just begun his reverse psychology routine with a slot machine when he caught sight of an elderly man who looked enough like Frank Cooper to be his father. Same size, same build, same chiseled features. Yet the man lighting a thin cigar down at the far end of the aisle wore the well-weathered look of a man in his mid-seventies. He had deep wrinkles at the edges of his mouth and eyes. A flimsy gray beard and hair parted right down the middle fit perfect with his old-fashioned eye-glasses and badly scruffed leather coat. The old-timer flashed a tentative, tobacco-stained smile at Val.

The first time Val saw Cooper, back in El Paso, he thought then that with any decent roll of the dice, his father could have become an actor. A little later that night in the casino, this impression would harden into absolute conviction.

When they teamed up at the blackjack tables, Val was amazed to note that Cooper had also changed his voice and manner. He now seemed rather frail, and moved and spoke with grave uncertainty. It was his facial transformation, however, that held Val's eye for most of the night.

Cooper always travelled with a small professional makeup kit, which he'd bought at a theatrical supply store in Las Vegas; a tiny investment, he told Val, that had paid for itself a thousand times over.

The kit even had an assortment of fake noses, but since Cooper had done his face fixing that night in the restroom of a service station, he'd tried to keep the remodeling job as simple as possible.

Val had changed his own appearance. It felt good to wear new and expensive clothes. Of course he couldn't lighten his skin, but Val knew that at least he now looked like a rich Mexican.

By eleven o'clock that evening, they were ahead by more than four thousand dollars. Most of the other people at their table hadn't been so fortunate. None had stayed for more than a few dozen hands before drifting away in search of better luck, or a more personable dealer.

The dealer was a cadaverous-looking, frozen-faced man with what Val considered all the endearing charms of a zombie. Yet Cooper had selected his table for exactly that reason, figuring that the nastier the dealer, the more inclined the pit boss might be to let him handle the table all by himself. But by the time Cooper and Val had hit the three thousand dollar mark, the pit boss was glancing suspiciously at them.

Several hands later, Cooper flashed a sign. Val immediately doubled down his bet, and a moment afterward, beat the dealer's hand by a single point. The pit boss began to circle their table. The large, big-shouldered man was dressed all in black. Yet there seemed something delicate about him. Finally angling in next to the red-faced dealer, the pit boss trained his soft eyes in Val's direction.

"Say, Pancho," he muttered past lips that barely moved. "Wonder if you'd mind playing at another table?"

The question sounded friendly, as if he might have simply asked a waitress if she minded warming up his coffee.

Val shot a furtive glance in Cooper's direction: a miscue that did not go unnoticed by either the pit boss or the dealer. Blue then made a mistake of her own. She'd been playing errorless ball all night, but by now she'd been standing behind Val for several hours in her high heels, and was exhausted.

"Hey, butt out, mister! My boyfriend can play any place he likes," Blue exclaimed loudly, though the pit boss stood no more than a few feet away. "Hell, still a democratic country, ain't it?" she persisted. "Home of the free, land of the brave, and all that stuff, right?" She sounded like a civics teacher grilling one of her less enlightened students.

Yet this mild outburst was just strange enough to let some steam out of the situation. The pit boss stood blinking at no one in particular.

"We're only asking the Mexican kid to move to another table," the big man murmured, making an effort to control his temper. "So why this big production number?"

"Say, you the one doing the dance routine," Cooper said in a high-pitched, peevish voice. "And all because this dark-skinned fella won a couple of bucks. Mexicans can come in with money, but can't take none out, that it?"

The pit boss stood chewing on his fleshy lips. By now, the conversation had attracted the interest of several people nearby. Most of them stared antagonistically toward Val for no other reason than the dark color of his skin.

"Then would you mind moving to another table, sir?" he said to Cooper. "This seems your lucky spot, as well."

"Yeah, real lucky, mister," Cooper softly said, fussing with his eye-glasses. "Only your definition of luck ain't quite the same as mine," Cooper muttered to the pit boss. "I lost more'n three hundred dollars in the last four hours, sitting in this so-called 'lucky' spot."

"Yeah, but during them same four hours, your Mexican side-kick here has taken us for more'n ten times that amount... So if I was you, old-timer, think I'd call it a night."

Then Val noticed a couple of stout-chested men, standing some thirty feet away, watching the scene with what seemed more than passing interest.

The scam had come to a skidding stop. Cooper started to awkwardly gather up what remained of his chips. "I don't work with nobody, mister... Truth is, us older folks just don't lose our money fast enough to suit you, do we?"

Several older people were following the conversation. But before the pit boss could muster a placating reply, Cooper slid off his stool and slowly started away, his feet stamping at the carpet with an uncertain cadence.

His sudden departure startled Blue. She began to hurriedly scoop Val's chips into her purse. "Come on, honey," she muttered, yanking Val's arm hard enough to make his ribs hurt even worse. "Let's try the roulette wheel. It's usually managed by a much nicer class of morons."

Blue's blast went a little wide of the mark. The pit boss was already drifting away from the table, though not before getting off a parting shot of his own. "Another dumb-ass mistake like this one," he muttered to the dealer, "and you're gonna be back parking cars again."

Val and Blue now headed for the parking lot themselves. But first they hurried over to the cashier's cage, where Val traded in his chips. Blue put the money into an envelope. Then she and Val started for the same door they had used coming into the casino. The plan called for Cooper to be waiting for them just outside.

Making the long walk across the casino, Val half-expected to be intercepted by another pair of fast-talking thugs pushing the old door prize routine. But the exit opened onto a canopied walkway that angled down to a drive-through lane. Several cabs sat parked nearby. When Val saw the relieved look on Cooper's face, he almost let out a cheer. They had made it safely away; sweet revenge for the defeat of the night before.

Then Cooper's smile curdled into a grimace. When Val glanced over his shoulder, he understood why. The two stout men Val had noticed earlier were standing just inside the door. Only they didn't look like spectators anymore.

Val's battered kidney sent him an urgent warning. Yet he wasn't nearly as frightened as he'd been the previous night. He figured Cooper would somehow get them all home in one piece.

Cooper hurried Val and Blue down toward one of the taxi-cabs. "When we get to the cab, you turn around, Blue... and hand me the envelope you put all the money in." His voice sounded deceptively casual.

As Blue got drift of the dilemma, her features froze solid. It seemed all she could do just to nod her head. Arriving at the cab, she went to her purse for the envelope. She started to fish through her oversized purse as Cooper, still sporting a steady smile, muttered: "But first dump the money out inside your bag. Then hand me the empty envelope."

This seemed simple enough. But with Blue so jittery, the procedure looked to Val only slightly less complicated than brain surgery. In trying to extricate the envelope, Blue first had to take out several geological specimens, as well as her little flash camera. She laid the rocks and camera on top of the cab.

Watching her made Val even more nervous than glancing back in the direction of the door. The two men had been joined by a third one. All three packed plenty of beef.

Finally, Blue handed the empty envelope to Cooper, who made an obvious display of stuffing it into the inside breast pocket of his leather coat. Then, as he patiently helped Blue reload her rocks, he gave Val and Blue their final instructions.

"Now you all take the cab back to the motel. And stay there. I'll hang around. See what them three stooges have on their so-called minds."

"You're not coming with us?" Blue whispered through clenched teeth.

"Naw, they'll bird-dog us back to the motel," Cooper muttered. "So I'll stay, try to cut 'em off at the pass."

Three against one seemed to Val pretty slim odds, especially when he remembered how badly beaten he'd been the night before by just one guy.

"No, I'm sticking with you, Cooper," Val muttered through clenched teeth. Val's mind had whipsawed back to the movies, and at this moment he saw his father playing the main role in "High Noon."

Val recalled how when faced with a big shoot-out, none of the townspeople, nor even the marshall's deputy, had managed to hold their water. Now, in a wildly different context, he was determined to hang onto his own. But Cooper apparently hadn't seen the movie.

"Please, Val, don't go stupid on me," he said quietly. "Them three bastards back by the door could get mean—and you ain't up to another beating, son."

"I'm staying with you," Val quietly repeated.

Cooper's mouth quivered slightly. Val wondered if that was a sign of deep annoyance or heartfelt gratitude.

Then, as Cooper closed the door behind Blue, he noticed her little camera on top of the cab. But no sooner had he handed the camera down to Blue, when she aimed it in the direction of the three men back by the door. Cooper smiled. Blue was about to buy him an insurance policy.

"Smile for the camera, boys," he said, turning toward the three men. Blue's flashbulb went off. Then she yelled to the cab driver. The cabbie had sensed the danger, and now stomped on his gas pedal.

After the cab peeled away, Cooper and Val started toward the convertible up at the far end of the parking lot. As they walked along, neither of them glanced back. The light grew dimmer as they moved farther away from the casino.

The convertible was sandwiched in on three sides, its front end facing a wall. Cooper walked Val over to his door.

"Get in, Val... Lock your door," Cooper muttered. "And no matter what happens, you stay in the car."

Climbing into the convertible, Val locked the door, then turned around. The three men were now about ten feet away from the rear of the car.

The man who had joined the others back near the main door of the casino said something to Cooper that Val couldn't hear. Val rolled the window down slightly.

"—Man, you whipper-snappers sure sore losers," Cooper was saying.

The main man grinned. But he seemed the only one of the trio with any sense of humor. "Well, old-timer, it does hurt bad as a toothache when somebody clips us cute for better'n thirty-five hundred dollars."

"Say, you boys ain't just sore, you're stupid," Cooper retorted. "I'm the monkey who lost money, remember?"

The main man's grin hardened into a sneer. "Now we don't fancy the idea of trashing a man your age, but we will if you don't fork over that envelope you're carrying."

Val couldn't see Cooper's face. But what he heard hinted of desperation in his father's voice. "You think the Nevada gaming commission's gonna endorse this idea of yours?" Cooper asked. "Remember, my lady friend has your mug shots on file—"

Cooper got no further. The first blow, a right hand to his face, staggered him badly. The second bruiser lurched forward to start jack-hammering Cooper's body.

In less than half a minute, they had forced him up the far side of the car. Cornering him near the front fender, they began to nail Cooper with ham-fisted blows.

Then he dropped from sight. The two big guys went to work on him with their feet, playing soccer, it seemed, with his head and body as the ball.

From inside the car, Val watched helplessly as the mayhem continued. He wanted to spring to his father's defense; but remembering Cooper's warning to stay in the car, Val simply said a prayer as his eyes filled with angry tears.

The leader stood watching the beating from the rear of the convertible. Then he noticed something which spoiled his smile. Slowly approaching the front of the car, he stared down for a long moment. "Well, looky here: if it ain't Frank Cooper himself, in yet another of his famous disguises... But let's see if we can make some permanent alterations."

The main man joined the kicking team.

Unable to control his emotions any longer, Val scrambled out from the other side of the car. But he hadn't wheeled around to the far side when one of the men came at him like a locomotive. Val tried to sidestep past him, but his arms seemed wide as railroad crossing guards.

Then Val heard Cooper weakly call out: "No, the kid's got a goddamn heart condition. Please, leave him alone, please—"

Cooper's voice stopped short. It sounded as if he'd been kicked again. The leader turned and nodded to the man who still had Val snared in his arms. The nod seemed a signal to the big man to go easy. Val almost laughed. The main man had actually believed Cooper's outrageous plea.

The second bruiser now rose from Cooper's side and handed something to the leader. After inspecting it, the leader tossed it to the ground.

"Well, fifty bucks in your wallet and an empty envelope in your pocket ain't gonna improve my own heart condition..."

The leader abruptly turned in Val's direction, a move that didn't much improve his own condition. Then he realized that the leader was staring at whatever was behind him.

A group of people stood off in the distance, watching. The main man glanced at the man holding Val.

"Try to search the kid and the car without further troubling them tourists, huh?"

Val felt himself moving again, though this time somebody else provided most of the locomotion. When they got past the door on his side of the car, the big guy opened it, shielding them off somewhat from the tourists. The man began his search. Val winced, remembering that his own money was still hidden in his boot.

But the big man never got below Val's waist. He was fat as well as big, and didn't seem to enjoy leaning over. The big guy finished frisking Val, and started to search the car.

As he leaned into it, Val thought of slamming the car door across his legs. But before he could do so, the man turned back around. "Car's clean. So's the Mexican punk," he quietly said to the main man.

The leader's feet flew in Cooper's direction again. "Yeah, I get the picture," he hissed. "So where do we find the bimbo who took the money?"

Val held his breath and waited for Cooper's answer. By now, Val was ready to propose a trade. Cooper's life in return for the money. But then they were suddenly saved, just as Val had been the night before, by a troop of tourists.

They had drawn close enough to the action to refuel their original suspicions, though from their angle of approach, Val knew they couldn't see Cooper. Val thought about waving them closer, but his bruised kidney made him decide on a safer course.

Glancing across the hood of the car, he waited for the main man to make his next move. The tourists came closer.

"It's okay, folks," the man called in their direction. "Just helping somebody fix a flat tire, that's all."

But the four men and two women continued to warily advance. The main man turned and glared down at Cooper. "Okay, you sorry son-of-a-bitch, you win this hand," he spat out. "But if I was you, I wouldn't try playing another one."

The leader then spun on his heels and stalked back toward the casino, both his bruisers barreling along right behind him. "Okay, sir, all fixed," one of the big guys called back. "But best you drive real careful on that spare. Could blow out at any second, hear?"

That sounded to Val like another warning, but it was bland enough to placate the tourists. They began to angle off in the direction of the casino. Val shot them an appreciative wave. If he lived long enough, he might have to change his mind about tourist-types. For the second night in a row, they had ridden to the rescue. If this kept up, he and Cooper might have to take them in as full partners.

Then Val remembered his current partner. Peering across the hood of the car, he softly called Cooper's name. No answer. He was probably dead by now, Val thought.

Slowly walking around the rear of the convertible, he saw Cooper lying with his head propped up against the wall, legs sprawled out over each other. The closer Val came, the worse Cooper looked. When his father slowly turned his face toward the light, Val almost vomited. It seemed Cooper's features had been shoved sideways. His fake beard hung from his chin like a piece of fungus, and some of the skin on his face seemed to have been scraped with a metal file.

Kneeling down, Val gently cradled Cooper's head in his arms. "*Dios mío*, oughta see what you look like, Dad," Val muttered.

Cooper didn't say anything right away. But at last he did open his eyes. "Oughta see what things look like from my angle," he gamely groaned.

Then he tried to smile. Only his features were no longer following orders. Val started to feel his father's arms and legs to check if anything else had been busted.

"Can you make it into the car?" Val said, still feeling for broken bones. "I'll drive us over to that emergency clinic... Way things are going, maybe we oughta rent a room over there. Geez, good thing Blue isn't here, she'd go crazy if she saw you like this!"

Cooper suddenly raised his head. "Forget the clinic, Val," he murmured. "Just get me back to the motel."

Val couldn't believe his ears. He pulled away a bit to get a better look at his father. Cooper squinted at him past two narrow slits now surrounded by purple-colored bruises.

Then Cooper tried another grin. "No, kid, I ain't suffered no brain damage... Just think I'm in better shape than must look like, that's all."

Chapter 27

Val had once wondered whether a man named Frank Cooper ever truly existed; the only proof was a tattered photograph of him standing out in front of the diner, with Val in his arms.

That picture had faded badly with the passage of time; yet for the last several years, it was the first thing Val looked at when he awoke every morning. He'd grown up thinking his past a puzzle with several pieces missing; but perhaps in his father's face he would someday find those lost parts.

Now, having found the person in the photograph, the missing pieces were slowly falling into place. Val figured if he could only stay alive for another week or so, he might at last possess a pretty good idea of who he was, and what made him that way.

At this point, however, a week seemed almost as long as a year. Already this one night seemed more like a month. Val felt old, and Cooper certainly looked it.

Yet by the time they limped back to the motel, Cooper was talking about returning to another casino that very same evening. Perhaps Cooper was right, Val thought. Maybe he was in better shape than he looked.

"God, he looks better with the blood," Blue whispered, as she continued to wipe off Cooper's face. She had been hurrying back and forth from the bathroom, rinsing out one washrag after another. Val was trying to strip off Cooper's shirt, but with the blood almost dry, it was like peeling adhesive tape off his hair.

Cooper flinched a time or two, though by now he looked too beat up to feel anything short of a head-on collision.

After Val finally managed to take his father's shirt off, and Blue had wiped the blood and loose gunk from his face, they sat staring at him. His head looked like a broken bust; seeing the deep concern in their eyes, he tried a reassuring smile, but it only seemed as if another piece had cracked off.

At that moment, so many emotions were swelling up inside Val, he thought his chest would burst. He felt deeply proud to be Cooper's son, proud his father had taken his own licking, and grateful that Cooper had saved him from taking another beating himself. When at last Val took his eyes off the wreckage, he couldn't resist a slight boast.

"Just want you to know, Blue," Val said. "It took three real big guys to do this to my father."

Blue seemed less than overwhelmed. "Yeah, and if he tries this stupid stunt again, all it'll take next time is one very small guy."

Cooper ventured another smile. "Aw, come on, Blue," he said, flexing his fingers as if to make sure they were still connected to his hands. "Ain't feeling near so bad as I must look."

Blue snorted with disgust. But Cooper already appeared anxious to get the show on the road again. Straightening up a bit, he muttered, "Well, think I'm gonna climb into another set of duds, then try one of them north shore casinos. They don't know my face so good up that—"

Cooper suddenly stopped. A shuffling noise came from outside the cabin. Val and Blue ceased breathing for a few seconds. Then they heard a second sound. Whoever was moving along the walkway outside kept on going.

"Goddamn you, Frank Cooper," Blue whispered in a trembling voice. "You get caught just one more time, and nobody is gonna know your face anymore."

Tiptoeing over to the window, Blue peered past its curtain for a moment. Then, realizing she still had a bloody towel in her hand, she returned to the restroom to rinse it out.

"And what good's it gonna do you, Frank," she asked from the bathroom, "to raise some more money—if by the time you get into that game in Reno, you've been beaten so blind you can't even see your cards anymore?"

Cooper had no answer. Neither did Val. Yet he sensed that his father's return engagement that night might soon become a moot point.

Coming back to the bed, Blue handed Val one of the towels. "Here, Val, you don't look so hot yourself. Now listen: I'm gonna go check if they have any first aid stuff up in the office. You keep your father here... even if you gotta chain him to the bed."

Moving to the door, Blue stood listening intently for any sound from outside. Then she turned and waved Val closer.

"And chain this door, too—and don't open it back up for nobody but me or the Red Cross."

Val nodded and started toward the door. But halfway there, something stopped him. It seemed that Blue was on the verge of making an important announcement. She took a deep breath, and turned to stare at Cooper. Val and Cooper stared back at her, waiting.

"...Okay, Frank. You win," she said quietly, her eyes glistening with tears. "Gonna loan you the money to buy into that game in Reno. But on one condition only: after you lose your own money, you get out of the game before you start losing mine."

Cooper studied Blue for a few seconds. Then he nodded. "Push comes to shove, Blue, I'll get out of that game, even if I gotta pretend I'm having a heart attack."

Picturing such an outrageous circumstance, Blue snickered and walked out the door. Val quickly reset the chain; then, after testing the main lock, he murmured a quiet prayer of thanks. But his sense of relief sunk the moment he saw the shrewd smile on Cooper's face: it was the same smile Val had seen him flash back in the casino's parking lot.

Suddenly, Val realized what the smile had meant then, and he knew what it meant now. The thought struck him like a blow to the chest. Slumping into a chair, he stared down at the carpet.

"...So that's the reason you didn't want to get fixed up before we came back here, huh?" Val heard himself say.

"Hey, boy, you gave me the idea," Cooper murmured. "And does beat the hell out of us taking another whipping, don't it?"

Cooper wasn't wrong, Val thought, though it didn't make the hustle look any more honorable. He had tricked Blue into coming up with the buy-in money for the poker game.

Yet he had paid one hell of a price, and maybe that made it almost okay. But at the moment, Val was no more sure of that than of anything else.

≫ ≪

That night Val had a vivid dream. He had never dreamt much in the past; maybe because he'd always done so much dreaming in the daytime, by nightfall his imagination was usually exhausted.

The dream unspooled in the diner back in Big Bend. It was snowing outside, very cold and dark. Val stood near the jukebox, dropping in one coin after another. But the music never came on. Over by the sink, his mother kept washing and drying a plate. The same plate, over and over again.

The little bell sounded over the door.

A gust of snow swept past the door. Then Cooper limped into the diner. He looked nearly frozen, his hair and face matted with snow. He held a mesquite stick in his hand, using it as a cane.

"You *cabrón*," Lupe said quietly, setting aside the plate. "Finally you come back, eh? Now that you are sick and nobody else want you."

Tears slowly filled Cooper's defeated eyes. He seemed to want to say something, but had lost the ability to speak. All that came from his mouth was a weak bleating sound, like that of a sick lamb who had found his way home too late.

He started toward Lupe. As he hesitantly moved farther into the room, Val kicked the cane from his hand. Cooper fell heavily to the floor. Lupe stared at him for a moment, then went back to washing and drying the same plate. Val began to weep.

Mortified by what he had done to his father, he knelt down next to him, and cradled Cooper's body in his arms. Then

Cooper slowly turned his head. With a start, Val saw that it was now someone else in his arms. It was Floyd.

Floyd looked up into his eyes and smiled gratefully. Val hugged his stepfather closer and continued to cry.

Chapter 28

The following morning, Val and Blue hauled Cooper into the emergency clinic in State Line. The same doctor and nurse were on duty who had been there two nights earlier, when Blue had brought Val in, but they didn't even seem to notice that Cooper appeared as if he'd been trampled by the same truck.

After the doctor finished fixing what Blue had temporarily patched up the night before, the travelers fortified themselves with a large breakfast, then drove to another motel about thirty miles farther north.

The beating Cooper had endured had finally taken its toll, and for the next twenty-four hours he did little more than sleep. Blue lingered nearby, like a nurse in an intensive care unit. Val sat watching the soap operas on TV, hoping they might have the same therapeutic effect on him that they had had down in El Paso.

The next morning, Cooper still looked badly battered, but with only another day to get to the poker game, he decided to start for Reno.

Val and Blue did most of the driving, and by the time they reached Carson City, they were again in desert country. The scenery turned bleak, the sky gloomy. Cooper slept most of the way. Yet even when he wasn't asleep, nobody had much to say. Everything had been settled.

Each of them had gotten what they wanted: Cooper, the game money; Blue, his promise to seriously consider going partners with her in a little nightclub; Val, his father's word that if he won big in Reno, he'd finally settle down in one place.

But Cooper's notion of buying a small ranch didn't really excite Val. What did delight him was his father's agreement that from now on, he and Val might forge a lasting relationship. Both Val and Blue had driven a hard bargain in trying to insure their deepest dream.

By mid-morning, Cooper had rekindled his own dream. Deciding to drive straight through to Reno, he figured they could make it by no later than high noon. And on this last leg of their long journey, Val chanced to ask his father a casual question that brought him an unexpected bonus.

"How'd you get into all this gambling stuff, anyway?"

The question, neutral though it seemed, appeared to catch Cooper's soft spot. Val assumed he had asked his father yet another question too personal to answer.

Val was driving. Cooper was up front with him, as Blue lie resting in the back seat. But once Cooper started to speak, she quickly forgot her weariness. Yet her interest couldn't compare with Val's. He had waited a lifetime to hear the tale his father now quietly began to spin.

≫ ≪

Cooper and his family had immigrated in 1905 to the United States from Ireland's County Cork. The trip on a tramp steamer took twenty-five turbulent, disease-ridden days. Several of the passengers did not survive the long sea voyage.

Finally reaching Boston, the Cooper family journeyed on to Kansas, where the family eventually settled in the tiny farming community of McPherson.

"But the so-called Promised Land failed to materialize," Cooper said, staring out at the bleached Nevada desert. "First we tried farming, but with little money and even less luck, that was a rocky road that soon turned into a dead-end street. Then things got worse. The cold and the hardship liked to have killed my poor mother. She was already frail, but it took both diphtheria and pneumonia to finally do her in..."

As Cooper paused for a moment, Val glanced over at him. His father looked as if he was remembering every painful detail of her death. Val had the eerie feeling his father had never spoken so openly to anyone in all his life.

"Well, with my mother gone, the old man started in to belt the bottle. Didn't exactly make things easier for any of us. But luckily, my older brother Thomas took me under his wing. Then along came the First World War, and Thomas headed off for France. But France was even worse than Kansas. Poor ole Tom took a shot of mustard gas, and though he seemed okay when he came home from the war, from then on, he was living on borrowed time. Of course, none of us knew this back then..."

"How much time did he have?" Val quietly asked.

Cooper didn't seem quite ready to discuss the subject. Instead, he digressed a bit to talk about his brother's sheep dog. The day Thomas Cooper left home to go off to war, they drove him to the train depot in a buckboard wagon. The dog Thomas had named Old Sam crouched in the back of the wagon, whining as if he knew exactly why they were headed for the station.

Back in those days, Cooper said, the train came through town only every Sunday morning, its steam whistle invariably heralding its arrival. Old Sam could always tell when the train was coming, and for the next two years he shuffled up to that station every Sunday morning.

Later the dog became so lame he could barely walk; yet every week, there he was, sitting on the platform, patiently awaiting the return of his owner.

Then one Sunday morning Thomas Cooper finally arrived back home from overseas. Spotting him, the dog hobbled forward. Moments later, Old Sam died in the arms of his master, having hung on just long enough to see him once more.

Again Cooper paused. Val had just swallowed the lump in his throat when his father took up the threads of the main story.

"Well, they say that death always comes in pairs. Couple of months after Old Sam died, my father was killed when a hay wagon overturned on him. He'd been drunk that morning... So now there was just me and my brother. But Thomas didn't give me much chance to grieve. He'd come back from the war all fired up about Mexico. Had read somewhere that Mexico was one of the few places left in the entire world where a hard-working man could still make a fortune."

Cooper interrupted the history lesson to light a cigarette. Val glanced in the rearview mirror. Blue had tears in her eyes. She had sensed the story would not have a happy ending.

"Yeah, my brother had big ideas. But like with most dreams," Cooper grimly continued, "they weren't about to come cheap. So for the next five years, Tom and I worked like mules at any job we could find... And on the day we finally raised our stake to three thousand dollars, we hightailed it out of Kansas, bound for the Mexican border. Then damned if our luck didn't get better when we crossed the Rio Grande River. Or seemed to, anyway..."

Val was following the story more slowly than Cooper told it. He wondered about Cooper's older brother and parents; after all, they had been part of his family, too. Would they have liked him?

"Anyway, in the long aftermath of the Mexican Revolution, the local governments were usually lasting little longer than some people take to change their minds," Cooper was saying. "And in all the confusion, good grazing land could often be bought for not much more than a dollar an acre. In the seven years that followed, my brother and I built up a fair-sized cattle ranch in the northern state of Chihuahua."

Hearing this, Val smiled. His mother had been born in that same state. For a moment he considered mentioning this to Cooper, but decided not to; he didn't want to derail his father's train of thought. It might be tough to get him back on the same track again.

"But in 1927 our luck began to run out. The hoof and mouth disease had grown rampant in that part of Mexico... It hit our ranch like a hurricane. Then came a long drought. Before it passed, we were as pressed for ready cash as our father had been the day we first arrived by tramp steamer into Boston Harbor... Then some rich Americans offered to loan us money. Only at some chicken-shit rate of interest. When we turned them down, they said they'd buy the ranch. But only for a fraction of what it still was worth. When we refused to sell, our so-called fellow countrymen pulled some strings. Bastards finally got the ranch for just a fraction of the original fraction!"

Cooper's eyes suddenly blazed with rage. He still seemed deeply rankled over the theft of the ranch, as if it had happened only the week before. Then he abruptly calmed down.

"Well, ole Tom took the loss pretty hard. Started to drink heavily, which of course weakened his already damaged health. Before six months had passed, his borrowed time came due..."

A slight mist settled over Cooper's eyes. Then he went on to say that for a long time after his brother's death, he wandered aimlessly through Mexico, harboring a wound that wouldn't heal.

Then, in late 1930, Cooper finally returned to the United States. Just in time, he said, to collide head-on with the Great Depression. Almost penniless and with no more than a ninth-grade education, his future now seemed little better than it had been back in Kansas. But he had mastered something during his years in Mexico, and that skill would soon prove sufficient.

"I'd been introduced to the game of poker by some of the old *vaqueros* who worked on our ranch. Them Mexican cowboys taught me good. But I'd always been sorta fast with figures. Anyway, it all made for a combined talent that I knew, as I drove out of Mexico for the last time, would someday lead me into gambling sure as a thirsty horse finds its way to water... And praise the Lord, it's a gift that's taken me through these past twenty-five years in a style neither my brother nor my folks ever dreamed existed."

Yet Cooper quietly added that despite his success, not a week had gone by in all those years that he hadn't thought about that ranch in Mexico, and the brother he'd been allowed to leave buried in the shade of a big tree along its western fence line.

Val realized now why Cooper had dwelt on the idea of their going into a little ranch together; he wanted to revive a dream that had turned to dust more than a quarter of a century earlier.

After Cooper finished his story, it went very quiet. Val sensed that his father had disclosed more about himself than he had ever done in all his life. The effort seemed to tire him. Closing his eyes, Cooper leaned back and a little later began to softly snore.

Val glanced into the rearview mirror. Blue's eyes were also closed, though he doubted she was asleep. Tightening his hands on the steering wheel, Val peered off into the endless desert ahead and said a silent prayer: Dear Lord, if that little ranch is somewhere in your deck of cards, please let it come up real soon. And not for my sake, but for my father's.

PART FIVE

Chapter 29

Like the battered remnants of a beaten army, they finally limped into Reno. The journey north from El Paso had taken four and a half days. Yet it seemed to Val they had been on the road for a full month.

Reaching the heart of the downtown area, Cooper checked them into a hotel that might have been a backdrop for a western set in the 1800s. This same old-fashioned, yet fancy establishment was where the poker game would be played the next night.

Cooper and Blue took a small suite, and booked Val into a single. By mid-afternoon, he was sleeping like a dead man. But just before Val fell asleep, Cooper's story about his past ran through his mind again. The tale had affected him in more ways than one. Val decided that if and when he ever got back to Big Bend, he would get himself a dog, and name him Old Sam.

But would the town look much different when he got back? What had it been like, Val wondered, back in the mid-1930s, when Cooper had stopped off there and first met Lupe?

It couldn't have been much more than a wretched little way station out on the lonely road between El Paso and Fort Worth. Probably pretty desolate, too, Val figured, what with the Great Depression and all.

Maybe Cooper had ambled into the diner late one afternoon, very hungry, but unable to afford more than a 25-cent bowl of chili. Lupe had probably slipped him free seconds, which might have triggered a conversation. Since Cooper spoke fluent Spanish, perhaps that's what first sparked her interest.

❊ ❊

"*¿Y de dónde vienes, Señor Cooper?*" Lupe asked.

"*De todas partes, Señorita,*" Cooper replied, wolfing down the chili. It would take too long to tell her all the places he had been, and at the moment his mouth was rather busy.

"*¿Y a dónde vas?*" Lupe wondered, always curious where people came from, and where they were headed.

"*¿Quién sabe? Soy como el perro que ha viajado a muchos lados, pero todavía no ha encontrado su hogar.*"

Cooper had been all over, but like a homeless dog, was still searching for some place where he might belong. This struck a responsive chord. Lupe had also travelled many miles, with much the same result.

Neither of them had family, home, or much of a job.

What developed later between Lupe and Cooper might have been in the cards from the moment they met. He had recently lost his brother; she had earlier been abandoned by her father. They were ready for each other.

Maybe all deep relationships were born by either death or desertion, Val thought, just before he fell asleep.

❊ ❊

They had agreed to meet for breakfast the next morning, but Cooper was still asleep when Blue got up. She decided to let him sleep in peace, figuring he'd probably get very little of either over the next twenty-four hours.

After Blue and Val put away a double order of ham and eggs, she asked him to come along to her apartment. She worried that her canaries might have died of loneliness while she'd been away.

Sitting right next to a tree-lined river, the old two-story wooden building seemed rather sedate for somebody in Blue's rowdy line of work.

Her own apartment was at the rear of the second floor, down a long, musty hallway. Many of the doors hung open, and as they walked down the corridor, several elderly people hurried out to greet Blue.

Most of these old folks had been fairly young when they had first come to Reno, hoping to strike it rich in the casinos which back in those early days had been little more than small, family-owned betting parlors. Now they stayed on, courtesy of Social Security, still trying to hit that one big number that had eluded them for most of their lives.

A few of these old-timers seemed the closest thing Blue had to a family; they also comprised her cheering section. Most still believed Blue was a singer with a talent that couldn't miss; this despite the fact that over the past twenty years, she had yet to hit a bull's-eye.

Blue's apartment seemed the biggest in the building, but was basically just one room, with a tiny kitchen and bathroom tucked off in two of its corners. Her canaries started to chirp the instant she and Val entered the room, though not because they could have been hungry or thirsty. Blue had left them enough birdseed and water to last for a full month.

The bottom of their cage, however, needed attention, and while Blue went about cleaning it, Val took a look around. The apartment seemed almost as messy as the cage, and the decor didn't help much. The place was furnished in a style that could be called Early Salvation Army. But there was one minor surprise.

Hanging over the fold-out sofa hung a large oil painting. Peering at it, Val wondered how Blue could have afforded to buy such an impressive picture.

She had read his thoughts. "Some old guy with a double dose of the uglies painted it," Blue said, as she relined the bird cage with fresh newspapers. "Been travelling from Santa Fe to San Francisco to sell his stuff, but had stopped off in Reno just long enough to lose all his expense money. He offered me the painting for one hundred dollars—but only if I threw in some naughty conversation as part of the deal. He was too old to engage in anything more strenuous. What the hell, I really liked the painting."

Val thought it very depressing. The picture was of four bedraggled Mexican workers coming out of a copper mine. Yet Blue claimed the painting could always cheer her up. It was vivid proof there were worse ways to make a living than the one she had been saddled with for the past twenty years.

After they left the apartment, Blue hurried back to check on Cooper. She wanted to haul him to another doctor, then run over to her bank to withdraw the money Cooper would need to buy into the poker game that night.

That left Val with time to scout out the territory. Reno was the raunchiest place he'd ever seen. Even Juarez looked tame by comparison. At only ten o'clock in the morning, it already seemed a carnival show had taken over the entire town. There were slot machines in every drug store, bowling alley, and restaurant. Even in the restrooms.

Some of the machines resembled bandits out of the Old West; indeed, the entire town seemed to Val something right out of a movie western, with everything and everybody several cuts out of the ordinary, and all connected in some way with the gambling fever that hung over Reno like radioactive dust.

The evidence of that mania was everywhere. Pawnshop windows bulged with whatever could be hocked: wedding rings, glass eyes, gold-plated dental bridges, even hernia trusses; which might be the reason, Val concluded, why he noticed so many toothless old men limping around town.

Then there were the bearded, flinty-eyed prospector types, sweltering in the hundred degree heat, who probably had pawned their lighter clothing, thinking it healthier to sweat in summer than freeze in winter.

In that summer of 1955, Reno was known as the "Divorce Capitol of the World." But it seemed many people had taken leave of their senses, as well as their spouses. Yet despite all the rowdiness, it made for a sad spectacle. Cooper had advertised Reno as one of the few places left in the entire country still wide open enough to accommodate the type of rugged individualists who had once tamed the western frontier. But now their world was changing all around them, and like the buffalo, this maverick breed of American was slowly dying out.

Cooper had looked half-dead himself the day before, but when Val returned to the hotel, it seemed his father might survive; at least long enough to make the poker game that night. The game had been set for eight o'clock. But by mid-afternoon Cooper already was chomping at the bit. One of the local doctors had pretty well mashed him back into shape. What he hadn't been able to fix, Blue did when she handed over the eleven thousand dollars she had withdrawn from her savings account.

"I left my last nine hundred dollars in the bank," Blue muttered with a mournful smile, tossing a bulging envelope onto Cooper's lap. "Just to keep my account open."

Cooper walked the envelope over to a table at the far end of the suite, where he spread out the hundred dollar bills as if they were playing cards; then, with the flying fingers of a bank teller, he counted the money.

"Good thinking, honey," he said, stuffing the bills back into the envelope. "Because you're gonna be re-depositing this eleven thousand dollars tomorrow morning."

Blinking a troubled smile, Blue walked over to the bar.

"Now, cowboy, I wanna go over things just one more time, so's later there won't be no misunderstanding," she said, pouring herself a glass of milk.

"I'm all ears, honey," Cooper said.

"Okay... you, Frank Cooper, being the party of the first part, do hereby agree that you'll use your own money first—then, if and when that's lost, you'll get out of the game before you commence to lose any of my eleven thousand dollars. Me being the party of the second part in this here contract. Fair enough?"

Past his patched-up lips, Cooper bared his teeth in what seemed a smile. "Honey, like I told you before, ain't planning to lose my money—but if it happens, I shall immediately bow out of the game. Even if I gotta pretend my ticker's just jumped off the track," he said, playfully tapping his chest.

"And on the outside chance you do win big," Blue went on, "this will be your final high stakes game. From then on, dollar slot machines gonna be your house limit. Correct?"

This last stipulation surprised Val. He doubted his father would agree to it. But Cooper was still smiling, though his drawl now seemed even slower. "Okay, I'll say it again, so's even Val, who claims he's slow at arithmetic, can get my drift: I clear fifty thousand or more tonight, my high stake gambling career is history. After that, I'll have smarter places to invest my money, and better people to bet it on."

Cooper's impromptu addition to Blue's so-called contract was a pleasant surprise. Val waited for him to elaborate, but Cooper had apparently run out of any further concessions.

The room became very quiet. Cooper sat still as a stone, his eyes fixed on something only he seemed able to see. Val glanced over at Blue, still encamped behind the bar, thoughtfully nursing her glass of milk.

Val walked over to the window. The mountains in the distance looked like gigantic pipe organs, and the tune they seemed to be playing was vaguely upbeat.

Okay, tonight we finally spin the wheel, Val thought. He had no idea where it would stop, but already he sensed that by the end of the game, his life would never again be the same.

Chapter 30

The seven players had journeyed to the game from all over the western part of the United States. Five were full-time, professional gamblers; the other two, gifted players with oversized ambitions. The game was being hosted by one of the professionals, a white-maned gentleman named Matt Logan, who seemed a member of that maverick breed that was slowly dying out. Rounding out this cast of characters was the dealer, a tiny man whose legs barely touched the floor when he was seated, and his son, who served as the relief man. Both seemed as solemn as a couple of priests about to conduct a sacrament.

The lamp hanging over the large gaming table was set low, partially masking the faces of the taller players. This lighting arrangement made the table look somewhat like a bright altar in an otherwise dimly illuminated area.

Indeed, the suite was almost sizable enough to house a small chapel; and when the game started at precisely eight o'clock, the room was packed with would-be parishioners. Most sat on stools, or stood some distance away from the felt-covered gaming table. Many seemed so somber, they could have been actually attending a church service.

At one end of the suite, saloon-style doors opened into a few small bedrooms; there, either the dealer or his relief man could grab a little sleep over the course of the upcoming night.

The rules were rougher, however, for the participants. Once a player missed three hands in a row, he stood to lose his entire stake. Hence, the winners would need stamina, as well as skill.

The game was being played with money, rather than chips. Every player had earlier proved he carried the required twenty-five thousand dollar entry fee in cash.

Even with Val's limited grasp of arithmetic, he knew there was at least $175,000 gathered around the table. Val and Blue sat perched on a small sofa, next to an open window about fifty feet away from the table. The room was very warm. Its air conditioner had not been built to cool off a suite with more than half a hundred nervous people. Beyond the window, a neon sign pulsated with the relentless beat of a metronome.

Watching the first two hours of the game, Val realized that the poker game back in El Paso had been penny-ante by comparison, as different as a donkey race and the Kentucky Derby.

The current track was so fast, Cooper already was down by more than three thousand dollars. He had lost most of that money to one of the nonprofessionals, a vile-mouthed man with manners to match. Val hated him for both reasons.

During the early part of the game, Val and Blue tried to carry on a conversation; but for the past hour, neither had said a word.

"So what the hell happened to your face, Frank," the white-maned man was saying, as he intently studied the cards in front of him. "Somebody's husband catch you poaching on his private preserve?"

Cooper seemed to smile, though with his mangled features, Val couldn't tell for sure. "Avoiding the issue, ain't you, Matt?" Cooper drawled. "I just bumped that last raise by three hundred American *pesos*."

The white-haired man grinned, then quickly raised one hand over his mouth. Logan had several teeth missing. Val grinned. Maybe one of the dental bridges he had seen in a pawnshop had once belonged to Matt Logan.

"I'll see that half-hearted raise of yours, and call," the old-timer muttered, flipping three hundred-dollar bills onto the bulging pile of greenbacks in the center of the table.

Val leaned forward. Cooper had yet to score a single pot, but from the look in his eye, it seemed sure he had this hand won. A hush came over the crowd. Cooper bent forward to lay out his cards. Val glanced back at Blue. Her lips were moving, but there was no soundtrack. Val figured she was praying.

"Pair of aces, gentlemen," Cooper softly said. "And I ain't even gonna use the one I still got up my sleeve."

A few of the other players plunked their cards down on the table as if they were wagering stubs on a horse that had just finished out of the money.

As Cooper happily reached for the pot, Matt Logan murmured almost apologetically, "Frank, that's a mighty pretty hand—but I'm afraid it can't beat my three little ole piss-ants."

Logan laid out his three deuces and then slowly raked in the sizable pot. Cooper seemed stunned. He had lost eleven hundred dollars on that one hand. But what immediately followed jolted him even worse.

The vile-mouthed player had also lost a fair chunk of money on the same hand and now smirked in Cooper's direction. One of the two non-professionals at the table, he had already won several thousand dollars. Most of it Cooper's.

From the beginning of the game, he hadn't seemed to like Cooper; now that he'd put away several shots of whiskey, his disdain became more demonstrable.

"Well, Mister Big-Time," the man softly snarled to Cooper, "seeing that horseshit look on your face is almost worth the grand and change I just fucked away on this last hand."

For a long and elaborate moment, Cooper studied the source of this insult. Val had picked up from previous conversation that the player owned a booming used-car business in Los Angeles. He also had a lot of muscle to go with his money, and was handsome in a slick sort of way, but with the darting, empty eyes of a man who'd sell his own grandmother a worthless clunker.

Staring at him, Cooper quietly growled, "Remind me, punk, when this here game is over, to step on that pretty little face of yours... That is, if you're still around."

Cooper and the car dealer were sitting directly across from each other, and if looks could kill, both men would have already been on their way to the morgue. But Val didn't think Cooper had anything personal against the man. Not yet, anyway;

instead, his father appeared more annoyed at his poor run of luck; the wise-ass seemed no more than a convenient urinal.

The stumpy dealer collected the cards, shuffled them, and commenced flicking out a new hand. "Now, folks, let's remember that we're all gentlemen and scholars. So shall we ante up and spin the wheel one more time?"

"Yeah, come on, Frank," Matt Logan muttered, raising his hand to his mouth again. "Still got a long night ahead of us."

Cooper seemed in vague agreement to the proposed armistice. But when he saw the car salesman sporting the same smile, he fired off a final shot. "Yeah, Matt, gonna be a long night—which should give me enough time to wipe the smirk off this sun-tanned, half-baked specimen sitting across from me."

Val and Blue waited with bated breath for the battle to start all over again. But then the tension slowly eased. The game went on. Studying his new cards, Cooper suddenly smiled.

However, Val knew that poker players seldom smiled for the same reason normal people do. He glanced over at Blue. She looked as if she had just avoided a serious accident.

"Think I'll slide downstairs and get another drink."

Val pointed toward the bar. "Hey, they have plenty of stuff right here."

Blue drained the drink in her hand. "Well, I can't sit here watching your father lose one damned hand after another. Like seeing him commit suicide on the installment plan."

Her remark rubbed Val the wrong way. The game was only in the first quarter, yet Blue already was trudging off toward the loser's locker room.

"Hey, he's only down by a little more than four thousand dollars," Val reminded her. "Still has almost the whole night to make a comeback, right?"

But Blue had drifted out of his range. It seemed she was no longer receiving signals. Instead, she sat staring at Cooper, as if seeing something she hadn't noticed before. Peering over at him, Val thought he saw the same thing.

Hooded by the low-hanging lamp, Cooper's eyes now had an unfamiliar, spiteful gleam that made them look almost fierce. His blue eyes, usually soft and kind, now seemed cold and cruel;

they seemed to belong to somebody else. Someone Val didn't want to know.

"... No, I ain't so sure your father can come back," Blue said under her breath. "Even if he does win the game."

Setting aside her drink, she weaved past the congestion, toward the door. Watching her, Val wondered why he had known beforehand what she had just said. He might have figured it out right then and there; instead he sat simply listening to the hiss of the neon sign outside the window.

➤➤ ◄◄

When Blue returned to the suite a couple of hours later, Val noticed that something about her had changed. Earlier, Blue had gone down to the hotel's casino, where she wandered around for a while. Then, feeling sorry for herself, she drifted into the bar of the hotel.

Blue commenced to drink, though alcohol invariably picked trouble with her ulcer. This time she was half-hoping the booze would kill her. But after she'd finished off her third sloe gin fizz, Blue heard a piece of music that caused her to abruptly stop drinking.

A young couple down at the far end of the bar were playing "Frenesi" on the jukebox. The same song Blue had sung at her last audition. Listening to it now, she stared at herself in the long mirror behind the bar. Blue didn't like what she saw.

The many arduous years she had put into her singing lessons back in Kansas trudged through her mind. As a young girl, she had possessed a special gift; yet she had spent most of her adult life tarnishing that same talent.

She had already lost almost all hope of ever recovering the eleven thousand dollars she had loaned Cooper; the ease with which she did so surprised her. The harsher shock came with the sudden awareness that despite an occasional auditioning attempt, she apparently had also written off her fondest dream.

The revelation jarred her like a soft jolt of electricity.

At her last audition, the peanut-shelling owner had said that he would like to have heard her voice five years earlier. Bullshit,

Blue now muttered aloud. With hard work and expert coaching, she could still turn those lost years into friends, rather than foes. By now, she had paid enough dues to truly understand the lyrics of those sad songs she loved to sing.

Oh, sure, it was probably too late to become a star, but with a little luck and a lot of practice, she still had a chance to become the next best thing: a headliner who could always be counted upon to give the public its money's worth.

Blue smiled at herself in the mirror. For the first time in a long while, she had a plan that didn't depend on the next man she might meet.

∗∗ ∗∗

Val followed Cooper over to the bar, and watched as he mixed himself a drink. On their way over, several people had muttered some words of encouragement to Cooper. They seemed to like, or at least admire him, which made Val proud. Yet he doubted Cooper had even heard them.

He also doubted that Cooper could turn his luck around. By now he had lost more than nine thousand dollars, and Val figured that despite those hopeful words to the contrary, any light at the far end of the tunnel was an optical illusion.

"Hey, the cards gotta change pretty soon," Val exclaimed, trying to sound more optimistic than he really felt.

Cooper took down half his drink in one swallow, and stood staring into the glass. "Well, certainly hope so. But sometimes you gotta spend a lotta money before you can make a lotta money."

The comment was too bland to argue with; instead, Val burst forth with a thought that had been festering inside him for the past hour.

"Yeah, but if you lose just another five thousand, you'll be into Blue's money, and then—"

"Hey, calm down, kid," Cooper interjected with a sour smile. "Let me handle the bookkeeping, okay?"

There wasn't much Val could say to that. It wouldn't have done any good, anyway. Cooper was already striding back to the gaming table. Val sighed; then, as if trudging off to join Blue in the loser's locker room, he shuffled toward his post next to the noisy neon sign.

When Cooper lost big on the next two hands, the locker room began to resemble a morgue. Finally, unable to take any more of the suspense sitting down, Val wandered closer to the table. Coming up behind his father, he glanced at the cards in Cooper's hand. It was Val's first pleasant surprise of the evening. Cooper was holding three jacks, and had yet to call for additional cards. This hand could be, Val hoped, the beginning of the end of his father's bad luck.

Then came a soft knock at the door of the suite. A pudgy man in red suspenders cautiously opened it. Cooper wasn't thrilled by Blue's return appearance. Neither was Val. The tension around the table already was thick enough to slice. Blue's brooding presence would only make it worse.

As Blue headed for the sofa, Val went over to try to cheer her up. But he wasn't that good an actor. He had barely settled down next to her when she said: "That bad, huh?"

"Well, yeah. If ole Coops don't win this hand, he's gonna be down real close to your money," Val quietly confessed. "But hey, he's sitting on something real special."

The last part of his report didn't make much impression. "Great," Blue muttered. "I got here just in time to watch him have his heart attack."

Hah, Val thought, it would probably be him who had the attack first. Especially if Cooper lost the play now in progress. The game began to slow down, the players' voices sounding like a record run at the wrong speed. Even the used-car dealer stopped running his mouth, though he still wore the same sly smirk.

The mood was so somber that Val and Blue, along with the other spectators, could have been medical students watching a brain-tumor operation. All Blue needed was a white coat to match her pale expression.

"...I'll kick that last raise another dollar," Michael of Los Angeles (as the car dealer had been dubbed) announced, tossing two five-hundred dollar bills into the pot. He had jerked the bills from his large roll as if tearing tissue out of a box.

Val had lost track of the size of the pot, but judging from the tension hanging over the table, he figured it must be one of the largest of the night. He also had no idea whether Cooper had improved his hand with the two additional cards he'd drawn.

The hour had crept past midnight. The old gambler hosting the game seemed to feel the strain. The white-haired man sat studying his cards for a full minute, before responding to the car dealer's last thousand-dollar raise.

"...Yeah, suppose I'll stay onboard for a while longer," Matt Logan uttered with a vacant smile, as he counted out the steep occupancy fee. "But the ride's sure getting bumpy, even for an old bronc-buster like me."

Now it was Cooper's turn to either match the last thousand dollar raise, or fold over. But when he hesitated, Val realized he'd been unable to improve on his three jacks.

Turning toward Michael of Los Angeles, Cooper tossed ten one-hundred dollar bills into the pot. "Well, guess I'll do about anything, including something stupid, to wipe that shit-assed grin off your face... I call."

Matt Logan laid his cards out first. "Two pair, gentlemen. Tens and aces," he said, making no effort to cover his spotty smile.

Two of the other players cursed and tossed their cards away like so much confetti. Val glanced over at Cooper. The tattered smile on his bruise-filled face almost made Val cheer.

"Sorry, Matt," Cooper muttered. "But two pair ain't quite enough to beat my trio of Jacksons." Cooper slowly laid out his cards, then reached for the first big pot he'd won all night.

"Hey, but even three Js can't beat my straight!"

The voice came from the worst possible place. Michael of Los Angeles. For a moment, Cooper looked like someone trying to catch the license number of a truck that had nearly side-swiped him. He took a deep breath and watched the pot pulled off in the wrong direction.

"Yeah, read 'em and weep, shit-kicker," the car dealer chortled, laying out his straight. "Like it says in the Good Book, 'Mine eyes have seen the glory of the Lord.'"

Val doubted the car dealer had ever once cracked open the Bible. But he didn't dwell on this for long; already a new game had begun. Cards were floating out across the table.

"Gentlemen, this will be my last hand for the next hour or so," the tiny dealer wearily announced. "But my relief man shall carry on in a manner I trust will be most satisfactory."

The moment had arrived for Cooper to pull his vanishing act. He was now down to Blue's life savings.

Val and Blue sat waiting for Cooper to make his escape. Then Blue caught his eye. She tapped her chest and rolled her eyes, as if to say that now was the time for him to simulate his heart seizure.

But Cooper didn't appear to receive the signal. He sat peering at her in a curious way, as if she were someone he'd met before, but couldn't remember exactly where or when.

Watching Cooper pull this pose, Val fought back the urge to stand up and loudly remind him of the agreement he had earlier made with Blue. The deal Cooper now seemed determined to forget.

Then someone said, "Hey, Frank, you in or out?"

Matt Logan had noticed that Cooper had not yet put up his ante for the new hand. A long moment crawled by. Cooper heaved a sigh, then flipped forward a five-dollar bill.

"Gentlemen, let's play cards," Cooper declared, in a voice loud enough for almost everyone in the room to hear.

Blue sat very still for several seconds; then, reaching for the drink she had laid aside hours earlier, she got up from the sofa and started toward the gaming table.

Reaching the table, Blue quietly said, "Well, Frank, I wrote off the money two hours ago. Now, maybe if I get lucky, I can do the same with you."

An odd thing then happened. Not a single player gave her more than a passing glance. It seemed she'd never spoken a word; indeed, as if she were not even standing there. Maybe they all thought if they ignored her, she'd disappear. But when Cooper realized this was not about to happen, he glanced up at her.

"Well, lady, perhaps by the time you sober up, things will look a little better to you."

Blue slowly circled the table, never once taking her eyes off Cooper. Then, coming up directly behind him, she calmly poured her drink down the back of his neck.

"Hey, cowboy," she muttered with a rueful smile, "things are already looking a little better." Then, amidst a roomful of startled expressions, she serenely started for the door.

Some of the spectators couldn't help smiling. But back at the table, the only man grinning was Michael of Los Angeles. Yet nobody said a word till Blue exited the room.

Only then did Cooper turn to the dealer. "Sir, excuse me for a moment. I seem to have developed a slight chill."

The little dealer suppressed a smile and nodded his assent. Cooper rose from the table, and made his way toward the nearest bathroom.

"Well, hurry it up, shit-kicker," chuckled the used-car dealer. "Because I'm sitting on another sweet-smelling hand."

Cooper was halfway out of his shirt when Val closed the bathroom door. Watching his father slowly struggle to get out of the garment, Val winced. The shirt seemed stuck to Cooper's skin in places where the bruises were still moist. It was painful to see. Finally, working the shirt off his back, Cooper began to wring it dry.

"That silly bitch," he snorted, as the last of Blue's drink dripped into the wash basin.

"Yeah, dumb, alright," Val muttered. "But heck, she was counting on you to get out of the game when—"

"Hey, kid, I can beat these guys," Cooper said, grimacing as he twisted around to dry off his back. Val grabbed a towel to help him.

"Yeah, but what if you don't?" Val lamely asked. "And it's all the money she has, all she's ever been able to save—"

Cooper spun around so fast, Val thought sure he planned to hit him. Instead Cooper just glared, as if keenly disappointed that Val had turned out to be no different from all the other fools he'd met in his life.

226

"Yeah, and so what if Blue loses a little money?" he quietly exclaimed. "Hell, all she's gotta do to make some more is chat up the next rich drunk she meets."

Val didn't know what to say, and wouldn't have said it even if the words had arrived in time. Cooper's rasping voice and raw expression frightened him.

Finally drying himself off, Cooper placed a fresh towel around his neck and got back into his coat.

"Hey, come on, pal," the car dealer's voice boomed from the main room. "Out here is where you get to take your bath."

Buttoning up his coat, Cooper strode out of the bathroom. The look on his face rattled Val. His father seemed to have no less than murder on his mind. Then Val caught a glimpse of his own face in the mirror. He didn't like what he saw: the guilty look of a coward idly standing by as a good friend was pushed closer and closer to the edge of financial ruin.

When Val returned to the main room, Cooper already was moving Blue nearer to the abyss. "I open with fifty dollars, and will take two cards," Cooper said to the dealer. The little man had apparently decided to stay at the table until things calmed down a bit.

Val could watch the game for only another few minutes; like Blue, he'd finally tired of standing sentry duty while Cooper went on destroying himself. Yet Val couldn't resist glancing at him one last time; he wondered if the two cards he'd just been dealt had done him any good. But for all Cooper's expression told him, it might well have been cut from a slab of granite.

Wiping the sweat from his face, Val started for the door.

Chapter 31

Blue had just punched up "Frenesi" again on the jukebox when Val wandered into the bar. By now the casino crowd had thinned out and the long, dark room looked bleak. Val thought Blue was in much the same condition. Sitting down next to her, however, he noticed that she hadn't touched the sloe gin fizz she'd ordered.

Val must have looked like he needed a drink himself, and the first thing Blue muttered was, "You're a couple of drinks behind me, so better order yourself a strong one."

Val signalled the bartender, who slowly crabbed closer.

"Bottle of your lowest-priced beer, please," Val said.

The hatchet-faced bartender eyed him hard. Val thought sure the man was about to say he wasn't allowed to sell firewater to either Indians or Mexicans.

"Well, young fella, let's see some I.D., just to keep me from getting hauled off to the hoosegow."

Vaguely relieved, Val went for his wallet and thought about Clarence. Before they left Big Bend, Clarence had altered the birthdates on their driver's licenses. Now, Val silently thanked his friend. He also hoped that the bartender's vision wouldn't prove perfect.

"Just had a birthday, huh?" he asked, holding Val's license under a thin cone of light.

Say something quick, dumbo, Val thought. Distract the guy before he pulls out his magnifying glass. "Yeah! Almost forgot—seems like a couple of years ago now!"

"Oh, this town'll do that to you," the bartender chuckled, handing Val back his driver's license. Watching him drift away to get the beer, he thought the man wasn't wrong about Reno. Val felt as if he'd aged ten years in the past five hours.

Turning back to Blue, he was about to feed her some baby talk on whatever subject seemed safe enough when her expression stopped him cold. She was staring wistfully into her glass, as if it might be a crystal ball.

"Yeah, the time does go by... but it's still the same old story," Blue murmured. "Seems like fifty years ago, Val, that I first came out to Reno, hoping to get the chance to sing my own rendition of that song..."

Blue seemed to be wondering, Val thought, how she could have been left standing at the dock when the boat had sailed.

"Hey, bet you're a real good singer," Val mumbled, patting her hand. "But how come you didn't keep at it?"

Smiling softly, Blue placed her hand over his. "Well, about a year after I came out here from Kansas, I developed an ulcer. I had thought only high-powered business types got them. Seemed comical, me having an ulcer. But it didn't feel funny at all. Then I felt even worse when I couldn't pay my medical bills... So decided if I couldn't sell my singing talent, I'd try pushing the one thing people did want to buy. Companionship and what sometimes, if I got unlucky, went along with it."

"So hell, you did what you had to do," Val said, grinning, though he wondered exactly how often Blue had gotten unlucky.

"But it was only gonna be for a few months. You know, just long enough for me to get back on my feet again... Instead, I ended up on my knees for the next twenty years. Praying, I might add. Hell of a twist, huh?"

Blue was trying to tell him something, Val realized, about the nature of dreams; how hard they die, but how easily they can become misplaced.

The bartender had brought him the beer, though by now Val had lost his desire to drink. So he simply sat making wet circles on the bar with the bottom of the bottle. He strained to come up with another topic of conversation. When he had first entered the bar, he hoped to avoid any mention of the game upstairs. Now it seemed the safest subject.

"But listen, what's to say your money's lost for sure?" he muttered to the wet circles. "I mean, Cooper does win a lot more than he loses, right?"

Given what he and Blue had witnessed for the last several hours, Val knew his remark must sound like the silliest of straw-grasping routines.

"Yeah, Val, your old man does win more than he loses... Yet, somehow he's never been able to turn his winnings into much more than just a way to buy into another game... Well, I'm not gonna make that same mistake."

Then Blue told him of the decision she had made earlier that night. Val tried to show some interest, but he had grown dubious of happy endings.

"But can we ever really change things?" Val asked, still making wet circles on the bar. "Just have to play out the cards we're dealt, don't we?"

"Yeah, that's true," Blue said quietly. "Can't change the cards. But we can switch to another game."

➤➤ ➤➤

By daybreak of the following morning, they had covered a lot of ground in an entirely new direction: Big Bend, Texas. Blue was a terrific talker, but when the mood was on her, she was an even better listener. By the time the sunlight crept into the bar, Val had told her the story of his life, such as it was.

She seemed genuinely interested in Bonnie and his mother, but when Val came around to Floyd, her expression went wistful. She thought he was one hell of a fine man; the more Val talked about him, the more he had to agree with her.

Finally, about six o'clock that morning, they trudged over to the casino's coffee shop; both of them out on their feet, but too keyed up to sleep and too scared to go check on Cooper. The coffee shop seemed the best available compromise.

An hour later, they were still encamped in a booth at the far end of the room. Val could barely keep his eyes open, but several cups of coffee had somewhat revitalized Blue. She was again picking at her cherry pie when they heard a familiar voice. "Great day in the morning, Blue, don't you ever get tired of feeding your face?"

Cooper stared down at them with an indulgent frown, as if they were naughty children who had stayed up past their bedtime to raid the refrigerator. Cooper also looked as if he should have gone to bed hours earlier; yet all things considered, Val thought he appeared surprisingly spry.

Blue shot Cooper a hostile glance and turned back to her cherry pie. "So what the hell was I supposed to do while you were upstairs losing all my money? Commit suicide?"

"Woulda been less fattening," Cooper chuckled, taking an envelope from his breast pocket. "Anyway, here's your eleven thousand bucks back... and another thousand for so vigorously reviving me with that damned drink."

Blue looked stunned. Val sported the same dazed expression. He couldn't have come wide-awake faster had he been told about the Second Coming of Christ.

"Man, I don't believe this," Val sputtered. "Mean to say you finally won that game?"

Cooper paused, then slid in next to Blue. "Naw, kid. Only did a little better than break even," he drawled. "But here's another thousand for you, Val... for that beating you took back in Tahoe."

Then, as casually as if he were tipping a waitress, Cooper dropped ten one-hundred dollar bills on Val's empty pie plate. Val started to sputter again. Blue, meanwhile, had recovered just enough to begin counting her money.

"Oh, dear God, there is a wizard after all," she gushed as her eyes filled with tears. "Lord, Frank, I been down here all night just eating dirt."

"Yeah, I been upstairs sampling pretty much the same menu," Cooper muttered, gently rubbing his bruised hands together. "But now I know I can beat those guys—and when we see them again over in Vegas, I plan to do exactly that..."

"There's gonna be another game?" Val asked.

"Yeah, some of the losers demanded a rematch. So, what the hell..."

This second surprise left Val and Blue almost as flat-footed as the first revelation. They grew quiet as tombstones. Another all-night vigil around a poker table seemed about as much fun as a visit to a cemetery.

Cooper read their faces as easily as if they were turned-up cards. His own expression grew somber. "Look, I said and did some things last night that ain't exactly making me pop my buttons with pride... Won't happen again. Hell, it can't happen again. The game over in Vegas gonna be a bit more modest, and I already got the buy-in price. Your own money, Miss Morgan, can go back into the bank and stay there."

Clasping his hands together, Cooper levelled his gaze on Val. "Told you last night, Val, even when I was way down, that those guys could be beat. Now I'm sure... and in this next game, I figure there's a damn good chance of finally winning that fifty thousand we talked about... And both you and Blue have earned the right to be around for the payoff."

Val felt a little lump rise in his throat. His father's words contained no great message; yet a few other things had lent strength to the speech. Val had never heard an adult apologize for anything; the sheer novelty of it impressed him. He was also remembering the ranch Cooper had lost down in Mexico, and the brother he'd left buried there.

But what gave Cooper's plea its power was the graphic proof of how hard he had struggled to get into the game that had ended only moments earlier. The evidence was in his bruised hands and battered face.

"Guess I'm just a little tired," Val said, with an undernourished smile. "But not anything some sleep can't fix."

Cooper's expression brightened. He gazed slowly over to Blue. When she wearily shrugged, as if to say she was staying on the team, he finally smiled.

"Well, you all ain't the only ones who could use a little shut-eye," he muttered, gently easing his body out of the booth. "We'll mosey down to your room, Val, about the middle of the afternoon. Map out our game plan for Vegas. Okay, partner?"

Nodding, Val made ready to follow him and Blue to the hotel elevator. Then he realized the waitress had not left them a check. "Yeah, sounds okay," Val said, looking around for her. "You all go ahead. I'll stay and grab the check."

Cooper smiled and started for the door. Blue paused for a moment. Looking down at Val, she gently touched his face; she was trying, it seemed, to thank him, though for what he couldn't tell. Maybe the encouraging words he'd said to her the previous night.

Some joke, Val thought. He hadn't believed a single syllable of what he'd told her. Even now, he couldn't quite believe that his worst fears had gone unrealized.

After Blue hurried off after Cooper, Val finally caught the waitress's eye. But the old gal didn't seem any better than he was at adding up a check. It took her a full minute to calculate the charge for two coffees and four pieces of pie. But Val let her slide. It was, after all, pretty early in the morning.

Pocketing his change, he left the coffee shop and started out across the casino. Most of the gamblers had by now slunk off to wherever they repaired to at this time of the morning.

The casino's dealers, however, still stood lurking behind their tables, their tired eyes scanning the sparse crowd for one more sucker. A couple of blackjack dealers nodded to Val. But he flashed a nothing-doing smile and kept moving. It felt good to walk through a casino without worrying about getting waylaid.

Reaching the elevator, Val punched its button. When the door opened, he shuffled in and pressed his floor number, then leaned back against the wall. But as the door was closing, a couple of men and two women jumped in at the last moment.

Val recognized the two men. One of them had been a spectator at the game; the second man was the used-car dealer who the night before had so badly fouled Cooper's mood.

The used-car dealer looked very drunk and deeply disgusted; over the course of the previous evening, he had lost his smirk. Val closed his eyes, hoping that when he opened them again, the man would be gone. But no such luck.

"Hey, Pancho," the car dealer barked, twisting his thickly-muscled body in Val's direction. "What the hell you looking so tired about? I'm the guy who stayed up all night losing all my money!"

Val had to open his eyes. He didn't have to grin, however. That was voluntary. "No kidding, sir?" Val murmured politely, secretly hoping the jerk might have to walk all the way back to Los Angeles. "But you were winning big when I left to—"

"So why didn't you take me with you?" the man said in a slurred voice. His blonde lady friend chuckled, though she must have heard this tired line a thousand times before.

The next question was the obvious one. "So who finally won the game?"

Some instinct instantly told Val he should not have asked the question.

The man's eyes suddenly glazed over, as if he were reliving a catastrophe. "Who won the game?" he repeated. "Tell you who won the goddamned game! That fucking friend of yours, that's who! More'n seventy-five thousand dollars, 'bout half of it mine. Sneaky bastard suckered the shit outta me!"

He looked mad enough to maul somebody, and Val knew he was the most logical candidate; Val was about to raise his arms to defend himself when the elevator stopped. The door opened and the foursome filed out, with the used-car dealer still cursing the world at large and Frank Cooper in particular.

Suddenly Val felt very strange. The conversation had ended so abruptly, that for a moment he wondered if it had actually taken place. Yet he knew it had. He also knew it wasn't something he could simply overlook.

As the elevator door snapped shut, Val punched the number for Cooper's floor.

Chapter 32

The only other time Val had felt so crushed was the night he first learned that his father had not died, but rather had simply deserted him and his mother. Now it seemed Cooper was at last truly dead.

Riding the elevator up to the top floor of the hotel, Val felt caught in the midst of a raging sea, yet aware that even bigger waves would soon engulf him.

Coming up to Cooper's floor, he stumbled out of the elevator like a sailor setting foot on dry land, and started down a long plushly-carpeted hallway. Reaching his father's suite, Val took a deep breath and knocked softly on the door. After several seconds the door opened just enough to pull taut its chain-lock.

"Open up, Blue," Val said in an urgent whisper. "I got something to tell you."

The chain came undone. The door opened, and there stood Cooper.

Muffling his surprise, Val cleared his throat and strode into the suite. The door to the bedroom was slightly ajar. Beyond it could be heard the shower running in the bathroom.

Val suddenly felt foolish. There was no place left to rush toward, no place safe to go. Stopping short, he clenched his teeth and stared down at the boots Cooper had bought him in Lake Tahoe. They didn't look so great, anymore.

"Kid, you look like I better have a drink," Cooper muttered, ambling toward the bar.

Studying the shine on his boots, Val said, "I've got a few things to say to Blue. Then I'm catching the bus back to Big Bend."

"Well, Blue's in the bathroom," Cooper said, pouring himself a shot of bourbon. "And knowing her like I do, you could probably be halfway home before she gets outta there."

Val sank down into a chair, putting Cooper on notice that he wasn't going anywhere until he'd said his piece. But for several seconds, Val couldn't muster up the courage to comment on even the weather. He hated himself for that.

"I am truly disappointed, boy," Cooper finally said, taking down the last of his whiskey. "Didn't figure you to run out on me like this."

"Why the hell not?" Val fired back. "You once ran out on me, didn't you?"

The return shot startled Cooper. Then he grinned. What had caused this shift of gears, however, was not Val's question. Cooper had noticed that the bedroom door was open.

"Look, Val, let me get into some fresh duds. I'll meet you down in the coffee shop. We'll get this all untangled, huh?"

"You won that goddamned game, didn't you?" Val blurted out.

The question caught Cooper like an uppercut. But experienced fighter that he was, it took him only a second to shake it off.

"Bullshit, boy," he growled. "Who the hell told you that?"

"Yeah, bullshit is right," Val yelled. "You won over seventy-five thousand dollars last night—and what does it matter who finally told me the truth? You didn't, because you didn't want me and Blue to hold you to all those phony promises!"

Glaring at Val from behind the bar, Cooper's patched-up lips quivered with anger. Val could tell his father had seldom had his nose rubbed in his own crap. It seemed to rile him worse than the beating he'd taken back at Lake Tahoe. Yet Val knew there was no escape for either of them.

Both were caught in the eye of a hurricane, with no recourse but to ride it out. He also knew that what he was determined to say next would probably blow his father completely away; and not anxious to go with him, Val clung more tightly to the arm of the chair.

"Anyway, if you don't tell Blue the truth, I will... But seems the least you owe the lady is to tell her yourself."

Some dark emotion seemed to fill Cooper's eyes. Coming out from behind the bar, he started forward. Val sunk deeper into the chair, hoping his father might consider it bad form to hit him while he was sitting down.

"And what about what you owe me, kid?" Cooper demanded to know.

"Hey, I'll give you back your goddamn thousand dollars, and everything else you ever gave—"

"Oh, keep the change, you little jerk," Cooper snarled. "I told you before, money's good for just keeping score, that's—"

Val vaulted from the chair, though Cooper now stood close enough to hit him. But Cooper's last remark had taken Val past the point of no return.

"Then let's really add up the score—and let's go way back in time, to eighteen years ago when you decided a few thousand dollars was more'n enough to bury me and my mother in the past, and for the rest of your goddamn high-rolling life!"

"Hey, I didn't even have to do that much," Cooper growled. "Not according to Texas law, anyway."

Val knew next to nothing about Texas law; but he was not about to allow his ignorance to slow him down. "Well, who gives a damn about Texas law? Hell, there has to be a bigger, better law somewhere, some law that says what you did owe me and my mother was just a little something of yourself! Shit, what would it have cost you to drop us a postcard every now and then? Damn it, we were people—not just a couple of worthless Mexican souvenirs you once saw back in a little town in West Texas."

Stopping to catch his breath, Val suddenly realized that part of the reason he had come a thousand miles was just to drop this garbage on Cooper. He also knew there was much more to dump.

Then tears started to sting his eyes. It galled him that he was breaking down in front of his father. He wanted Cooper to know he wasn't the only tough bastard in the family. Yet the tears seemed to strike his father harder than the words.

"Aw, hell, kid, please don't go to crying on me," he said. "Last time I saw anyone I truly cared for cry was my brother the day we was pushed off our ranch... "

The memory seemed to trigger an emotion Cooper couldn't hide. The fire left his eyes, and a curious wistfulness now came over him.

"Kid, you won't believe this... but when you was born, you and your mother were really about all I had left in my life. My brother had died, we had lost the ranch, and I didn't have a friend worthy of the name in the entire world... I wanted to stay in touch with you and Lupita. Hell, I needed to, but it just seemed something always came up that kept me from..."

Cooper's voice trailed off, yet it seemed his sentiments were still reverberating somewhere deep inside him. Val sensed that he had his father on the ropes. Yet Val wanted to keep on hammering him. Harder and harder.

"Yeah, something always came up that was more important, like a poker game! Right?"

A helpless shrug was all Cooper could muster. He had lost his will to fight. Now was the time, Val figured, to swing with his knock-out punch.

"But you know what's really sad?" Val muttered, wiping his eyes. "Doesn't matter how much you win, because it'll never be enough... You're like some sick fool who can't stop eating, even when his stomach is bulging out with food. You got a bad disease, Cooper... a disease worse than cancer."

Cooper had wandered over to the window at the far end of the room. Val figured it was safe to make his closing statement.

"Funny, most of my life's been spent feeling sorry for myself because I never had a father. Fate had sure short-changed me. My mother, too. But now I see that you missed out on a lot more than my mom and I ever did. You got the sorriest excuse for a life of any man I've ever known."

Cooper sank into a chair and sat peering out at the blue foothills in the distance. Val felt strangely disappointed. He wanted his father to say so much more than he had, to finally set free his feelings. But Val realized that Cooper was incapable of confronting the truth; instead he had become an expert at simply ignoring it.

All the cannons had at last been fired. But the effort had torn Val up worse than Cooper. Val dreaded having to replay some of the scene for Blue.

Then he saw that she'd saved him the trouble.

Blue was standing just inside the bedroom door, fully dressed, with her pink suitcase at her feet. She had obviously heard most of the conversation.

Cooper took a brief shot at blustering his way out; but he was too smart and too tired to put much steam into the effort. "Well, Blue, guess you heard that the kid here is fixing to blow a real good thing."

"No, Blue, don't buy any more of his bullshit," Val said. "He was lying all along to both of us. Saddest part is, maybe even to himself."

Tears slowly came into Blue's eyes. "Yeah, deep down, Val, I sorta suspected your father had won that game. But thanks just the same for coming up to tell me."

Val waited for Blue to unleash a barrage of her own; but when she remained silent, he decided it was time to climb down off his soapbox. Yet he didn't want to leave without giving Blue a hug and telling her how much he'd miss her. But all Val could manage was a stiff handshake.

"Well, next time I come to Reno, hope I see your name up in lights on one of those big signs."

"No, Val... you're not ever coming back here, honey," Blue whispered with a solemn smile. "But want you to know that from now on, every time I walk into an audition, I'll be thinking about you."

Blue's words were the nicest anybody had ever said to him. *Smile, you dummy*, Val thought to himself, *say something gracious to the lady*. But it wasn't any use, so he simply started for the door.

When he got there, though, Val couldn't resist turning to take one last look at her. She hadn't moved an inch. Val sensed that she wanted to walk out with him, but some stronger impulse was holding her back. At that moment, Blue seemed one of those lost souls who can love only men who mistreat them. Gently opening and closing the door, Val started down the long, dimly-lighted corridor.

Chapter 33

Back down in his own room, Val phoned the bus station. A Greyhound was leaving in forty-five minutes bound for Santa Fe. From there Val could catch another to El Paso, then make a third connection to Big Bend; three buses, thirty-six hours, but at least he wouldn't be walking home broke like some of those Paiute Indians Blue had told him about.

After hurriedly packing his bag, he was headed for the door when the phone rang. Probably Cooper, wanting his money back, Val thought. But it was Blue, calling from down in the lobby. She had walked out on Cooper. Val was pleasantly surprised, but wondered aloud why she hadn't left with him earlier.

"Dammit, Val, I still have some feelings for the bastard! If you and I had bailed out at the same time, woulda been blasting him with both barrels of a shotgun... Anyway, main reason for calling was I didn't want us parting company without at least exchanging addresses. Okay?"

Yet even after they did so, Blue seemed reluctant to say goodbye. She needed to talk, Val figured; and hell, if it was that important to her, he could always take a later bus. He had the rest of his life to make it back to Big Bend.

Blue went on to say that after Val left Cooper's suite, the room had gone as gloomy as a funeral parlor.

"Well, Miss Morgan," Cooper had finally muttered, "you thinking about making the same mistake Val did, just remember this here town can be mighty cold to an unattached lady like yourself."

"Oh, don't worry about me, cowboy," Blue said, taking up her suitcase. "I've gotten pretty used to dealing with people with poker chips where their hearts oughta be."

Cooper had slowly come to his feet and reached for his wallet.

"Well, here then. Let me least give you a little something toward that dream of yours," he said, a hint of derision in his voice. "A little piano bar, right?"

Blue had reached the door, but turned back for a moment. "No thanks, Frank. Hang onto your money. All you got left, cowboy."

Cooper had frowned, but made no immediate retort. Blue tried a cheerful smile, and walked out the door.

She hadn't made it halfway to the elevator when Cooper caught up with her. They walked along in silence for several seconds before he finally spoke.

"Blue, please... Let me at least give you something for your time. Hell, it's just money. But like you said, it's all I got. Come on, do me that favor, will you?"

Blue kept chugging along as fast as she could lug her heavy suitcase. She knew if she stopped once, or even looked over at him, she might change her mind about leaving.

"No, thanks. See, you gotta understand something: you've already done me a favor big enough to last me a lifetime. That is, if I play it smart... which of course I probably won't."

Cooper had seemed confused, which was not his natural state.

"Okay, Frank, let me spell it out for you. See, it's like this," Blue continued, still stalking down the long hallway. "Been you of all people who made me realize that I been running on empty for a long time... You made me see just how important it is to hang on to some sort of dream. But I guess that's what usually happens when you meet somebody who don't have a dream of his own anymore..."

The elevator was standing open when Blue got there. Moving into it, she started to press the button. But the expression on Cooper's battered face stopped her short. He had looked as forlorn as any luckless old prospector she had ever seen.

Blue suddenly wanted to leave Cooper with an encouraging thought. "Come to think of it, Frank, you do have something more than just money," she said with a fragile smile. "Got yourself one hell of a fine son... So why don't you catch up with him, and say goodbye proper-like, huh?"

Then Blue had pressed the elevator button. The door started to close. "Happy trails, cowboy," she whispered. "Thanks for the ride."

❧ ❧

She had done the right thing, Val told Blue, in leaving Cooper to his own troubles. She was one terrific lady, and deserved far better cards than the ones he had dealt her. Val also said that while he appreciated what she had said to him, he wasn't crazy about running into his father again. Like Blue, Val was afraid that if he did, he'd change his mind about walking out on him.

Besides, Val had a bus to catch. Wishing him luck, Blue promised to write. Val said he hoped she would, but didn't plan to place any serious money on it. Blue laughed. "But that is one bet," she said, "you could safely win."

Chapter 34

After buying his ticket, Val ambled across the bus station to a phone booth, and counted out his loose change. He wanted to call home, though he knew it was the worst time of the morning to do so. The phone rang several times before his mother answered.

"Yes, highway diner, hello!"

"Hi, Mom, it's me. Your former headwaiter."

"Val, *¿dónde estás, hijo?*"

"Up in Reno, Nevada," Val quietly said, hoping a soft tone of voice might make Reno sound a bit closer to Big Bend. "Anyway, didn't Clarence tell you that—"

"*¡Sí, pero todavía estoy muy enojada contigo que fuiste tan lejos sin darme una llamada!*"

"But Mom, it all happened so fast, I never had time to let you know," Val exclaimed, wishing now he'd sent his mother a telegram instead of calling her. Then a commotion came over the line. Lupe was calling to somebody.

When she came back on the line, her voice dropped so low Val could barely hear her. He guessed that she didn't want Floyd to overhear the conversation.

"Well?" Lupe asked.

"Well, what, Mom?" Val knew exactly what she wanted to hear.

"*No seas tonto, Valentín,*" she said. "*¿Como fue todo con tu padre?*" She sounded almost afraid to ask how things had gone with his father.

Val could have answered her question in a dozen different ways, but knew it would cost him more than that in dollars to do it over the phone.

"Tell you about it when I get home, okay?"

"Tell me now, Valentín."

This was the second time she had called him by his real name; and experience had taught Val that whenever she did so, she usually meant business. "Well, things went okay. He's a real big spender. Wouldn't let me pay for anything!"

Over a long pause, Val sensed that his mother was smiling. But he had lied to her. He had paid plenty.

"But still with the gambling, eh?"

Val chuckled. "No, ma'am. Way he plays, it's not much like gambling at all. He never loses."

Another long pause. Val knew what was coming next.

"And he is married now?" Lupe finally asked.

The term 'mercy killing' flashed through Val's mind. Hell, even a wounded animal deserved to be put out of its misery. And besides, what was another lie, more or less? Val planned to tell her many of them when he got home.

"Yeah, Mom. He's married. Sort of, anyway. She's a singer. Real sweet lady. You'd really like her..."

For a long moment, the line went deadly quiet. Then Val heard a faint sigh. "Anyway, Mom, just called to say I'll be home tomorrow night. Okay?"

Yet another long pause. *"Bueno, está bien,"* Lupe finally said, responding, it seemed, to more than his travel schedule. "Everybody need someone. Even Frank Cooper..."

Val could almost feel his mother at last giving up the ghost that had haunted her for so many years. He felt a sudden pang of guilt for having lied about his father being married. But it was only a brief attack and soon passed.

"Is there something I tell to Bonnie?" his mother asked. "She been calling here almost every day since you leave."

"Yeah... tell Bonnie I'm coming home to let her know exactly what she can count on," he muttered. "Then think I'd like to do some more traveling."

"¿A donde, hijo?" Lupe asked in an unsteady voice.

Val could almost see the frown on her face. He also sensed that there were several customers stacked up near the register, all waiting to pay either their checks or their respects.

"California. Gonna get a job out there," Val said, speeding up the conversation. "College can wait, Mom—and there will always be some schools around. You know, if I ever change my mind."

"...But Bonnie and the baby?" Lupe quietly asked. Heavy frost seemed to form on the line.

Taking a deep breath, Val hurried on. "Mom, please listen to me. If I go home and marry Bonnie now, it's not gonna make anyone happy. Not in the long run. Not even you. Because all that'll do is just keep her from finding a good man who can really love her. A man like you found in Floyd."

There was another silent lapse. "Well, *hijo*... maybe you right... and thank you for saying this about Floyd," Lupe managed to mutter. "And now for sure thank your father for all he do for you, eh?"

"Yeah, and you tell Floyd for me he doesn't have a thing to worry about. Tell him he has the 'legend' beat hands down, okay?"

Another pause.

"What legend you talk about, Valentín?"

"Hey, gotta go, Mom. The bus is leaving!" Val sputtered, and then softly hung up the receiver. The bus wasn't really pulling out, but Val figured whatever else he and his mother had to say to each other could be done in person a lot less expensively.

After hanging up, Val lingered inside the phone booth for a few moments. He wondered what Floyd's reaction might be when Lupe relayed the message to him.

A voice was droning over the loudspeaker. First call for Santa Fe. Val stood waiting just outside the phone booth for the operator to ring back with the additional charges. But she never did. It seemed a miracle he'd been able to complete the entire conversation, pauses included, within the three-minute limit.

Val reached down for his suitcase, but somebody's banged-up hand got there first. Val recognized the bruises.

"Hope you haven't already bought your ticket," Cooper said, with a lopsided smile.

Val nodded blankly. But Cooper didn't seem to catch his air of indifference. Val wondered if perhaps he was already sending out mixed signals.

"I'd like to give you a lift. Far as El Paso, anyway," his father drawled. "Might give us a chance to talk things out."

By now Val wasn't so angry anymore, which made his dilemma all the more dangerous. He knew that Cooper could probably talk a grizzly bear into changing its mind.

"Not much more to say," Val replied, taking his suitcase from Cooper's grasp. "Besides, already bought my ticket."

Val started toward the boarding area. Cooper ambled right along with him. Val felt strangely flattered by his father's persistence.

"So how is little ole Lupe doing these days?" he finally asked, a hint of sincere interest in his voice. "That was your mother you called, wasn't it?"

"Little Ole Lupe is doing just fine!" Val said, clenching his teeth. But Cooper didn't catch the abrasive tone in his voice. Val suddenly realized how totally exhausted his father must be.

"She ever get married?"

"Long time ago," Val declared, hoping to seal shut the subject.

"Is she happy, Val?" Cooper quietly asked. "Or like most of us, just pretending?"

"Sure she's happy," Val barked back. "Her husband's a damned fine man... and he's taken a lot better care of her than some people I could mention."

But Val meant what he'd told his mother to pass on to Floyd. He was a better man than Cooper; and in previously believing otherwise, Val now saw that he had himself wasted a lot of years.

He tried, however, not to waste any more time in getting to his bus. As he and Cooper walked, Cooper took out his wallet.

"Well, now here, Val," he said. "Want you to take along a little extra cash, just in case you get stranded somewhere."

Stopping short, Val studied him for a moment. Cooper didn't look so almighty powerful anymore; simply a middle-aged man whose future now seemed pretty well used up. Blue had been right when she'd said that all Cooper had left was his money.

"Look, get something straight," Val said, trying to keep his voice as level as his gaze. "My mother has spent eighteen years waiting for some sign that we meant a little something to you. So all this kind attention of yours comes a bit late."

Cooper seemed stuck for an answer.

Then a voice announced the final boarding call for the Santa Fe bus. Cooper quickly fell in step with Val. As they walked out the door, he struggled to get something off his chest. "Okay, Val. I plead guilty to all charges," he finally said. "But you know, sometimes a woman can fall in love with the wrong man. Some dumb bastard who ain't necessarily a bad guy, but just ain't been bred to be a house pet. So the match is doomed from the get-go. But just because something didn't last forever don't mean it can't be of some value to a man, does it, son?"

A lump formed in Val's throat. Despite all the barricades he'd put up around himself, Cooper had managed to reach his heartstrings again.

A moment earlier, Cooper had mentioned the possibility of Val becoming stranded. Now, Cooper seemed marooned himself. No place to go, and the rest of his life to get there.

"I'm glad I found you, if that's what you're asking me," Val said, trying to smile.

A wry grin formed over Cooper's bruised features. "Well, bless you for saying that, son," he murmured. "Even if you don't really mean it."

Val stopped dead in his tracks. "Hey, listen, Val Cooper doesn't say nothing he don't mean."

Cooper chuckled, though Val doubted he thought the mimicry very amusing. They moved under a canopied loading dock. The bus to Santa Fe sat waiting, its motor softly growling. They walked up to the rear of the line of passengers who were boarding the bus.

When Val turned to say goodbye to Cooper, he was amazed to see tears in his father's eyes.

"Dammit, boy, sure gonna miss you," Cooper muttered. "Best gambling partner I ever had."

That sounded to Val like the finest compliment Cooper had ever paid anybody in his entire life.

"Well, thanks... But I hope you never have to work so hard again, just to get into another lousy poker game."

Cooper made a feeble effort to laugh, then turned and stared toward the foothills in the distance. He and Val had come close to the head of the line before he finally spoke again.

"What would you say, Val, to us walking out of here right now, and go shop around for that little ranch we was talking about? What would you say to that, huh?"

A sudden pain stabbed Val in the chest. Sweet Jesus, there was a time when he would have given anything to have heard those same words. Why the hell was life so goddamned unsynchronized?

"Well, Cooper, I'd have to say we were about eighteen years too late."

A rueful smile came over Cooper's battered features. "Yeah, guess I had that answer coming to me."

They were nearing the head of the line. Fishing his ticket out, Val turned to shake hands with his father.

"Oh, almost forgot. My mother wanted me to thank you again for giving her the down-payment on the cafe. Said she'll always be grateful... And I want to thank you, too. This has been the most interesting time of my entire life... and maybe someday I'll look back on it as one of the best."

Cooper took Val's hand in his. Then, in almost the same motion, he put his arms around him and quietly said, "I just wish to hell it'd been in me to do a lot more for both you and your mother. But now you give little ole Lupita a big hug for me, will you? She was quite a wonderful lady, your mother..."

Val thought for a moment. "Yeah, she still is a wonderful lady."

There seemed nothing left to say or do, so Val climbed onboard the bus. Placing his suitcase on an overhead rack, he settled into a seat next to the window. Cooper stood a few feet beyond it, looking up expectantly. He hoped Val might yet change his mind.

As the bus slowly pulled out of the station, Val glanced back and waved. Cooper was still rooted to the same spot. He looked like a man with no other place in the entire world to go.

Chapter 35

About four hours out of Reno, Val began to mull over all that had happened since that night at Saint Jude's Church, the evening he'd discovered that his father was still alive.

Back at the bus station, Val had told him he was glad they'd finally gotten together. What he didn't say was that if it hadn't worked out, it wasn't really anybody's fault. Not even Cooper's. A serious disease had kept him from being all Val wanted him to be; to blame him for that would have been like faulting a man with polio for the limp in his walk.

Nor could he blame Blue for having been caught in a trap for most of her adult life. He only hoped she might someday get out of it. But leaving Reno that morning, Val would have bet against that ever happening.

The first big surprise, however, was waiting back in Big Bend. Val thought sure his mother would insist on hearing a full account of his adventures with his father.

Lupe had asked Val to take a long walk out in the hills behind the diner, something she had never done before. But he had just barely begun to tell her about the first time he had met Cooper when Lupe cut him short.

"He and this lady, are they happy together, Val?"

Val sighed and peered out across the barren mountains he hoped he might soon be able to forget. "Not exactly, Mom. He's not the easiest guy in the world to be in love with... or maybe you already noticed, huh?"

Lupe chuckled ruefully, and turning abruptly, she started back toward the diner. Val went on talking, but he could tell that she wasn't interested in hearing much more of the story. The saga of Frank Cooper was like a book she'd finally finished, and was now placing back on a shelf along with all her other ones. Val was happy for this.

Then Lupe announced that she and Floyd planned to close down the cafe for a few weeks, and take a trip to Chihuahua City.

"You been wanting to take that trip for as long as I can remember. But why now?"

"I still have *familia* there," Lupe said quietly, as they trudged closer to the diner.

"Yeah, I knew that, Mom... But why now?

Val realized that maybe his mother's shame and embarrassment were now gone. They had almost reached the diner before Lupe answered Val's question.

"Because it is time, Valentín," she said, smiling. "It is finally the right time."

A few days later, Val asked Floyd about the trip, and was surprised his stepfather seemed so willing to go into all the details. Floyd saw the trip to Mexico as the honeymoon he and Lupe had never taken. He told Val that right after Val had called his mother from Reno, she had just hung up the phone when Floyd called out: "Hey, you still working here? Honey, we got customers!"

As Lupe walked over to the partition, she had a flirtatious sparkle in her eyes. In their eight years of marriage, Floyd had never seen that look before. She reminded him of a pretty young woman he might have just met at a dance.

"Listen to me, Floyd," Lupe murmured with a coy smile. "Just because you the best cook in West Texas no mean you can go so crazy on me, eh?"

Her manner flummoxed Floyd. He quickly laid out some food platters on the pickup shelf.

"Anyways, that is Valentín on the phone," Lupe said, passing the steaming plates back to old Juana. "He coming home tomorrow night, and oh... he say you nothing to worry about.

He say you beat the legend with the hands down. Now, Floyd, what he mean with that?"

Floyd knew exactly what it meant. "Oh, hell, Lupe, who knows what that young fella ever means about anything he says. Now, come on, let's get some food over to them truck drivers before they go to chewing on the table legs!"

Laughing, Lupe had reached through the partition to gently touch Floyd's face; a small gesture of affection, yet one she had never made before. Then, her tray loaded with ham and egg orders, she started toward a table filled with grumbling truck drivers.

Watching her go, Floyd had stood thinking about things in general, and Val's message in particular.

As Floyd finished his story, Val laughed and asked: "So then what did you do?"

"Won't believe this, son," Floyd said with a sheepish smile. "But I started to hum that goddamned "Wild Goose" song of yours!"

≫ ≪

Val felt pretty friendless as he mapped out his trip to Los Angeles. Clarence had already gone off to college. So just before Val left town, he went down to the local dog pound and got himself an animal: a spirited little terrier, white with brown spots. Val planned to christen him "Old Sam," after the dog in his father's story. But the name didn't seem to suit the secondhand terrier. Val settled on the name "Spunky."

The morning they pulled out of Big Bend in the '47 Mercury coupe Val bought with some of the money Cooper had left him, he felt strangely sad. The dog seemed to pick up on his mood. They resembled a couple of pallbearers; the dog with his mournful eyes, Val with his mopey manner.

But once they hit the highway, the dog seemed to quicken to the open road. It would take Val a little longer. For the entire thousand miles out to Los Angeles, he couldn't shake the feeling that despite all that had happened that summer, he hadn't done much better than break even.

Yet he finally made it out to the land of palm trees, swimming pools, and fantasy factories, though from his tiny one-room apartment in the shabbiest section of Hollywood, the studios still seemed as far away as they had back in Big Bend.

He eventually landed a job at a film laboratory, and was soon sending a little money back to Bonnie every month. She had given birth to a baby girl, whom Val wanted to name after his favorite singer. But Bonnie didn't think 'Blue Cooper' had much of a ring to it, so they settled on the name of Catarina, the name of Val's Mexican grandmother.

Val had been in California for about six months when Bonnie wrote that she was engaged to be married. Her fiance was from a little town nearby.

"He's an engineering student in his senior year at Texas A&M," Bonnie wrote. "And he doesn't excite me, Val, like you once did. But he's a real good-hearted guy, and he's crazy about the baby. Best of all, though, he's already been offered a job in Houston after graduation..."

So Bonnie would be getting out of Big Bend, too. Yet the letter saddened Val.

Someone else would be at Bonnie's side when their little girl took her first wobbly step, and there perhaps to pick her up after her first day at school. Many years later, Bonnie's husband would probably walk Catarina down the aisle of some church to turn her future over to another man.

Soon after Val got word of Bonnie's impending marriage, he received another letter. Lupe had sent it to him from Big Bend. Blue Morgan had written to say she was about to open up a little music theater in Reno.

"It's only the third lead in the musical, but it's my first professional engagement in many years. See, what happened is that my singing coach finally informed me that while my voice was not quite good enough for the nightclub circuit, it was more than adequate for dinner theater. The little truth-telling toad also told me I was a better actress than a singer—something, I gotta admit, I have long suspected!"

Blue went on to say that soon afterwards, she had signed up for some acting classes and now that the first professional job had come her way, she felt almost ready.

"But it wasn't easy, Val, to give up my dream of becoming a headliner, though I am now starting a new career that might at least allow me to hang onto my self-respect. But then, hell, I'm just happy to have an option, something that poor bastard of a father of yours has never been lucky enough to find..."

Reading over her letter, Val mused that maybe happiness didn't always mean getting exactly what you wanted, but rather in appreciating what came your way. Who was it, Val wondered, who first said, "Life is what happens to us while we're out making other plans."

Val wrote back, wishing Blue the best, but making clear that as far as he was concerned, Blue had already made the grade. Val hoped someday he could say the same about himself.

Many years later, standing at the bay window of the home he had just rented in the Hollywood hills, Val realized that in one respect he had succeeded, though not because he had finally made a career for himself as a screenwriter. He was proudest that he had managed to be with his daughter for most of the major moments in her life.

And it would take years after that, when he began to write about the events of that summer which had forever changed the course of his life, that Val would at last understand he had done a great deal better than break even, after all.